Evald Flisar

Enchanted Odysseus

Translated from the Slovene by
David Limon

Texture Press
Norman, Oklahoma
2016

EVALD FLISAR (1945, Slovenia). Novelist, playwright, essayist, editor, globe-trotter (travelled in 96 countries), underground train driver in Sydney, editor of (among other publications) an encyclopaedia of science and invention in London, author of short stories and radio plays for the BBC, president of the Slovene Writers' Association (1995 – 2002), since 1998 editor of the oldest Slovenian literary journal Sodobnost (Contemporary Review), since April 2015 President of the Slovene PEN Center. Author of 14 novels (nine of them short-listed for kresnik, the Slovenian "Booker"), two collections of short stories, three travelogues, two books for children, and fifteen stage plays (eight nominated for Best Play of the Year Award, three times won the award). Winner of the Prešeren Foundation Prize, the highest state award for prose and drama, and the prestigious Župančič Award for lifetime achievement. Various works translated into 38 languages, among them Bengali, Hindi, Malay, Nepalese, Indonesian, Turkish, Greek, Japanese, Chinese, Arabic, Czech, Albanian, Lithuanian, Icelandic, Romanian, Amharic, Russian, English, Dutch, German, Italian, Polish, Spanish, etc. His stage plays are regularly performed all over the world, most recently in Austria, Egypt, India (three different production in two months alone), Indonesia, Japan, Taiwan, Serbia, Bosnia, Bulgaria, Belarus and USA. Attended more than 50 literary readings and festivals on all continents. Lived abroad for 20 years (three years in Australia, 17 years in London). Since 1990, resident in Ljubljana, Slovenia. His novel *My Father's Dreams*, published by Texture Press in 2005 and recently by Istros Books in London, UK, has earned him a place at the European Literature Night, an annual event at the British Library that features 6 of the best contemporary European writers. Another of his novels, *On the Gold Coast* (published in English by Sampark, Kolkata, India) was nominated for the most prestigious European literary prize, the Dublin IMPAC International Literary Award. It was listed by The Irish Times as one of 13 best novels about Africa written by Europeans, alongside Joseph Conrad, Graham Greene, Isak Dinesen, JG Ballard, Bruce Chatwin and other great literary names. In June/July 2015 the author completed a three-week literary tour of USA, reading at the Congress Library in Washington and SUA convention in Chicago, attending the performance of his play *Antigone Now* at the Atlas Performing Arts Center in Washington, speaking at the Slovenian Permanent Mission at the United Nations. In January 2016 he was one of the speakers at the largest literary festival in the world (Jaipur, India), together with Margaret Atwood, Colm Toibin, Colin Thubron, Aleksandar Hemon, Stephen Fry and other illustrious names.

*t*P
Texture Press

Evald Flisar

Enchanted Odysseus

Translated from the Slovene by
David Limon

Texture Press
Norman, Oklahoma
2016

ENCHANTED ODYSSEUS
Copyright © Evald Flisar

Translation copyright © David Limon
David Limon has received a grant from the Slovenian Book Agency.

Originally published in Slovenia (European Union) as *Začarani Odisej* (Maribor: Založba Litera, 2013). Shortlisted for Kresnik, the Best Novel of the Year Award.

**Published in the United States by
Texture Press, 1108 Westbrooke Terrace, Norman, OK 73072.**

Editor
Susan Smith Nash, PhD

Cover design
Arlene Ang

Published with the financial assistance of Trubar Foundation, Ljubljana, Slovenia.

ISBN 978-0692693940 (Texture Press)

Printed in the United States of America.

**Texture Press
Norman, OK 73072
USA**
texturepress@beyondutopia.com

*'What is truth?' said jesting Pilate,
and would not stay for an answer.*

Francis Bacon

1.

Greetings, Dr. Krauthaker. I heard that you were coming to Singapore. Wonderful! After a long time we'll be able to talk face to face once more. I no longer enjoy looking for a cybercafé and waiting for a free computer from which to send you my latest report from the field (as we agreed to call them). While I had to inform you about the paths I had taken, as demanded by our agreement, looking for internet access was fun. But since my case is no longer a top priority for you (and you have perhaps even stopped reading my mails), I type in my Yahoo password with a feeling of guilt. I'm afraid that I may be harassing you – someone who has done more for me than a mother would do for her own son!

Unfortunately (as you well know), you are the only one who I can talk to about my accident. Anyone else would reject me as a madman.

If you erase the messages even before opening and at least skimming them, then my words are wasted, I am aware of that. But the hope that perhaps it is not like that spurs me on to keep sharing my experiences with you, although less often than at the beginning. I am frequently driven to the nearest cybercafé by the hope that you might have replied and given as the reason for your silence lack of time, illness or absence. That would delight me like nothing else.

The feeling that I am completely alone would vanish.

Do you remember the enthusiasm with which we began? Yours was even greater than mine, since you hoped that my case would make you one of the greatest neurologists of all time, perhaps even bring you a Nobel Prize nomination. You never said that out loud, but it was written all over your face. Your dark eyes literally glowed! And mine, too, for you filled me with hope that you would help me to find my way back to myself. To that self who was there in time and space before I forgot who I was.

You said that my return would be full of danger and the result uncertain. You promised that you would steer me in the right direction as much as circumstances allowed, but that such a case of amnesia could not be found in the medical literature. Do you remember how desperately I clung to the lifebelt you offered me? When just over a month ago you severed contact and changed your phone number I thought that without someone to constantly relate my life to, I would never find the willpower to return to myself. The plan for this return was drawn up by you, Dr. Krauthaker. And the plan was that I would sail with you as the captain of the vessel back across the unknown expanses to the realm of the known.

After the shock, that lasted several days, I thought that you had unexpectedly disappeared without trace because that was part of the *plan* for my return. Maybe you wanted to help me find myself, to learn to live without support. In one of your last emails you even mentioned such a possibility. You wrote that the loving mother bird, at a particular moment, shoves the young one out of the nest so that it learns to fly. But Dr. Krauthaker – you pushed me from the nest too soon!

Tell me: what does a lonely middle-aged man do when he cannot entrust his unbearable anxiety to someone who will genuinely listen? Find a prostitute and pay her to lend an ear? To find a woman who will receive his verbal ejaculation with professional commitment and if she can feign interest, so much the better?

So don't blame me for deciding to seek a sympathetic pair of ears among the healers of wounded egos. One who knows how to fake the gleam of genuine interest in her tired and often hostile eyes, so that men are not even aware that it is not real.

10

I was lucky. Since you know Singapore (I read that you will be attending the world congress of neurologists for the third time), I won't need to describe in any detail the district of Geylang. Perhaps you have sometime availed yourself of the services of the attractive girls of every nationality standing on the street corners. And if you have not, then I recommend that you do so – you won't regret it. Chinese, Indonesian, Vietnamese, Thai, Malaysian, Indian, even Ukrainian (and even Black!) – you will find everything on the streets of Geylang. Plus a host of hotels that rent rooms for an hour or two or three, depending on your requirements. And your stamina.

It was there, Mr. Krauthaker, that I headed when the consequences of your silence became unbearable. At first I really did think of telling all to some stranger in a bar or to one of those that I met professionally as part of your rehabilitation plan. But after some thought, I chose a prostitute.

Why?

The answer is clear. In front of a woman to whom you are prepared to show your sex organ and even to shove it inside her, you feel no embarrassment. Intimacy is inherent in the nature of the exchange. Not only physical, but psychological. Her eyes will never linger on your organ with contempt (what she really thinks of it she knows how to conceal all too well). And it is even less likely that she will show any contempt for what you are telling her. The essence of the agreement is that she makes it possible for you to express something and you pay her for that.

When I say I was lucky, I mean to say that I came across a woman who was not a whore in the usual sense of the word. She was educated and well-read, a teacher by profession, who had left her three children at home in Java and come to Singapore for six months in order to earn as quickly as possible enough money for their education. And she acted in accordance with her "short-term" employment plan: she was quick, decisive, economical; she knew that she needed to make use of every minute to earn money. Late in the evening as I was walking along the streets of Geylang, avoiding the alluring looks

11

from the girls lined up along the pavement at twenty metre intervals, she suddenly stepped out of the darkness, took me by the arm, kissed my cheek and said: "I know you're looking for me. Shall we go to the nearest hotel?"

She was slender, quite tall, with beautiful features. But I was tempted, Dr. Krauthaker, by something else: that without any embarrassment, almost with pride, she was wearing glasses. Women with glasses have a quality which leads you to hope that their head is not empty or filled with stereotypes – that they have at least some intellectual capabilities, enough perhaps to be able to talk about things that are not usually present in the female brain.

You will probably wince at this display of male chauvinism; so did I. What were my experiences with women in the life to which my memory will not give me access? Was I really unlucky enough to encounter only the dumb blondes of magazine jokes? Or had a woman who played a central role in my life – my partner, maybe my wife, the mother of my children – worn glasses? And because of that, was my trust of bespectacled women a kind of reflex, one of the few that had managed to slip past the wall of forgetting? Not only that: women wearing glasses arouse in me a strange agitation that is most reminiscent of the sex drive. Perhaps that was the main reason why I did not object when the young lady emerged from the darkness and took my arm.

When, in the reception of the "love hotel" with the rather unusual name (Ismarus), I hired a room and had already paid for it, it occurred to me that an hour would not be enough and so I extended it. When I was paying for the extra hour, the young lady reached for the passport lying on the counter and opened it out of curiosity. "Oh, Mr. Youngson!" she exclaimed. "Australian," she added, sounding almost disappointed, and threw it back down.

She did not put it back down, but actually threw it. Even the receptionist looked taken aback.

In the fear that she'd had bad experiences with Australians, I immediately corrected her: "An Englishman who has lived in Australia for quite some time."

She shrugged, as if in relation to the favour I was expecting from her this was not of the slightest importance. She took the key and went along the corridor towards the room, in which she had no doubt been many times with clients of whatever nationality, with genuine or forged passports and with sexual needs of every kind, definitely including some perverse ones. She gave no sign of what she thought about me extending the agreed time to two hours.

When we first got to the room I went to the toilet to relieve the pressure in my bladder. When I emerged she was already lying naked on the bed and she held out towards me a packet of condoms. For her, this was business: instead of me it could have been anyone at all (even you, Dr. Krauthaker). And she wanted to carry out her work like an efficient, precise secretary, who means to ensure that her boss does not waste any time.

Mr. Krauthaker, since we are both grown men I will not trouble you with a detailed description of the attractions she had to offer. I know that you have a well-ordered sex life and so anything of that nature would not only be superfluous but impolite, even immature. I shall tell you only that I almost succumbed to the logic of the gesture with which she offered me the packet. After all, that was the intention that had brought us into this room.

But in the end my desire to unburden myself proved stronger. When I asked her to get dressed because I only wanted to talk, she was at first disappointed. That is how I interpreted the slightly weary expression on her face. Oh no, one of those, she seemed to be thinking. But in spite of that, she put her clothes back on in a flash. She sat on the edge of the bed with her back towards the wall mirror in which we could have watched ourselves in a badly acted and even more badly directed film about a man and a prostitute who with mixed feelings get involved in something slippery instead of obscene. Something that the very next moment one of them might regret.

You know how it is, Mr. Krauthaker: relations between people are least painful when each knows what to give and what to expect.

"There was no need to take a room just to talk," she said. "We could have gone for a coffee in the nearest bar."

"I wouldn't have been able to relax there. Neither would you. I would like to talk about very personal things."

13

I discerned a look of concern on her face. Obviously the kind of guy who gets aroused by talking about sexual perversion. An impotent type who might be masking a potential killer: which woman would not feel concerned? She moved so that she was facing the door. To stop her from leaving I quickly pulled out my wallet and counted out five hundred Singapore dollars onto the bedspread. (The usual price for an hour of fun in Geylang, Dr. Krauthaker, is one fifth of that!)

But instead of calming her, I confused her even more.

"Put your money away," she said. "We'll go for a coffee to the bar round the corner. My treat. You can have half an hour, even an hour if all you want to do is talk."

I reached for the banknotes, folded them and almost forced open her left hand.

"Take it," I said. "I'd like you tell me as much as you can about yourself. About your life, your memories of the past." I closed her fingers over the money and pushed her hand towards her.

She opened it and exclaimed: "Five hundred dollars to tell you about myself?"

"Exactly," I said. "I'm interested in your memories. It doesn't matter which, as long as they are clear and picturesque. About good things and bad. About your childhood, adolescence. Your parents and school. And your first love. The injustices you have suffered. Please."

Perhaps she was convinced by my pleading look. Perhaps she sensed in my tone of voice that my words arose from a genuine need, from a deep distress. Or perhaps it was the money that tipped the balance. It really doesn't matter: the main thing is that she began to talk. At first, in rather a forced manner and with silences, as if she was passing on information to an official who was filling out a form for her, and at times almost as if she was suspected of something and needed to offer proof of her innocence.

I found out that her name was not Suni, as she had told me on the short walk to the hotel, but Njoman, and that she was not from Java, but from Bali, which she was reluctant to admit because prostitutes

14

in Indonesia are usually from Java, even on Bali. And young women from Bali never come to Singapore with that intent. She was thirty-two years old. She had left behind at her mother's in Ubud three children aged ten, eight and six. They had lost their father, a surfing instructor, who before the eyes of his pupil and other swimmers had been carried away by a large wave. Thus she had come to Singapore on her own: so that her modest wage as a village teacher would not prevent her from offering her children all that they had become accustomed to.

Six more months and she would return home, she added. And forget about Singapore as if it had never happened.

"Interesting," I said. "What about memories?"

I was not looking for details, I explained, I was interested in all the pictures, all the films, that she carried in her head and which every now and then were triggered as stories from life that told her who she was, where she was from, who she was connected to, what she had dreamed about as a child and which of her dreams had come true. Memories of rain, of heat, of the first time she walked to school. Her first sexual encounter, the birth of her first child – that kind of thing.

Dr. Krauthaker, you wouldn't believe how these words loosened her tongue. She talked non-stop for the next half hour. She made no effort to link together the fragments she came out with, rather there erupted from her a chaotic flow of memories and impressions and opinions and judgements and self-judgements. As if she had been suddenly overcome with the need to tidy the fragments of the past into a drawer, to clear her mental space and to clarify who and what she actually was.

Oh, how much she enjoyed it. And how I enjoyed it (and suffered) with her!

She talked of how as a girl she helped her grandparents to plant rice on the terraces. And of the babbling of the water in the irrigation channels that ran to the fields and then down the slope; and about the smell of wet earth and the mud in which she waded up to her knees; about offerings to the gods that she and her grandmother took to the village temple; and about the fiery cloud of smoke hanging above the erupting volcano of Gunung Agung. And also about her school

15

years in Denpasar, where she was never happy – and a thousand other details, Dr. Krauthaker, that I will not enumerate since they would mean nothing to you.

The pain that smouldered inside me from the start increased with every word she spoke and soon became a real flame. Particularly when she spoke of the relationship between her parents, who concealed from Njoman and her two brothers that there was no real love between them. And then how her mother sold cheap souvenirs on the beach in Kuta, while her father took tourists on trips around Bali in a rented Toyota. And her education. She learned the basics of English from tourists, so it later seemed natural to her to choose that for her studies. She was a good teacher and the pupils liked her. If the sea had not swept away the father of her children, she would still be teaching in the village not far from Ubud.

And then she asked me to tell her something about myself. Imagine, Mr. Krauthaker: that *I* tell *her* something about *me*!

I told her that could tell her nothing about myself, because I didn't exist! There was no *me*. I was a kind of robot devoid of content, of memories, of history. Of course, at one time I'd had those things, but now I wandered through space like an empty shell, like a vampire who has no choice but to feed on the memories of others.

Naturally, she failed to understand me. So I described to her the incident on Bali in more or less the same words that I described it to you, not long after it took place.

How on the beach at Kuta I had waded into the waves between the two flags that indicated where you could swim, so that the surfers who had taken over the rest of the sea could surf in peace. How one of the young heroes, still a novice, had drifted among the swimmers and how his surfboard had hit my head. How the people on the beach who saw this happen immediately ran to pull me out of the water and carried me to the nearest sunbed. How I lay there unconscious for fifteen minutes, while the young surfer knelt in the sand, weeping loudly. His instructor, who was supposed to keep an eye on him, kept trying to reassure him that it was not his fault.

16

And how you, one of my rescuers, desperately sought transport to the hospital, while your wife stayed with me and kept the curious at bay.

I told her, the young woman in the hotel, that I had no memory of the incident and that I was recounting only what I heard from you when I regained consciousness in a private clinic in Sanur and the brain scan showed that I hadn't suffered any brain damage. Apart from bumps and bruises, I was suffering from concussion. But not only that: I could not remember a thing. Not only the accident that you described to me, but nothing before it. I didn't know my own name; I didn't know who I was or what had brought me to Bali.

I told her, Mr. Krauthaker, how you had taken control and told the clinic staff that you were a neurologist, a professor of neurology, no less, at a university in Sydney, specialising in all types of amnesia, including the retrograde kind that had evidently followed my collision with the surfboard.

Since I was wearing only a swimming costume and nothing belonging to me was found on the beach apart from some sandals, you surmised that I had come from one of the nearby hotels. You immediately asked the police to find out if any of them was missing a guest. It soon turned out that all the hotels were full – it was the height of the season – and that none of them was missing a guest.

That seemed to you highly unusual. You demanded that the police widen their enquiries to the whole island, on the off chance, however unlikely, that I had come to Kuta by taxi or with a rented car from the other end of Bali with nothing other than a swimming costume and sandals. But nobody reported anyone missing.

And so it seemed that I had fallen onto the beach from the sky.

I told all this to the young woman in the hotel. I know that you told me I should not talk about my condition to a complete stranger. You said that people in general are dishonest and that sooner or later I would come across someone who would try to take advantage. But after what she had revealed to me, she no longer seemed a stranger. Besides which, I had bought two hours of her time so that she could listen to me and I wanted to see her reaction to my words.

17

It was different from what I had expected. To start with she listened to me with feigned politeness, then with growing interest and then with increasing concern. Eventually her face showed unmistakable fear. She suddenly jumped up and ran into the bathroom. And there, Mr. Krauthaker, she threw up. She left the door open and I heard very clearly her vomit splashing into the toilet bowl. I did not know how to explain this.

Then she turned on the tap, rinsed her mouth and gargled, gasping from the effort. You yourself must have vomited at some time in the past, Dr. Krauthaker, and you know how unpleasant it is. When she came back into the room she averted her eyes, rummaged in her handbag and made a great show of looking for paper tissues. She used one of them to wipe her mouth, as if she hadn't already done this with a towel in the bathroom. I remained silent as I waited for her to recover. As she said nothing for quite some time, only staring in a preoccupied way at the carpet, I commented: "It was probably something you ate."

She suddenly spoke. She wanted to know whether I *really* didn't remember anything about the incident on Bali, whether I'd *really* heard about it only from others. And how did I know that the described incident *really* took place? How did I know, Dr. Krauthaker, that you hadn't lied to me? Imagine: you lying to me. My benefactor, my doctor!

"To what end?" I asked.

"You have an Australian passport!" she exclaimed. "Why do you say you don't know who you are?"

The young lady thought that by obtaining a name I had also obtained an identity!

You and I know that a passport in the name Napoleon Bonaparte would not transform me into the French conqueror. And the fact that you supplied me with five passports in five different names does not mean I *am* five different people. I'm still hollow; I'm still just a shell. But the circumstances did not seem to suit a long explanation. I could actually feel that she was suddenly afraid of me: either me or my situation, or something that I had told her. It was fear that had led her to throw up. Perhaps she had remembered that the sea had

18

swept away her husband on that same beach, where he was a surfing instructor.

But how could the waves carry away a surfing instructor? That wasn't clear to me. Surely a prerequisite for the job is that you are a better than average swimmer? And if you are not, but you are still teaching people how to surf, you can't be much of an instructor, because it can happen all too easily that an inept pupil takes you in the wrong direction, towards the area reserved for swimming, rather than surfing. And where the pupil's surfboard can by the by crash into the head of one of the swimmers. For which Poseidon, out of a sense of justice, takes revenge by dragging you down into his underwater lair.

For instance.

Or you surrender yourself to the waves out of a feeling of guilt.

"I don't want the money," she said, nervously putting the banknotes on the bed.

I got the feeling she was suddenly in a hurry.

At first, it seemed that I would lose nothing by allowing her to flee. After all, I had got what I needed: for the first time since the accident on Bali I'd been able to tell another person my story eye to eye – to a real Other, not to some email address that could be concealing, as you yourself know, almost anyone.

But above all, like a vampire I had sucked from her some of her memories. Since my only spiritual food became the memories of others, I need people more often than they are willing to present their throats to my fangs. The tension inside me had subsided slightly; to share a secret with at least one person was always salutary. But I wanted to pay for the service – that had been the agreement.

But she did not want the money; she kept on pushing it back towards me.

"No, no, no," she kept repeating.

And I: "I insist and will keep insisting until I get my way."

"Okay," she said. "On condition that we do what we came here to do."

And she began to strip in nervous haste. And to strip me almost at the same time. She removed her skirt with her left hand and with her right almost ripped the shirt from my back.

19

What could I do, Dr. Krauthaker? You know how considerate we men are. Women quickly take pity on us. It seemed odd to me that she was doing this (a normal woman would have taken the money and run). So, I succumbed faster than I should have.

A few moments later it was too late: she had already skilfully aroused me, she had already climbed on top of me, with measured movements she was already doing her job and, it seemed to me, with particular attentiveness. As if she really wanted to earn that money. Or as if she wanted to apologise, to console me for the wrong that had been done to me? Or as if she wanted to divert my attention from the thoughts flashing through my mind? Who knows? She rolled onto her back, pulled me on top of her and said: "Carry on!"

And then, Dr. Krauthaker...

I'm sorry, I'm writing to you from the airport and they have just called my flight: I'll continue as soon as I get to a computer.

2.

Dear Mrs. Krauthaker, Milly, I see on Yahoo, our mutual friend, that it is three months since I wrote to you. Your reply was so short that it did not seem worth responding to.

"Carry on!" you wrote.

According to a book I was reading today, that is the answer that Buddha gave to the question what is the meaning of life. You no doubt had something else in mind, since for you the meaning of life was always idleness, shopping, enjoyment, manipulation, deceiving Dr. Krauthaker, deceiving those with whom you cheated on him (including me), taking drugs, both soft and hard, and planning mischief, mainly small scale, since you are not exactly overflowing with imagination. But occasionally something worse. Forgive me for being frank.

What did you have in mind when you ordered me to carry on? Perhaps the task you gave me when we said our goodbyes in Sydney – and I forgot about it? Although it's not clear to me whether that task is connected with what I did in a Singapore hotel and I have no doubt at all that the incident in Geylang is not among the occasional memories that have made their way into my brain from books that I read or films that I saw at God knows which point in the past. This incident happened.

And if it did, you're probably wondering why I didn't end up in one of Singapore's prisons.

Or perhaps sentenced to a life in prison. Or shot!

The answer is an extremely simple one. As you undoubtedly know, your husband, officially my doctor and benefactor, supplied me with five forged passports with different names, nationalities and, of course, identities. When the Australian Kevin Youngson became aware he had committed the act that someone had ordered him to commit, he did not linger at the scene of the crime. He realised in time that if he was discovered he would not only lose his passport, but that *all* of his identities would be lost with it. (And he would then really be No-one, whereas with his false identities he was at least Someone.) I calmly walked past the receptionist onto the street and gestured to the nearest taxi. (The receptionist probably thought that the professional young woman, after completing her work, was showering; how could he know that she was lying in a pool of her own blood?)

Mr. Youngson went to his hotel, The Strand (one of the best in town, as you know), paid the bill, walked the long corridor to his room, stuck on a bushy moustache and the blond wig of a Swede named Sven Lindgren, stuffed his belongings into a suitcase and a carry-on bag of the permitted dimensions, took a taxi to the airport and asked for a seat on the first available plane out. He boarded and after a thirteen hour flight landed in Amsterdam.

And so now I am writing to you as Sven Lindgren, in case you don't know who I am. For each false *me* has his own email address. Otherwise it would lead to misunderstandings and great confusion; in the end my notes would be so much waste paper. Although I cannot pretend that they are not half made up, they still offer me a safe refuge, at least until I remember who I really am.

And what am I doing in Amsterdam? I am living in a commune composed largely of ageing hippies, who have through a series of strange coincidences adopted me as their own. We succumb to the mild intoxication brought on by controlled consumption of various drugs. We also have sex (don't imagine that on leaving Singapore I embraced celibacy). The rest of the time I wander around the city.

And think.

I am gripped by a painful feeling that I am the victim of forces that I cannot comprehend and that everything is not as it seems. Or as I *think* it is. I will not disagree with the idea that human life is ruled by fate and that fate is a chain of coincidences that are crossroads on our path through space and time. But the fact that when my accident occurred on a beach in Bali there was a world expert on amnesia at hand requires further clarification, don't you agree? How can it be that the right person was in the right place at the moment when fate decided to rob me of my memory through a stupid mistake made by a novice surfer? And with that to rob me of my life? For what is life other than an album of memories to which we add new photographs as we move through time?

Although we were very close, you never indicated that the story the two of you told me about my accident was not quite accurate. There are two possible explanations for this: either it is true, or you know how to pretend just as consummately as all the others who launched me into a new life.

You seem to have been born, my dear Milly, with a capacity for pretence. Did we not once have sex on the living room sofa while Dr. Krauthaker was upstairs writing one of his scientific articles about me? You never even asked me whether I fancied such a thing, you simply climbed on top of me. And since men, as you well know, can't help getting aroused at the right kind of touch, you took possession of me *before* I had the chance to ask myself whether I even wanted it to happen.

And when you heard Mr. Krauthaker coming down the stairs you fastened my zip and pulled your skirt over your knees as if you had just served me coffee. Which you had, conveniently, shortly before, and it was still standing on a tray on the table.

"Darling, would you like coffee, too?" you asked when Dr. Krauthaker entered the room. And you held out a cup towards him, while I (I don't know if you noticed) quickly put a cushion on my lap to hide the erection which hadn't had the time to subside.

"Darling, would you like coffee, too?"

I was stunned at the negligent tone of your words (you even yawned as you said it). I was overcome with the suspicion that you

23

were not so much concealing our sexual contact from your husband, but rather concealing from me the fact that you and he had agreed it in advance. And that Dr. Krauthaker had even suggested it. Perhaps as part of his research into my condition.

There are so many puzzling things that I am sinking beneath their weight. Why, for instance, do I speak English with an Australian accent if I am speaking with an Australian, with an American accent if I am speaking with an American, with an English accent if I am speaking with an Englishman (and that includes English regional accents), with an Indian accent if I am speaking with an Indian, with a South African accent if I am speaking with someone from Johannesburg? And why do I speak with an appropriate foreign accent if I am speaking English with a Russian, a German, an Italian, a Spaniard, a Dutchman?

That I could just about understand: I recently read somewhere that George Orwell also had a similar gift of unconscious mimicry. But why do I speak French when I meet a Frenchman, Japanese when I meet someone from Japan, Finnish when I meet a Finn, Slovene when I meet a Slovene, or Spanish when I meet a Spaniard, a Mexican or an Argentinian, with all the local variations? Where do all these languages come from? Was I a polyglot in my previous forgotten life? Some kind of wunderkind, like that poor soul (I've forgotten his name), who spoke twenty languages fluently, but could not say anything sensible in any of them?

Or did the supposed collision of a surfboard with my head, in addition to destroying my memory centre, at the same time activate some kind of genetic matrix that we carry inside us and which enables us to learn languages?

Is the Tower of Babel something that we bring with us to this world? And the words that later become our mother tongue simply pour into the appropriate mental vessel that is already connected up to grammar?

Perhaps you are asking yourself why I am writing about this to you, who are most likely bored by it. The reason is not difficult to guess. Because my polyglotism is unusual, to say the least, for now I dare not mention it to people who might be able to explain it. Not even your husband knows about this skill of mine, although he was taken aback when in the hospital on Bali I spoke more fluent Indonesian than he. And because he spoke with an Australian accent and I did the same, he supposed that I was Australian by birth. Which is why he was even more determined to take me into his care. Even I became aware of my multilingual abilities only gradually, when I left Sydney and began to meet people who spoke other languages. As the number of languages that I understood and was able to speak grew, so did my surprise. Which quickly became astonishment.

And finally fear.

Do you understand my need to talk about this? And to someone who will at best shrug and say: so what? Whatever I am and whatever I *was* in the life I do not remember, I would never want to be a freak investigated by international experts – from linguists to psychologists, from anthropologists to psychiatrists – not to mention the suffocating interest of the media, who would feverishly follow the story.

Perhaps in the forgotten life I wasn't a completely ordinary person. Perhaps I stood out in some way. I probably did; my mode of expression and my way of thinking show that I was not completely without education. But in the life that has been granted me now I would rather be No-one and live incognito. And that, surprisingly, I am and that is how I am living. Primarily thanks to your husband and his mysterious colleagues who supplied me with five false identities. That is very handy, for when one of them gets into difficulties, I can quickly transfer to another. I can also do the same when I grow weary of one of them. As far as this goes I am grateful to your husband. Tell him that when you speak to him.

At the same time ask him why he never gets in touch any more. Has a clumsy surfer also crashed into his head and robbed him of his memory? I'd hoped that we would see each other in Singapore, but fate decided otherwise.

The thought that my consciousness is merely the cumulative content of Yahoo messages is not a particularly pleasant one, but it is at least something. Without that, I would just be a living robot. Perhaps I will succeed eventually in uncovering the code in which you send me instructions. I will awake from forgetfulness, remember who I am, uncover the two of you, send you to prison. Or, if you are by any chance in Singapore, to the gallows. I won't pretend that the thought does not fill me with delight. Although there is no evidence, I am convinced that you are both involved, you and your blessed neurologist. Partly together and partly each in your own way. And that it is you who are responsible for the murder of the prostitute and that he may not even know about it. (Maybe he was involved with her and you wanted her out of the way.) Was the code that triggered the events the words "Carry on!"?

I also thought of the possibility that I recognised the young woman as the wife of the surfing instructor who was indirectly responsible for one of his pupils crashing into my head. And that triggered within me a desire for revenge to which I, incapable of reflection, too quickly succumbed. That would of course change the whole story: it would mean that the accident really *did* happen, or at least that deep inside I *believed* it did. But also that you and your husband do not have malicious intentions, and *really* do want to help me.

With regard to that, there is another possible explanation of the fact that no-one on Bali missed me. They looked for a record of me only in hotels and private rooms, thinking that I was no doubt an Australian tourist. But what if I have a house on Bali, as you do? A house in which I live, unlike you, without servants. And I came to the beach in only swimming costume and sandals because I came on foot.

Impossible? Far from it. So I can never decide which of the unclear, ambiguous stories that make up my post-traumatic *me* are true. Nor which is the most likely – I lean first towards one and then towards another. And it's possible that all the actions that I think you have put into my mind originate from my own inclinations. Perhaps they arise from a forgotten identity or subconscious like a sudden explosion, compelling me to do something that later I can find neither explanation nor excuse for.

At the Lotofaga Club, where I spend a lot of my time in Amsterdam, the majority of the members and their guests see me as a lucky man. In their opinion, I have managed to travel quite a long way on the path to total oblivion. Some admire me; all envy me. For them the aim of life is to forget, not to remember, for memory is a source of pain, disappointment and empty desires that can never be realised. This gives birth to new desires and transforms them into illness. Only in the embrace of oblivion is it possible to find refuge from the storms and tempests with which the consumer society fills our heads with only one aim: to survive. If you wish to be a victim of that world then you are mad, so the only path to health lies in the gradual weakening of the memory until you are no longer clear who you are and your identity sinks into the amorphous collective where we are all brothers and sisters, and we are aware only of the fact that we exist.

This is also the only way that we can shrug off the imparted inhibitions and moral restraints that forbid us to do almost anything that is natural. Such as sex with anyone we choose, or group sex, or sex with the under-aged, or zoophilia, or enjoying good food, alcohol, drugs – all of which are not only permitted in this club, but are daily practice. Lucky is the one who knows that he is, but not who and what he is. For if you do not know who and what you are, you are relieved of all responsibility, which is the most pleasant state to be in.

It's not completely clear to me how I became a member of Lotofaga, since the event has already begun to be eaten away by forgetfulness because I didn't send myself an email in time (which I regularly do). I have a hazy feeling that it began with an encounter at the airport, where a young Dutch woman by the name of Margaretha Cornelia greeted me as the uncle who was supposed to have been travelling from Singapore on the same plane. She hadn't seen this uncle since she was a young child and hoped to recognise him from the photograph she had with her.

I must say that Sven Lindgren looked very like this uncle. Maybe even I would make the same mistake in similar circumstances. Moreover, people don't always look the same on every photo and the differences between her uncle's picture and mine were so small that for a moment I even hoped that, thanks to a generous quirk of fate, I had found out who I was and could return to the life that had been concealed by oblivion. It was not surprising that I invited her for coffee in the airport café and then bombarded her with questions.

As soon as she showed signs of concern I told her what had happened to me.

And then, Milly, *then* she said that she wished it had happened to her. And she invited me to join the Lotofaga Club, where for a few days I was an object of curiosity and amazement. And of course, as someone new, constantly invited to take part in their games of pleasure, although, as you yourself know, dear Milly, I'm no Adonis.

Margaretha Cornelia, God knows why, latched onto me in a special way and was jealous when I had sex with others. She gave as her reason the fact that she was only at the beginning of the path and that my state was something that, all being well, she would achieve in a year or two. For now she was still working at some company in order to earn money (including for others more advanced than her who had already abandoned the habit). But the hope that she would reach the stage where the thought of poverty ceased to frighten her helped her.

Lotofagas are educated members of the middle or even upper middle class – people who think it natural to exploit others and who are extremely shocked when they realise that they too are being exploited. For this reason conversations with them are at times inspiring, but never as intense as in an amateur debating society. The basic rule of coexistence is that we politely agree with the opinions of others, even if we think precisely the opposite. Perhaps the moment will come when I no longer want to leave here and I will succumb to complete oblivion. Perhaps I will make use of the credit limit on all the cards that Dr. Krauthaker has equipped me with and enable the Lotofagas to revel in pleasure, idleness and a blessed absence of memory for the next half century.

Perhaps. For every once in a while, but ever more frequently, I am forcefully struck by (in the eyes of Lotofagas) an extremely sinful desire to regress to my real identity (regardless of the fact that they claim every identity you have at a given moment is real – even the identity that you say is false).

For now, dear Milly, I don't know which way the scales will tilt. I don't even know if I'll keep writing to you. I don't even know whether you will bother to reply. If I'm honest, it seems best if we sever contact, since you will never tell me what I don't know, you will never help me get back to what I was before I became No-one. Nor will your husband. Be prepared for the day, perhaps soon, when I will disappear without trace.

And go to hell, both of you!

3.

I'm going to bed, Mr. or Mrs. kleinebilly@yahoo.com. I picked out your address from the mass circulating in virtual space like fragments of lost meteorites. Why? Because every so often, it's good to send an SOS into unknown parts of space. Perhaps someone will decipher the message, send a considered reply and reveal something important, perhaps a solution to the puzzle or at least a consoling greeting. For after all space, even the virtual kind, is infinite and because there is an infinite number of puzzles there is also an infinite number of solutions. Is that not so? Sooner or later the puzzle and its solution find themselves in orbit together.

That's how it should be.

But let's leave that for now. As I said, I'm going to bed. And every time I go to bed I am overcome by an endless feeling of gloom. And I wonder how I went to bed in the life that is no more (which is no more in every sense, but what matters is that it is no more in my memory). What we remember is still ours, isn't it, kleinebilly@yahoo.com? Whenever I go to bed I speculate where (and with whom) I went to bed before my head became a void. And what I did during the day. What annoyed me the most, what gave me most enjoyment? Did I have ambitions? What were they? Was I happy, content with life?

Speculating brings no answers, but does pass the time. Perhaps it may even train my imagination. In the absence of hard facts, perhaps my imagination will tell me which direction I should take in order to find my way home.

When I ask where my home might be, the most obvious continent seems to be Europe – at least as the place where I came crying into the world. Although in today's mobile world many people for a variety of reasons find themselves in different parts of the world – Americans in Europe, Europeans in Asia, Asians in South America – my feeling is that my childhood and growing up most likely took place in Europe.

Not because of my appearance, which is so general that I could be Swedish, English, Hungarian, Greek, even German, Russian or Czech, although perhaps none of these convincingly enough. But also not convincing enough for anything else. Some nationalities you recognise the moment you set eyes on a person. I'm not that lucky. If I was, then I could narrow down my search to one country. I am an assortment of indistinctive features, due to which I completely disappear in a crowd. This is handy if you are involved in some business where it is good if you are as unnoticeable as possible, but it is not so good if you are nursing the hope that someone will recognise you on the street, come up to you and say: "Hi, how are you?"

Truth be told, I cannot shake off the hope that it will happen. Fortuitous encounters occur a number of times in life; more often to some, less often to others. I'm sure that this has already happened to you, kleinebilly@yahoo.com. If I want to find out who I actually am, then someone must *recognise* me – there's no other option. That the convulsive grip of amnesia will suddenly loosen on its own seems increasingly unlikely.

When I think of the education that I must have acquired somewhere or other and the profession I practised, nothing suggests itself as more likely than anything else. The fact that I know my way around airports and travel the world as if it is an everyday matter does not prove that I did that in my previous life; these days, everyone who has been on holiday in a foreign country can do that. Similarly, most people today have no trouble with computers, mobile phones and credit cards. And surprisingly, I have not yet come across any object or product whose purpose baffled me: amnesia has clouded my memory only of events, names and people. The fact that I speak more than twenty languages and can convincingly copy any accent suggests that something catastrophic took place in my head.

31

But in spite of that, my ability to recognise basically all the coordinates of reality has remained untouched. The only thing missing is the feeling that what is happening is happening to me. Because I don't know who I am, it seems that I am going through life on emotional autopilot. Nothing touches me really deeply, let alone in a fateful way. Feelings are short-lived; the memory of new events, meetings and facts fade in five or six days.

If you ask me why I am travelling round the world and who is financing my travels, I can only cite reasons in which I do not entirely believe. I am serving someone, there's no doubt about that, and someone is making it possible. My doctor, Dr. Krauthaker, a world renowned expert on less well known forms of amnesia, assures me that I wander from place to place because the long route may in fact be the shortest way home to myself, to what I was. If I am here today and there tomorrow, I will sooner or later remember something, however small. Perhaps my memory will be torn from the claws of oblivion by a passing glance at the church where I attended mass as a child; perhaps I will hear the voice of someone who was once dear to me.

Dr. Krauthaker and his colleagues are convinced that it is best for me if I am constantly on the move, here today, there tomorrow. And that I try everything possible, embark on a range of different adventures. Sooner or later some event will align with something that I have stored in my inaccessible memory bank and that event will be the key that unlocks the door. It might be an event or it might be a person who reminds me of one of the key people in my lost life. Of my mother, father, brother, wife. Or perhaps a son or daughter.

From the start I had to send Dr. Krauthaker reports from the field, describe in detail what I was doing and what was happening to me. At first I did this out of enjoyment, then out of a sense of duty, then habit and then the fear that I would otherwise be left hanging in empty space, without contacts or support. That has now started to happen. Dr. Krauthaker no longer replies. Perhaps he's dead, perhaps he was murdered by his wife, perhaps they've both died in a road accident. Or they have committed a crime about which they are being interrogated somewhere. Perhaps they have decided that there is no longer any space for me in their life.

It's true that in my travels around the world I have collected quite a lot of yahoos and hotmails and holders of other email addresses for occasional or regular correspondence, but none has any connection with my secret. So I can only talk to them through a wall of pretence that I know who I am. That brings me no pleasure. Although I am (because I have to be) 90 per cent fabricated, I would like to be at least 10 per cent *me*.

Being myself is the only thing that can make life out of life. And so I cannot (and may not) settle down. I have become the embodiment of the journey, I was told by one of those I came across while carrying out my duties; I think it was a professor of literature at New York University. How and why I know him I can't recall, I would have to go through the correspondence in my inbox. Maybe I was asked to do an interview with him, since I finance my travels round the world through journalism.

Yes, through journalism, kleinebilly@yahoo.com. But not *only* journalism. I can hold onto the odd secret for now, can't I? I receive commissions from unknown clients at the address info@media.com and payment in accounts at an international bank under five different names. They pay me on time and generously (I've even managed to put something aside for a rainy day). I send my articles to different addresses and every so often I come across one of them in some newspaper or other, usually at an airport while waiting for my next flight. If the articles did not have the by-line of one of the five names supplied by those who watch over me, then I would have no idea that I was reading something I wrote myself, since after five days, as I've already mentioned, I forget everything I've done and experienced. Almost always what I am reading is something new, unknown.

It is evident from the lists that I have emailed to myself in order to have at least a virtual memory of my life that I have already written about everything imaginable. Including, I see, about the general popularity of Facebook and mobile phones in Africa, and how South Korea, almost unknown at the end of World War 2, is now the world's thirteenth largest economy. Also how in the 9th century the richest

33

and most powerful country in the world was China, under the Tang dynasty, which was based in Chang'an (now Xian), which had a million inhabitants (a figure that London achieved only a thousand years later!) The other great centre of civilisation was Baghdad, the capital of the Abbasid caliphate. I'm sure you've read *A Thousand and One Nights.*

And how did these two kingdoms become rich? Through trade, business.

Interesting, eh? It increasingly seems to me that *everything* is business and *only* business. A group of people do business with me, I do business with others, they with someone else, we all buy and sell – that's all that we do. And perhaps we even do business with ourselves, selling to ourselves ideas, convictions and assumptions that sooner or later we must pay a high price for.

Perhaps none of this interests you. Perhaps you are a hairdresser who reads only gossip magazines, or a retired miner who collected stamps and now some madman is sending long stories to an address that you used only for exchanging greetings with your grandchildren. And these stories are pretty hard to believe!

But it's not important, even if my writing causes you no more than anger, it at least helps me; because I don't know you, I can trust you. And that is more than you can imagine, for in spite of all the memory loss there is something I do remember: that I can trust no-one. That everyone has some kind of plan for me.

In spite of the unknown waters I sail in most of the time, there are certain things from the past – to which I have lost access – which are clear enough. It seems impossible that in my forgotten life I did not have the skills (or characteristics) that I have now. It is not impossible that in my previous life I was what I am now. Maybe I was employed at *The Times* in London, or at one of the less well known newspapers in a less well known country. Maybe I travelled the world under my own steam or in line with instructions and commissions. Maybe I was a freelancer and offered my articles to different publishers. If in my previous life I was, for example, a pilot, football player or computer programmer, then I wouldn't have these skills. Maybe I was even a writer; maybe I wrote ten or twenty novels.

Under what name? I once spent three days in a row searching the shelves of Barnes & Noble in New York and looking at the photographs of authors on book covers in the hope that I would find mine among them. Another time I surfed the internet, looking at the photographs of journalists, but without success.

With regard to my characteristics, I can confirm that I am primarily phlegmatic, although this is not my natural state, but rather a kind of stunned amazement at the hand that fate has dealt me, as well as at all that I experience on my travels. I quickly lose my temper, so it seems that my natural disposition is probably more choleric.

I was told that I would be able to get nearer my true *self* through habits: the food that I like, the way I dress, the music I listen to. But none of this has been any help. As far as food is concerned, I'm so easy going that I eat almost everything that is put in front me, I don't object to anything. As far as clothes go, I feel equally ill at ease in a track suit as I do in an elegant suit and tie, and I am most relaxed when wearing nothing at all (but of course, I cannot go about the world naked).

Music of all kinds gets on my nerves; I experience it as malicious, aggressive noise. The only exceptions are pop songs and compositions that express deep, moving sadness. These are very dear to me, since they nourish my chronic melancholy, which is the foundation for all my feelings, its presence increases the more happiness I see around me.

Longing for what has sunk into oblivion is undoubtedly one of the reasons for my chronic sadness. To a large extent it is caused (or deepened) by the nature of the world in which I have to function in the hope that I will find a way back to myself (and perhaps to a different world, or a different understanding of *this* world, since I assume there is only one world and we see it in the way that we are capable of seeing it).

Perhaps to you, Mr. or Mrs. kleinebilly@yahoo.com, the world is different from how it is to me. Perhaps it is more or even completely how I wish it to be in my moments of romantic inspiration: without violence, deceit, lies, poverty, ignorance, exploitation, hypocrisy and terrorism. I assume that you read newspapers and watch television, as do I, usually in airport lounges and hotel rooms. I have to say that what my colleagues report on often gives me the feeling that I don't want to report on these things myself. Nothing is more likely to give you indigestion than bad news for breakfast, don't you agree?

Unfortunately, I have no choice, for the gods on Olympus have sent me around the world in order to uncover crime and wrongdoing, and terrorise people with them as punishment for turning their backs on the gods. We are but flies, which the gods kill for their sport – I remember the words vaguely from something I heard or read. And because the gods are too lazy to punish us themselves, they have come up with a perfidious system that compels us to punish each other, every day anew and in a thousand different ways.

Perhaps the melancholy that permeates every last cell of my body is a normal reaction to the way the world reveals itself to me. Perhaps even a glimmer of optimism would be a sign of mental simplicity or even one of the first symptoms of schizophrenia. Perhaps "the power of positive thinking", which the new-age messengers from Olympus offer in thousands of different forms on bookshop shelves, is merely one of the ruses that the gods make use of in order to win our trust, so that they can punish us even more severely. Do you agree, kleine-billy@yahoo.com, that it is better to live *without* hope, than to cling to false hope and then lose it?

Since we're speaking of Olympus (and angry gods), I can't help mentioning love. But when I say love, do we have the same thing in mind? Only yesterday I read and noted (I have the list in front of me) that the Ancient Greeks had a number of words for love and that each one expressed a different emotion. (Maybe I'm telling you something you already know, but no harm done.) The word *agape* referred to altruism, compassion; *ludus* was the playful mutual affection between children or lovers for one night; *storge* was felt between comrades or fellow warriors who went through great hardship together; *pragma* was the deep and lasting affection between spouses; *mania* was obsession, while *eros* was purely and only sexual love, often linked with *mania*.

36

And it was because of manic sexual desire, which takes over a man's reason and reduces him to an almost bestial level of existence, that Plato and Aristotle, each in his own way, placed at the apex of emotional life mature friendship – the only thing that can guarantee *ataraxia*, spiritual calm. Only friendship can protect us from the obsessions of jealous Eros. However, all this is by way of introduction to something else I'd like to say. Regardless of the fact that most of the time I feel like an empty shell in search of suitable content, I do have emotional needs that seem to be part of this shell. I like being alone, but I don't want to be lonely.

Although I am.

I have a desperate need for the company of people who understand me, who believe me. Whom I can trust. Who give me the feeling that they think me deserving of their affection and that they enjoy my company, needing it no less that I need theirs. The sexual needs that I have (they actually belong to the impersonal body, the mass of instinctive drives that are not me), can be satisfied without difficulty: I can go somewhere and pay. I don't remember when I last did that – perhaps I never have. For sex is after all an encounter of two people, albeit careful, albeit lacking in trust, albeit engaged in coitus only because of opportunity or momentary lack of control. Even when there is no money involved, sex can be business.

When I consider what kind of love I experienced in the life which is now behind the doors of oblivion, I perceive as the most favourable option *pragma*, which succeeded *eros*, preserving its essence, but also adding to it. I do not picture love in my previous life as a series of affairs, but as a convivial relationship with a beautiful (above all, beautiful in spirit) person of the opposite sex, with whom I am inextricably linked by various projects, from the most elevated to the most banal, from children that we both enjoy, to planning our monthly budget together, to deciding that the dripping bathroom tap needs replacing. Two people together, two people against the world. Two romantic comrades with a shared goal: to preserve and strengthen what they have.

Boring?

Possibly, but this is precisely what I miss most. Perhaps because I had it before and the memory of familial happiness, although erased from my brain, remained somewhere in the cells of my bodily tissue. For memory is certainly not located only in the brain: some transplant patients report remembering events that they have never experienced, but they did happen to the donor, be it of kidney, heart or bone marrow. The memory of everything that is "me" is perhaps present in every cell of my organism, while the brain is merely a kind of control centre or condensed summary of the memory data that is stored in the cells. A kind of filter that lets through only what is essential for survival; all the rest is stored in the cells of the body, since the excess of memories and impressions would smother our consciousness.

In connection with this, kleinebilly@yahoo.com, I would like to tell you something very unusual. The messages in my inbox show that after fleeing from Singapore I flew to Amsterdam, not for any particular reason, but because that was the first place I was able to get a ticket to. I ended up (the details wouldn't be of interest) in the Lotofaga Club, where they worship the god of oblivion and indulge in every possible kind of drug in order to distance themselves as much as possible from their identities. I could have stayed among them and revelled in what they strive for, but which I was granted. I could have stayed there without feeling that I must move on or that by returning to myself I would achieve more than another encounter with the pale, useless, perhaps even unpleasant shadow of what I was.

Why didn't I stay?

Although in their circle life seemed uncomplicated, it lacked something essential. Excitement, uncertainty, danger! All that might cause us to wake in the middle of the night, bathed in sweat. I was surrounded by too much of what I am myself, but in the form of a mirror image. They were *fleeing* from responsibility for themselves and the world, whereas I am *looking for it*, as well as for self-awareness. Their arguments (à la Valéry) that the end of the world was nigh and it was best to leave it to its demise, as any attempt to save what is already lost would be a fruitless waste of time, did not convince me. Their dogmatic, at times aggressive, defence of the philosophy they had chosen as their *raison d'être* repulsed me, sometimes even frightened me.

So it was a little more than a month before I decided to escape from their island. When I think about it now, it seems that I was compelled to flee by one thing in particular: amidst all their mutual tolerance, kindness, affection, enjoyment without jealousy or blame, not once did I encounter an action which could be described as an act of love. Do you know what I mean, kleinebilly@yahoo.com? For a genuine act of love, you need conditions that are unfavourable to love.

It is strange but true that I found the evidence for this among Muslim terrorists on the Philippine island of Basilan. It began with the instructions I received from info@media.com, my invisible employer.

"Travel to Manila," I was ordered by my nameless boss, whose identity is a complete mystery to me. "From there, take the fastest route to the southern island of Basilan and in the capital Isabela City contact Manuel Pedrosa, the owner of a fishing tackle shop. He will take you to the interior of the island, where in the middle of the jungle are hiding the members of the Muslim rebel group Abu Sayyaf, supposedly connected with Al Qaeda. Do an interview with the leader of the group, it's all been arranged, ask him what they're fighting for and why they are using terrorist strategies. Try to get as many photos as possible and write a report, it can be in the form of an adventure diary. Don't worry about your safety: the group *wants* to clarify its goals."

4.

To be honest, I would rather avoid such assignments. I am not very fond of human scum who in order to achieve their goals kill innocent people, including children. But the assignment came just at the right time; it gave me a plausible reason for withdrawing from the Lotofaga Club, where the forced bonhomie and compulsory sensuality had begun to smother me. Besides which, I must comply with instructions from info@media.com in order to make a living. I'm not sure what I'd do if money stopped appearing in my account. My efforts to return to myself would come to a halt, I would be stuck without money or food in some God forsaken place, I'd have to look for work to pay for a roof over my head. For a man of fifty (plus some) that wouldn't be simple: more than likely, I'd end up as a beggar, since my savings would dwindle away in less than six months.

So, I took the first available plane to the Philippines, flew from Manila to Zamboanga on the southern island of Mindanao, hired a motorboat to get to Isabela City on the smaller, neighbouring island of Basilan, knocked on Manuel Pedrosa's door and introduced myself as Alfred Haidacher from Berlin (one of my five identities). I had been announced under that name and spoke English with an appropriate German accent.

Manuel Pedrosa, a fisherman and, judging by his flattened nose and battered face, possibly a boxer in his spare time, spoke Spanish. I pretended not to understand the language. I wanted to give myself an advantage: if my hosts spoke with each other in Spanish, they wouldn't know that I could understand them. Of course, Manuel Pedrosa also spoke Filipino, a language that is a slightly adapted form of Tagalog, one of the 176 languages spoken on the Philippine archipelago. I was surprised to find that I understood nothing and that my polyglotism was not complete. This filled me with the hope that the catastrophe that had befallen my brain was not as extensive as I had feared and that my multilingualism was not a supernatural phenomenon.

Manuel Pedrosa wasted no time; we went up river in a motorboat towards the centre of the island. After a good hour and a half we disembarked and made our way through the humid tropical jungle towards the hidden camp of the Abu Sayyaf rebel group.

It was a long and difficult walk, and I won't bother you with the details, kleinebilly@yahoo.com; if you enjoy adventure stories, you'll soon find one in the nearest library. The Muslim rebel camp was in a clearing in front of a rock face in which there was a large cave; the arched entrance to the underground was overgrown with thick greenery. Five pathetic bamboo huts stood in a semi-circle in front of the cave; in the middle, a blackened cauldron hung from two forked supports, in which the rebels evidently cooked their meals. I was scared that they would invite me for lunch and out of politeness I would not be able to decline.

Fortunately, nothing of the sort occurred. When we reached the clearing, we were surrounded by bearded, armed men with far from friendly expressions, who searched us, and took away the tape recorder I'd planned to use for interviews and my digital camera. They let me keep my wallet, the passport in the name of Alfred Haidacher, my wrist watch and the small tin of anti-mosquito spray. After an intervention from one of them, I also got my camera back. Then they pushed us towards one of the huts and we had to sit on the ground in front of it.

"What is happening?" I asked Manuel Pedrosa.

He replied that it was routine. He was calm: evidently he had been here many times before. He exchanged a few words in Tagalog with one of the dozen armed men standing in a semi-circle, watching us.

41

One went towards the cave entrance and disappeared inside. I reflected how wise I had been to leave the other four passports and credit cards in the hotel safe in Manila; if they had found them on me, their trust would have evaporated in a moment. And if I told them my story, they would probably shoot me on the spot as an obvious madman.

The men were of various ages: the youngest was barely twenty, the oldest could easily be ten years older than me. They were almost all dressed in black, wearing creased, tattered trousers and collarless shirts; maybe this was their uniform.

The next moment, there emerged from the cave an unusual apparition. A man, emaciated and almost two metres tall, which is unusual for a Filipino, with only one eye. I don't mean literally: he could see with his left eye, but his right eye was covered with a black patch, like a pirate. I later found out that his eye had been pierced by a bullet fired by a Philippine army sniper during a skirmish. The bullet had exited the back of his head, but it had not (can you imagine?) damaged his brain. At least not so that you would notice.

This apparition came towards me with the ease of a man accustomed to giving orders rather than receiving them. His left eye fastened onto me and beneath his moustache his mouth twisted into a mixture of a smile, curiosity, mistrust, welcome and threat. That was how I interpreted the expression in his one eye. My fear deepened. But it was unjustified, since the rebel leader ordered his soldiers to withdraw and spoke briefly in Tagalog to Manuel Pedrosa, who took his leave.

And then, the one-eyed man indicated that I should follow him.

When, at the end of a long underground corridor, we reached a large, vaulted space, a scene met my eyes that at first seemed unreal. Leaning against the rear wall was a row of upright mirrors, of almost equal size, some of them cracked, but overall intact enough to clearly reflect everything, even myself and the one-eyed commander. And not only us, as I quickly noticed. Facing the mirrors, tied to stakes driven into the ground, were eight people: two men, three women, two teenage girls and a boy of around six or seven. They were sitting

42

on the earth floor, with their legs out, their arms bent around the stakes they were leaning on and fastened with thick wire that was cutting into their flesh, almost enough to draw blood.

The two men were priests, two of the women nuns, and all four white. The other four were locals: judging by her uniform, the woman was a nurse, the girls were school girls or students, and the boy, who could be mixed race, was just old enough to be starting school in the autumn. All of them were dishevelled and dusty, and all just hanging onto life – I got the impression that they could barely open their eyes when they saw our reflection. Of course, the whole time they were also watching themselves slowly dying. They were terribly dehydrated. Cruellest of all was the fact that in front of each of them was a dish of water, which they could not reach.

What kind of man would come up with such torment? I looked at the one-eyed commander I was supposed to interview, but he did not return my gaze. Clearly, what I thought of this was not important to him; he had received me only so that he could use me to convey his message to the world. I began to feel slightly nauseous, especially when I saw in the mirrors the desperate way the eight pairs of eyes were looking at me. The one-eyed monster (I had not the slightest doubt that the stakes in front of the mirrors were his idea) ordered me in broken English to take as many photographs as possible.

I began taking pictures of the hostages from every possible angle – from the front, in the reflection from the back – and with them the one-eyed fundamentalist sadist, who was not aware that I was doing so. I thought it wonderful that I could not only inform the world media about his cruelty but also supply them with his photograph. When the digital camera was full and I could take more only by erasing some of them, my one-eye host commanded me imperiously: "Carry on!"

He was used to giving orders.

He did not know that he should never have uttered those words.

And how could he have known? It's a mystery to me, too. All I know is that it triggers in me an incomprehensible reaction that I later regret, but that I cannot resist. Quicker than I could consciously follow, I pulled from a hidden slit, protected by three transverse bands,

43

in the sole of my left shoe a knife like a scalpel and with it I stabbed the stunned abductor of innocent people, first in the heart, then in the neck and finally, in the stomach. And then, for good measure, in the right eye so that he would die completely blind.

That, kleinebilly@yahoo.com, *that* was an act of love.

Then with the same knife I cut through the prisoners' ropes, freeing them.

But had I really freed them? For now it seemed that I had no idea how to get past the gunmen in front of the cave. In a moment it became clear that every single one of us was condemned to death, preceded by torture. I hadn't acted particularly smartly. But for the reasons I've given, I couldn't act in any other way.

So, let's die, I said to myself and, knife in hand, I moved towards the mouth of the cave.

I felt someone's hand on my shoulder. It was one of the three male hostages; judging by the faded and creased dog collar, a Catholic priest. A Filipino. He pointed past the mirrors towards the dark part of the cave. I followed him and the others followed me. Through a stone arch, he turned into a quite low, narrow tunnel, where all of us who were more than 150 cm tall had to bend over. He turned and said in English, with a barely discernible accent: "They brought us through this tunnel."

I pushed him aside and took the lead. I didn't want to risk anything, especially the lives of the rescued hostages. Scrambling through the low, winding tunnel, where there was no light, demanded all my attention. Luckily, it did not take long: after three minutes, the exit appeared in front of us. I asked the priest to keep the others back, and crept forward. I assumed that the entrance to the tunnel was guarded. And it was; through the branches awkwardly camouflaging the entrance, I could see two armed terrorists with automatic weapons. But they did not look too dangerous; they were holding their guns in a very light grip, they were leaning against a tree trunk with their mouths open, both asleep. What else would they be doing in the tropical heat in the middle of the jungle, where they were, who knows why, guarding the entrance to the cave. It probably never occurred to them that the entrance could also be an exit.

Lack of imagination cost them their lives.

I'm not apologising, kleinebilly@yahoo.com. The lives of innocent people are worth more than those of fanatics who are willing to kill for their deluded aims. I wanted to help the hostages to safety as quickly as possible, get to the port, board the ferry, return to Mindanao, fly to Manila, collect my things and leave the Philippines. And above all, to avoid the army and police, for the story of how I had single-handedly rescued eight hostages from the hands of Abu Sayaff would quickly find itself on the front pages of the world's newspapers. And the question would arise: who had saved them?

Alfred Haidacher? Kevin Youngson? Sven Lindgren? Trevor Morris? Kostas Asimakopulos?

What would Dr. Krauthaker say to this?

Such an outcome would do me more harm than good, so I asked the hostages to find their own way home. After three days trudging through the jungle, I came across a large village, from where I was able to take the bus to Isabela City.

In the Philippines, those embarking on a ferry journey run a great risk that they will be swallowed by the sea rather than reaching their destination. I will offer some evidence, kleinebilly@yahoo.com.

The worst accident happened in 1987, when near the island of Minoro the ferry Dona Paz collided with a passing oil tanker. More than 4000 people died in what was the worst maritime accident in peacetime. A year later, near the island of Leyte, the ferry Don Marilyn went down with 250 souls. In December 1994, in the Bay of Manila, a Singapore cargo ship collided with the ferry Cebu City, causing 140 deaths. Four years later, south of Manila, the ferry Princes of the Orient went down with 150 people. In 2000 the cargo ship Anahanda sank near the southern island of Jolo; it overturned because there were too many people on board and 150 drowned. Four years later, not far from the Bay of Manila, Islamic extremists attacked Superferry 14, killing 116. In 2008 the ferry The Princess of the Stars overturned in a typhoon not far from the island of Sibuyan. Of the 850 on board, only 57 survived.

And so on. And so on.

Anyone who wants to achieve anything on this earth before departing it should probably steer well clear of Philippine ferries. Most of them cram in twice as many passengers as the vessel is designed for. Ferries find themselves in the midst of tropical storms so often that one would think they had deliberately sought them out.

But there are more than a thousand ships in the Philippines and they don't all sink. What's more, there is often no alternative mode of transport. Regardless of my reservations, in Isabela City I got on a ferry to get to Zamboanga City on the much larger neighbouring island of Mindanao, from where I could fly back to Manila.

I don't know why I chose the Estrella del Mar, for there were ferries sailing every half hour. That was the way it was – it was the first to sail. And because a ferry tips over in the Philippines on average once a year it did not seem possible that it would happen precisely on that day. Moreover, the weather did not look threatening and it was not the typhoon season.

I only began to feel anxious when there seemed no end to the number of passengers embarking. None of the ticket collectors at the gangplank stopped them, although they knew that the upper deck was getting increasingly crowded and we were already standing shoulder to shoulder – in the hot sun, without shelter. It was hard to believe that there were fewer people on the lower deck, which was covered. When the flow of people failed to stop I decided to make my way back to dry land and wait for the next ferry. But it was too late: the wall of people in front made it impossible to get through. And even if I had wanted to, I had nowhere to go for at that moment the gangplank was raised and the Estrella del Mar was ready to sail.

I have never before been in such crush of people (except perhaps on occasions that I don't remember). The thought that I would be forced to stand there for the ninety minutes of the crossing, breathing in the odour of strangers, filled me with rage; I almost cursed out loud. Especially when I realised that I hadn't brought with me even the smallest bottle of water. I guessed that dehydration would only be a matter of time. I felt like hitting myself on the head because I hadn't hired a fast motorboat for my return to Mindanao, as I had done on the way to Basilan. I'd envisaged being on a standard ferry with a bar, in which I could sit down, order a bite to eat, read the paper, use the toilet.

When we left the port and Isabela City slowly sank behind the horizon, the children on deck, squashed between the grown-ups' legs, began to whine, to cry and the little ones even to scream. My fellow passengers, locals, seemed to think this was nothing special and remained indifferently calm. Obviously they were used to worse things. Whoever survives, survives; whoever dies, has been taken by God.

Why can't I think like that, kleinebilly@yahoo.com?

I won't go into detail about the journey towards Zamboanga, which took more than an hour and a half; you have no doubt at some time travelled by ferry and wondered why at times, time passes too quickly, while at others, it hardly ever moves. With no shelter from the scorching sun, in the mass of passengers squashed so tightly together that it was difficult to breathe normally, I felt a number of times that I hadn't really survived the encounter with the one-eyed guerrilla and that what I was experiencing on the Estrella del Mar was a journey to hell, if not hell itself. I could not imagine worse torture than sailing for hours, squeezed among a sweating mass of people. It was a good job that the sea was unusually calm, actually suspiciously calm, the calm before the storm, although the sky was clear as far as the eye could see and there wasn't the slightest sign that the weather would take a turn for the worse.

But my sense of foreboding rarely turns out to be a consequence of the anxiety that we all carry inside us, so I was not surprised when the surface of the sea began to ripple; I knew that we were sailing into a powerful current between Basilan and Mindanao. It was more than five days since my arrival on Basilan by motorboat and so I couldn't remember how badly the current had tossed us around. And even if I did remember, a motorboat is less susceptible to disturbances on the surface of the water, so it is possible that the current did not strike me as anything special.

47

Now it was different. The white tipped waves were getting higher, colliding with each other and, of course, the sides of the ferry, which began to sway and at times to shudder, so that we passengers had to hold onto each other to retain our balance. During one such sudden jerk, a local woman, a head shorter than me, wearing a red hat, was thrown backwards and crashed into my chest with such force that it hurt.

How much more must it have hurt her! I instinctively grabbed hold of her to stop her falling. During the collision, her red hat had slipped from her head; I loosened my grip and reached for it with my left hand so that it wouldn't fall onto the dirty floor. At the same moment, she also reached for it with her left hand.

She was quicker, my hand landed on hers. Actually, it didn't so much land as grabbed hers, since I was trying to catch her hat. The feeling did not last long as I withdrew my hand immediately. But the unexpected contact with her hot, clammy hand excited me, as you can imagine, kleinebilly@yahoo.com. Have you ever received an electric shock? Not a fatal one, but strong enough to feel it in every tissue of your body?

That is roughly how I felt. My body was flooded with lust. And when she turned her black-haired head and thanked me with a grateful, albeit slightly uncomfortable smile, I saw that I was close to (so close that the passengers behind me had pushed me a number of times into her pert backside) a Filipino woman – not one of the average looking ones who were squashed on deck together with their fathers, grandfathers, husbands and children – but a beauty who had not yet reached the age of twenty. My excitement, believe it or not, led to a spontaneous erection.

"Muchas gracias," she breathed. "De nada," I replied, shaping my mouth into what was supposed to be an encouraging smile, but was probably more like a grin. Then she turned back round, put the red hat back on her head and paid me no more attention. But a spontaneous erection, as you possibly know, is an awkward thing. It doesn't subside just like that, but stubbornly persists in the unconscious hope that part of the female anatomy will leap to its assistance – a mouth, a vagina or at least a hand. Unexpectedly and against my will, I found myself in a situation that I did not like one bit.

(Although at the same time, hand on heart, I liked it very much!)

The waves were ever higher, the ship was rising and sinking with increasing violence, I couldn't move even an inch, so it was inevitable that my hard on, more persistent than ever, would every now and then press against her body, most often against her left buttock, since she was standing slightly to my right. She said nothing, she did not turn around, she knew all too well that she could not move anywhere. I thought that she must be feeling incredibly embarrassed. And she probably was, until the sea began to bump, crash and slam with such force against the sides of our vessel – overloaded as it was by a factor of three – that the passengers began to panic. The possibility that the ship would tip over no longer seemed so far-fetched.

This clearly had an influence on the beauty in front of me. More or less automatically, it seemed, and in spite of a rational decision not to do so, she reached behind her with her hand, felt around with her fingers and, when she found what she was looking for, gave my erect penis such a strong squeeze that it almost hurt.

And how happy I would have been if it had!

Then she withdrew her hand; not so much because she had realised that she had done something inappropriate, but because, perhaps against her will, her hand had been affected by the ship jumping when it was hit by a high wave. I expected her hand to return, but it didn't. And how could it; even its young owner had probably become aware in shock that we were surrounded by Filipino Christians, who are known for their religious ardour, and that among them there must have been quite a few Muslims, since Mindanao is a largely Muslim island. From them, she could expect nothing less than a public stoning for her sin.

"Sorry," she said barely audibly, but loud enough for me to here; and this time she spoke English, probably so that as few people as possible in our immediate vicinity would understand if they happened to hear.

I bent over and whispered in her ear: "My pleasure."

She said nothing, but she did something unexpected: she deliberately pressed herself against my hard on, which still had not subsided. This time, too, it seemed she was doing it against her will. The fear that the ferry may overturn and that she may die before she had really started to live, had evidently released in her young body all her natural hormones.

But her fear, it turned out, was superfluous: the dangerous current between the islands was already behind us and the surface of the water was already so smooth that you could roll a ball across it. And half a kilometre away, we could already see the port. We all breathed a sigh of relief. We shall land, life shall go on. We shall still experience (as well as duties) something pleasant.

Then from the opposite side of the upper deck we suddenly heard terrified shouts and expressions of distress, as well as calls for help in Tagalog, Spanish and English. Our half of the deck was flooded with anxiety, which was quickly transformed into a physical crush.

"Fire!" we heard, "Fiego!", "Sunog!"

In a moment it was clear to us all that fire had broken out on the other side and that the threatened passengers wanted to move to our side as quickly as possible. But there wasn't even enough room for a nineteen-year-old girl's red hat to fall to the floor. The pressure was so bad that it transformed us into a mass of flesh and bone squashed against the railing, which began to buckle and break under the weight of bodies. I instinctively knew that, due to the sudden transfer of weight to one side, the ferry would tip over and all of those who did not jump off in time would be trapped underneath – drowned, dead, liberated from this world for ever.

The girl with the red hat turned to me and, almost accusingly but at the same time in a warm pleading voice, as if she was clinging to her father, said in English: "I'm going to die!"

"No, you won't!" I said. "What's your name?"

"Maria Mindoro," she whispered. "My father is very rich!"

This was not of much help to us at that moment. I grabbed her hand (the one that she had used earlier to grab something of mine) and pulled her after me, while I tried to elbow my way towards the rail from which the more intelligent passengers were already jumping.

"Jump!" I told her. "Quickly, now!"

"I can't swim!" she yelled, tears running down her cheeks.

"I won't let go of you!" I assured her.

I picked her up, as light as a feather, and threw her into the sea. It took me a long time to forget how desperately she waved her arms in order to find something to hold onto. I immediately hurled myself over the railing and, due to my greater weight and consequently greater speed, I splashed into the water almost at the same time as her, certainly in time to put my hands under her arms and lift her head above the surface.

I immediately began to drag her away, using my left arm to push our bodies away from the frightening mass that was the Estrella del Mar, from which more and more terrified people were jumping, some hand-in-hand with their children, others clutching luggage as if in this mortal danger it was necessary to save their dirty laundry, boxes of chocolates for granny, and things which they could easily replace at the nearest market. I saw that the Estrella del Mar was tilting ever more alarmingly and that at any moment it would tip over on top of us. Its movement also revealed the scene on the other side of the deck, where the passengers were desperately trying to escape the flames; they were shoving and striking each other without mercy in order to gain an advantage for themselves.

Less than a minute later, the ferry finally tipped over, drowning beneath it hundreds of passengers. It also caused a series of waves which gradually carried Maria Mindoro and myself (as well as quite a few other passengers who had jumped in time) further away than I would have managed by tirelessly waving my left arm. (With my right, I was still holding Maria Mindoro, who had lost consciousness, above the water.)

We were picked up by one of the first boats that rushed to the rescue from the port.

5.

Dear Dr. Krauthaker, unfortunately, the interview with the terrorists turned out differently than expected and so I am sending you a report on the subsequent events in the Philippines.

As the rescuer of the delightful Maria, Mr. Mindoro installed me on the third floor of his villa, or rather mansion, as the house was truly on a grand scale, in a comfortable, spacious room with a view of the sea and the sandy beach a hundred metres below. I was immensely grateful to him because the whole adventure – the sinking, the rescue, the fear of death that I had never felt so strongly – had totally drained me. I felt as if I needed a hundred years' rest.

Although certain things in the villa were rather confusing, due to my tiredness (and doubtless gratitude), I did not pay them much attention. It seemed odd that Mr. Mindoro and his daughter were living in such a spacious house alone – actually, with an armed guard in front of the main entrance, a gardener, a driver, two cooks and three serving maids, a cleaner and a room maid, a caretaker who knew how to repair everything from a lock to a hundred-year-old camera, and a number of others with unclear duties who sometimes hung around, but with no other family member, no wife or mother, no children or brothers or sisters – just father and daughter, a respectable and brilliantly knowledgeable gentleman and his quiet, extremely quiet young daughter who, in fear that I would do her an injustice, I would not want to describe in any more detail but by saying that it would be hard to find any man who would not pause on catching sight of her (and whose heart would probably also miss a beat).

Since I was a guest in the home of one of the politest people that I had met since my accident in Bali (and possibly in my inaccessible previous life), to begin with I didn't wish to show excessive curiosity. After all, even Mr. Mindoro did not expect, let alone demand, answers to questions such as who I was, what I was doing, why I was on the ferry that sank, where I was heading, whether I was in any hurry or not. And, above all, why I had risked my life for a girl that was a complete stranger, albeit stunningly beautiful, but nevertheless – how many people today would risk their life for someone else?

It's good that he didn't ask me this and similar questions, for I could only have answered them with evasion, which Mr. Mindoro might have perceived as impoliteness. And so the first three days we avoided personal questions and during meals or cocktails by the pool in the middle of the lush tropical garden we talked primarily about the weather, the state of the world that was heading relentlessly for perdition, although we didn't know whether this was according to God's plan or the Devil's, and about Christianity, most particularly Catholicism which, it rapidly emerged, was the most important thing in Mr. Mindoro's life. But we spoke about all of these things in a non-committal way; it was more or less a chance conversation in which we jumped from one topic to another, following associations, without ever trying to get to the bottom of anything.

It was actually only Mr. Mindoro and I who talked. Although Maria was present at almost all of our conversations she was largely silent: perhaps she slipped in a word here and there that was unconnected with the current topic.

This wouldn't have bothered me if she had not stared at me the whole time (and when I say the whole time, I mean it literally) with a deeply solemn expression. At first I thought she was doing this out of gratitude because I had saved her from a certain death and she could think of no other way to thank me. But when her staring went on and on, not just the first, second and third day but also the fourth,

I began to think there must be something wrong with her. And why had she decided to travel on a crowded ferry, when she could easily have hired a fast comfortable motorboat? Had she run out of money? Whatever the reason, it was odd.

It did not escape my attention that Mr. Mindoro noticed my surprise, but he accepted it as something quite normal. He seemed to feel no need to explain anything. And since no explanation was forthcoming, I began to speculate as to the reason for Maria's persistently solemn gaze, which was literally fastened on to me.

Gratitude for saving her life? But that is usually expressed differently, don't you agree, Dr. Krauthaker? Infatuation, because she was not capable of showing ordinary gratitude? Highly unlikely. In the Middle Ages, half a million dashing knights would have slaughtered each other to win the favours of Maria Mindoro, while I am a corpulent middle-aged man of average appearance, almost invisible, except when I am seized by anger and begin to run amok, which I can't afford to do too often. It is true that beautiful women fall hopelessly in love with talented artists of average (and even below average) appearance, but I am far from being an artist and even less talented (more than anything, I am the product of *your* talent, Dr. Frankenstein!)

It was quite clear that there was another reason. In spite of my curiosity, I didn't want to probe Maria's secrets, since in view of her father's exceptional hospitality that would be impolite. Nor did I want to bother him with questions which he might perceive to be aggressive or even fishing for gratitude. I had no choice but to wait for him to say something himself, to give me a hint, to rescue me from my increasing discomfort which, it was not difficult to see, had not gone unnoticed by him.

Of course, I could have somewhat constrained my politeness (which had never been so over the top) and ask him in a friendly way where his wife was, whether he had any other children, how he had become so prosperous, what Maria did (apart from ceaselessly staring at me in a solemn fashion as if I had just landed from Mars), what kind of business he had been in (I assumed, given his age, that he was retired), what he had studied and similar banal things that people exchange information about when they first meet.

But the taciturnity of father and daughter was too great for me to succumb to curiosity and perhaps offend them, so I persisted with the non-committal conversations instigated and led by the grey-haired Mr. Mindoro. A few times, I was tempted to strike up a conversation with one of the maids, who gave me a friendly smile every time we met. But whenever the opportunity arose, I was overcome by a feeling that this would be devious. So I abandoned the idea. I knew that in a few days I would be moving on; he who is travelling home cannot rest.

If anyone had told me that all the mystery would eventually be unravelled by a priest, I would not have believed him. What can priests do these days other than ritually bless the gullible? He was not there on the first day, nor on the second, he was expected on the third, and on the fourth he joined us for lunch on the terrace beside the pool. Padre Romero, Mr. Mindoro called him and it seemed that they knew each other well, that they were friends.

That he was a priest I deduced from his collar and from the word padre, with which Mr. Mindoro addressed him. Judging only by his appearance I would have placed him in a completely different profession, perhaps a second-rate actor, since he spoke with a sweet, mellifluous voice – too sweet – suitable for television ads (and maybe for the pulpit, how would I know, for since the accident on Bali, I had not crossed the threshold of a single church).

Moreover, Padre Romero radiated the kind of enthusiasm characteristic of used car salesmen; he tried the whole time to be persuasive, while at the same time striving to ensure that no-one noticed his efforts. In so doing, he of course (how could he not) betrayed the very thing that he was trying to conceal. One way or another, I did not include Father Romero among those whom I would trust without serious reservations. Although I did allow for the possibility that the impression was a false one.

And so the conversation could not be a relaxed one, everything remained within the borders of formal politeness and small talk, during which no-one dared express a serious personal opinion about

55

anything. Although a number of times I was on the verge of opening up the theme of paedophile scandals in the Catholic Church, at the last minute I always bit my tongue. Besides which, throughout lunch, which lasted a good two hours (and which was, perhaps because of Father Romero, even more sumptuous and delicious than the first three days), Maria Mindoro stared at me with the same religious fervour as she had since my arrival – perhaps even *more* ardently. Even though I tried to give the impression that I wasn't noticing this, it did hamper my efforts to inject some levity into the conversation.

And so I soon realised that, with the exception of Maria, who was staring at me openly and without embarrassment or fear of this being noticed, everyone at the table was trying to create an impression that would convince the others that there was no hidden agenda behind their words.

All this formality began to tire me and I felt a desire to be elsewhere. At the same time, I sensed that the hidden agenda (which I had increasingly few doubts existed) would in one way or another come to the surface in the end.

And it did. Straight after dessert and coffee.

First, Padre Romero praised me for my extremely Christian and selfless act, and for my great courage in risking my life for a complete stranger, and how it had clearly been God's will that Maria and I should find ourselves on the same ferry on the day of the catastrophe, for such things could not be mere coincidence; it is always God who decides whether we are to remain on Earth or to join him.

I could find no answer to this that would not be at least implicitly polemical, so I remained silent. Padre Romero gave me an opportunity to respond, perhaps after reflection, but when I showed no sign of doing so, he carried on. How happy Mr. Mindoro and his daughter were that I was a guest in their house, he said. And how they both wished I would stay as long as possible. And how they hoped (and he with them) that my obligations did not compel me to leave too soon.

After these words, I could not, of course, remain silent. I decided not to beat about the bush, but to be as frank as I could at that moment. Perhaps somewhat more: to be completely frank. Sadly, I said, my free time was not unlimited and I had extended it beyond the permitted level already. The next day, or at the latest the day after, I would have to move on. But I was grateful for the opportunity to rest for a few days and forget about everything that awaited me.

The response was silence. Mr. Mindoro sighed and bowed his head; Padre Romero shuffled restlessly on his chair and stared at a point above my head; Maria (I couldn't resist a glance in her direction) frowned and looked down at her lap. Evidently no-one was satisfied with my predicted departure.

But they can't have expected me to remain as their guest for a month or even a whole year? I had nothing to complain about, quite the opposite, but five text messages demanding that I get in touch and report what had happened in the rebel camp was a clear enough reminder that I served someone, that I had obligations to those who regularly transferred money to me, not only for day to day living, but also for the odd luxury.

Besides which, I was on my way to "myself" and comfortable lazing around in Mr. Mindoro's luxurious villa would be more of a halt on this path than a step forward. Particularly because in relation to his daughter I began to feel dishonourable intentions that Maria, as young as she was and a devout Catholic, could not satisfy, regardless of her devout staring which I felt, God knows why, as more of a threat than a promise.

Well, I added to break the silence, I could stay an extra day or so, and thank you for the hospitality. But what I had done (and done more reflexively than premeditatedly) in no way committed Mr. Mindoro to offer me limitless privileges. I was afraid that I had already begun to abuse his gratitude - afer all, I had been a guest in his house for four days!

Mr. Mindoro was first to respond. He said that he had to be honest and tell me that it wasn't just a matter of hospitality, which was of course of prime importance; there was something else, perhaps more important. Only Padre Romero could explain in more detail, since the priest was involved in the matter, but not as emotionally as he himself was.

Then Padre Romero carefully wiped his lips with a silk serviette, crossed himself, got to his feet and asked me if I had visited the grave of Maria's mother, who was buried among the palms on the rise above the house, beside the chapel that Mr. Mindoro had had built after her death.

No, I said, I haven't. I didn't even know that Maria's mother was buried close by.

I looked at Maria and saw that tears were running down her cheeks. She suddenly jumped up with such violence that her chair turned over, banging on the paved ground. She rushed towards the door to the house as if pursued by a monster or even Lucifer. Even though the door was open she slammed it behind her with such force that it almost came off its hinges. Mr. Mindoro bowed his head and said nothing (although he could not conceal he was extremely upset).

Padre Romero gestured for me to follow him.

He led me behind the house and along a winding path through the plantation of coconut palms on the rise behind it. The path was longer than I'd expected, but eventually we stopped before a neat little chapel with orange plaster walls and a slightly kitsch statue of the Virgin Mary in an arched alcove. When I looked closer at the statue I flinched slightly; the face of the Virgin was so reminiscent of Maria Mindoro that it was clear the sculptor had used her as a model. Maria had also been her mother's name; on the gravestone beside the chapel was carved: Maria Mindoro, 1970 –2010, rest in peace. The gravestone also bore, as was usual here, a photograph of the deceased. A photograph of the daughter, I thought at first, so great was the similarity between them.

Padre Romero knelt before the grave, not before the chapel, crossed himself and in a singsong voice recited a prayer in Spanish. I stood like a statue beside him and waited for him to finish. He got to his feet and looked at me without any sign he was offended that I hadn't joined him. Even if I had known how and wanted to, I would not have been able for the similarity between daughter and mother had stunned me too much. "Yes," said Padre Romero. "It's hard to say which one is buried here."

Dear Dr. Krauthaker, I continue where I left off (in between, there was a power cut and then I could not get an internet connection on my iPad, the signal was too weak, perhaps because of the remote location). As a matter of fact, I am surprised that it is possible at all to connect to the internet in a house which is at least ten kilometres from the nearest coastal village, and on the Philippines. My zigzag path "home" keeps surprising me; the world is not what I had imagined.

What I had imagined when? In my inaccessible life?

I don't know, Mr. Krauthaker. I don't know where the things I carry in my memory come from; some of them are certainly from before, some of them have been stored since you sent me on my journey "home". One way or another, in this report I am passing on things that will at the very least stun you; in the worst case, you will conclude that I have succumbed to psychosis and am experiencing hallucinations.

None of that, Dr. Krauthaker. What I state here is the honest truth. Unusual, for sure, but haven't scientists recently discovered something even more unusual, that not only is the universe infinite, but that there are an infinite number of universes? When we stood before the grave of Maria Mindoro (Maria's mother) as well as before the chapel devoted to the Virgin Mary (with a statue of Jesus' mother which was the exact likeness of the girl I had saved from the sea), Padre Romero asked me whether I had ever heard of someone being possessed by a demon. Had I ever heard of exorcism?

I replied that I knew roughly what he was talking about. "Well," he said, "then listen to Maria's story. Not the one who is buried here, but the one you rescued from the sea."

Your scientific mind, Dr. Krauthaker, will not allow you to believe what he told me. Nor did I, at least not at first.

He told me that three years earlier Maria Mindoro had been possessed by a demon. And he, with God's blessing and according to his will, had been trying for the last two years to exorcise it. Three years ago Maria Mindoro, a mild and exemplary girl raised in the spirit of Christ, had begun to disturb those close to her with profane and blasphemous statements. Then she had begun to yell obscenities during mass in his church, to the embarrassment of those present and to the shame of her father and mother, who was then still alive. Once, during mass, she had raised her skirt and started to pant as if approaching sexual climax. Could I imagine how her father and mother had felt?

Then at home, in the middle of lunch, she had begun to vomit an enormous quantity of nails. And the next day an even larger quantity of pins, which fell from her mouth onto the plate so quickly that in thirty seconds they outnumbered the uneaten rice. And the next day blood. Then chicken feathers. And then stones, coins, coal, dog excrement, pork and balls of cotton. While doing this she had growled and barked like an animal. At times she behaved as if she was experiencing an epileptic attack; twice she had risen from the ground and floated in the air for two minutes. Her eyes had protruded, she was paralysed as if turned to stone; four men had been unable to move her limbs. Her stomach had spontaneously bulged and remained like that for so long they all thought she must be pregnant.

She was. With a demon.

Mr. Mindoro only called for Father Romero's help when one day Maria vomited up a live eel. She had immediately taken it to the cook and ordered her to grill it for supper, when before the eyes of her father and mother she had eaten it with enjoyment. By then things had gone so far that not even Padre Romero, an experienced exorcist in his previous parish, could do no more than try to keep up with them. But events were becoming ever more bizarre. Maria began to speak in languages she had never learned. She recited verses from the Aeneid in Latin, she cited Homer in Greek and the Ramayana in Sanskrit. She survived a month without a scrap of food or a drop of water. She threatened her mother with a kitchen knife, her father with a hammer.

You are the Devil, she said to him. You are the Devil's wife, she said to her mother.

And how had Padre Romero gone about his task?

He said that in the Philippines possession was quite a common phenomenon, as it was in all countries where Catholicism prevailed. In his previous parish he had gathered quite a bit of experience, but not enough to cope with the demon possessing Maria Mindoro. There, over a period of ten years he had successfully dealt with two cases. The first was a young man who was obsessed with masturbation, bestiality and unsuccessful attempts to get his own sex organ into his mouth. In so doing he had damaged his vertebrae, but this had not stopped him. No animal in the vicinity was safe from him. The evil that had possessed him forced him to do the most disgusting things before the eyes of as many people as possible. Traditional methods of exorcism – such as threatening with a crucifix, slaps, jumping on his chest, blows with a stick – had no effect. In the end Father Romero had managed to shove his fist through the possessed one's mouth and down his throat to his stomach, forcing the demon to flee through his anus.

The other difficult case was a fifteen-year-old girl who over a period of three months vomited up four hundred litres of blood – not only in the house of the grandfather and grandmother who since the death of her parents looked after her, but also in the crowded market place and in church during mass, where she always spun round so that the blood splashed as many worshippers as possible, preferably men, and even the statue of Jesus on the altar. The faithful in the parish demanded that he do whatever he could think of to save the girl from the demon that had possessed her.

And he really did employ about a hundred different methods. He was dogged, he really laboured, on a few occasions he became so exhausted that he had to cancel mass. All without success. He thought the girl's condition was worsening. And then he decided to do something that God would probably send him to hell for, as a guest of the demon that he succeeded in driving out, but he had no other choice. He bribed two vagrants to kidnap the girl, take her to the jungle and rape her until she stopped vomiting blood. This they did. And she stopped. When she returned to her grandparents she was the most placid and amiable fifteen-year-old you could possibly imagine. Since then she had not missed a single mass, she had joined the church choir, liked helping others and had become a real angel.

Of course, he never told his congregation how he freed her from the demon because they would certainly have lynched him. They would not have understood the principle of fighting fire with fire and that sometimes a lesser evil may defeat a greater one. Let God be the judge of what he had done with the best of intentions. And if he should have to pay a price after death, he would pay it without feeling badly done by. The girl was now happily married with two children and he had heard that the family never missed a church event. In spite of this, he had long suffered from a guilty conscience; he had felt increasingly bad about it and in the end he had to request relocation to another parish. And here Maria Mindoro was the first and so far only case of possession.

And also the first that he could not cure.

Before I had seen Father Romero as a phoney priest, saintly without true faith, but now I thought there was a madman standing beside me. Or at least someone who belonged more in a psychiatric institution than the pulpit of a Catholic church at the start of the 21st century.

"I know that it all sounds almost incredible," said Father Romero. "But I assure you that I have not fabricated even the slightest detail. After all, I am the servant of God. And I have told you all this only because I want to ask you, in the name of Mr. Mindoro, for a favour."

I replied that any favour I did for Mr. Mindoro would be a personal thing between him and me, and that I didn't need an intermediary. And with regard to the cases he had described, I had my own views, which were regrettably considerably different from his. Since I was not particularly well up on this kind of thing, I could not contradict him with scientific arguments, which one way or another I had never placed much trust in. But in spite of that, I could say that all his examples were "medieval" and that it was almost impossible to believe that nowadays, at a time when reason had banished superstition or credulity, at least among the educated, so many such phenomena could occur. Certainly not as many as in the case of Maria Mindoro.

Surely these days such cases were the domain of psychiatry which, as far as I knew, even the Church itself now recommended. And if something like this or something similar happened to someone it was necessary to divert the victim of possession to the nearest suitable institution, where in the majority of cases they would be diagnosed as suffering from hallucinations.

I couldn't even imagine the polite, quiet and well brought up Maria Mindoro being capable of vomiting nails, chicken feathers and dog excrement, let alone a live eel, which she would then want to eat grilled. I didn't want to offend him, but why was he trying to convince me of something that today even a five-year-old child would doubt?

Padre Romero did not take offence; on the contrary, it was what he had expected and so he did not hesitate with his reply. And that reply, I must admit, surprised me greatly.

He said that I probably didn't know this, but it was a proven fact that that in Italy, the seat of the Catholic faith, in spite of all the progress in science and psychiatry, a million people a year still visited exorcists and this seemed to them quite normal, just like a visit to the dentist. Among Protestants there were few cases of possession, but there were also few in the distant past, while Muslims are not even familiar with such cases. Why was the Devil, who of course they knew as Satan, so fond of Catholics? Perhaps because of their spiritual superiority? Which for the demon that takes them over means a greater prize? Or because of lack of faith, due to which they were less well protected from devilish assaults?

Think of it, Dr. Krauthaker! That was what Padre Romero said. Then he said a number of other things which indicated, if not proved, that I was not dealing with a madman. He said that in Hebrew Satan means "opponent" or "prosecutor" and that the Bible often sees him as a tool in the hands of an angry God. Satan is a mirror image of Jehovah as judge and patriarch, the divine prima donna who needs to be placated with gifts, while Jesus is God as lover, comrade and advocate before the court.

Why, then, did some prefer the image of an angry God, threatening punishment?

Because some people, without knowing it, were masochists. And all masochists carry inside themselves, built into their psyche, a feeling of guilt for something that they have supposedly done, though they know not what it is. The image of God who will punish them and save them from this feeling of guilt is more attractive than that of the God who forgives them everything from the start because he is also of flesh and blood. Possession is an extreme expression of a feeling of guilt and anxiety, the point at which the masochist, just like the neurotic, expresses his guilt and at the same time disowns it. If guilt is rooted in the body, then obviously it comes from a foreign force that has moved there and so the possessed one is convinced that he is not guilty of the crime for which he feels guilt. Perhaps possession is an autoimmune disease.

I was struck by the thought that perhaps I was victim of the Devil or perhaps his emissary, who had seized my brain and cut off access to my memories of life before the accident on Bali. Perhaps he had pushed the end of the surfboard that the clumsy learner had crashed into my head. And perhaps he was not clumsy: perhaps Satan himself had been standing on the surfboard and bumped into me deliberately. Perhaps I had provoked him with some action or other in my previous life.

But that was only a fleeting thought, Mr. Krauthaker. Don't imagine that your patient has suddenly succumbed to superstitious delusions. Although with his next words Padre Romero surprised me even more.

He said that he knew the idea of possession was in contradiction with the modern concept of personal autonomy. For it allowed the possibility that at a certain level we did not belong to ourselves. The ownership of myself, my past, let alone my fate, was not the same as ownership of a house or car. Even the most scientific psychiatrists and psychologists acknowledge that there are destructive forces in our subconscious that we cannot successfully control. And which can sometimes turn against us for unknown reasons.

On a certain level, Dr. Krauthaker, people do not belong to themselves. When I heard that I could hardly stop myself hugging Father Romero and confessing to him.

"I, Padre Romero," I wanted to shout, "*I* do not belong to myself!"

For the fact is, Dr. Krauthaker, I belong to you.

You are the devil who has possessed me and usurped my goals, my motives, directing me on a path that suits you and not me. It's true that I don't vomit up nails or dog excrement, but I carry out assignments in every corner of the world that all but the most heart-less scumbags alive would baulk at. And I carry them out because you have succeeded in convincing me that this is the only way back to the life I lost and the only chance that I might sooner or later start belonging to myself again.

Of course, I could rebel and stop doing what I am doing. I could face up to the fact that I will remain to the end of my days just a fragment of a man, just the sum of the experiences of the last few years. I could disappear anywhere in the world and what would you be able to do? Nothing. Of course, I would stop receiving money in my bank account and that money (I admit) is enough for a pretty comfortable life in hotels around the world. But I'm sure I would find work, even without references. Badly paid, I'm sure, but I'd survive.

Why don't I do that?

Evidently I've sold my soul to you, Dr. Krauthaker. I serve you blindly in the belief that your prediction (given without any guarantee, it's true, but with optimism) will eventually come true. Why I am doing this is a question that recently bothers me more and more. After all, what have I lost apart from my memory of a life which is one way or another no more? And which I could not relive? And which may be such that to the present, temporary "me" it would be a source of shame and a burden?

Why can't I terminate our agreement? Especially since you no longer reply to me. As if you had attached me to you! There's no particular need to mention that I hate you. From the bottom of my heart. Nor is there the slightest doubt that I need you. I keep looking for possible parallels for our relationship in history, in world literature, but I can't find one. Our relationship, Dr. Krauthaker, is unique. Have you already written an article about it, published it in a scientific journal? Perhaps you have already lectured on my (our) case around the world, without notifying me. After all, why should you let me know?

One way or another, beside the grave of Maria's mother Padre Romero confided some pretty unusual things. He assured me that

65

since my arrival the manifestations of Maria Mindoro's possession by a demon had ceased and perhaps even vanished forever. It was possible that my presence had cured her. Since I came to Villa Kirka the girl had given not the slightest indication that anything was wrong with her. Her ardent stare was no doubt embarrassing for me, but perhaps it was merely her way of showing gratitude, for she certainly knew that my presence had rescued her from the Devil's claws.

Mr. Mindoro, who even in his wildest dreams did not imagine anything like this could happen, was bursting with gratitude. At the same time he was afraid (and how could he not be?) that after my departure things would return to their former state and that a demon would once again occupy Maria Mindoro's stunning body. And certainly also her soul, which had since early childhood been mild, kind and God-fearing, albeit, considering her parents great success, unusually simple, although in this regard, too, within the parameters of what was normal.

In other words, Padre Romero continued, Mr. Mindoro was asking me – and not just asking, but *begging on his knees,* to extend my stay at Villa Kirka. If I had obligations that were not primarily connected with people but more with earning a living, he was prepared to pay me an allowance for an unlimited period. And in addition to the allowance, the level of which I could propose myself, a financial reward that would not disappoint me. Mr. Mindoro was extremely wealthy and so even a large amount would not leave an appreciable hole in his personal finances.

The ideal outcome, of course, would be if I fell in love with Maria, proposed to her, married her, stayed with her to the end of my life, had children with her, created a family. In this case, Mr. Mindoro was prepared to sign over to the two of us ninety per cent of his assets. He was aware, Padre Romero emphasised, that this may not be possible, for it was not excluded that I had a family elsewhere. It would seem impolite to ask about this. But even if this were the case he was prepared, if my family did not mean everything in the world to me, to pay for the upkeep of my spouse and children twice as much as I was capable of providing, even if I was in reality richer than him.

That my presence or physical proximity, or perhaps the selfless gesture of saving her from the waves in which, as a non-swimmer, she would certainly have drowned, had freed Maria from her demonic possession, it was for him the central event in his rich, colourful and in every way exemplary life. And so for him no sacrifice was too great to enable his daughter to live a normal and happy life.

What would you have done in my place, Dr. Krauthaker?

I could have avoided you forever; I could have stayed in this remote but endlessly beautiful spot, married Maria (a fifty or older man with a nineteen-year-old girl, but why not, I would not have been the first or the last). I could have forgotten about the inaccessible past (can you guarantee that I will ever make contact with it?); I could have opted for a peaceful, boring life, in the luxury of a comfortable mansion in the Philippines, for the kind of family life that I had perhaps never had. I could have made use of one of the five forged identities you furnished me with and become married. I could have said: "My home is here; my life is that which I live." And everything would have been hunky dory.

Or not.

In spite of my uncertainty I decided to remain at Villa Kirka. "Although sooner or later I shall have to leave," I warned Father Romero. "And I can't commit to any specific timescale."

He replied that this was completely clear to him and Mr. Mindoro, who found out the result of our conversation at the grave of Maria's mother, also nodded agreement. Although he was a talkative person, he had never said anything to indicate his daughter's problem. But he could not conceal his unbounded satisfaction when Padre Romero whispered to him that I intended to stay.

And the news also filled Maria, whose melancholy kept bordering dangerously on despair, with good cheer. Or even with unconcealed delight. For the first time since I set eyes on her on the deck of the ill-fated ferry, her beautiful features displayed an innocent, genuine smile, full of gratitude for my self-sacrifice.

But perhaps it wasn't a case of self-sacrifice.

I am no less selfish than the majority of people and far from any kind of saintliness. I stayed because of the hope that the angelically (and also sensually) beautiful Maria would reward me with the act which was the only thing she could reward me with. That one evening, night or early morning she would silently creep into my room and slip into my bed.

Of course, this might have unforeseen consequences. One of them might be an even worse outbreak of her possession. Perhaps these thoughts and desires had been planted in me by Satan, who was waiting to possess my body through hers. Perhaps he had set a trap so that he could become your partner, Dr. Krauthaker. Insofar as he isn't already.

Why, in spite of this, I agreed to an extended stay at Villa Kirka is not completely clear to me. The desire for sex with a young girl certainly wasn't the primary reason, since such desires are not characteristic of the creature, equipped with five false identities and passports, that you have sent out into the world to carry out for you (or rather for your Mafia mob, which perhaps numbers more than a thousand) dangerous and dirty work.

But what might the other reasons be?

I must admit that I did not burden myself too much with this question. For notwithstanding, something natural had remained in my nature: a desire for physical contact with members – of course, as beautiful as possible – of the opposite sex. That you did not succeed in robbing me of this and similar desires can be confirmed by your darling wife. (If you expect me here to apologise for my inability to resist her attempts to steer my sexual organ into hers, you are going to be disappointed; you can discuss that with her; just as I am a victim of *your* manipulation, I was also a victim of hers.)

The fact is that I had not erred when I assumed that Maria Mindoro wanted to thank me for my victory over the demon within her in a way that even a young girl could assume would suit a man of my years. Had I erred when I awarded myself the prize for my services? Can even a man of my years be vain enough to exaggerate his own attractiveness?

Certainly, although at that thought even my temporary, false self was offended. Something within me still remained connected with what I had been before – with the feelings that all men have. But I was wrong: not only because this wasn't a matter of attractiveness (which in any case, as far as women are concerned, is very relative), but of something much more important. It was a matter of sickness and health, life and death, freedom or enslavement.

Around three in the morning I was awoken by a strange sensation. Imagine, Dr. Krauthaker, that in the middle of the night you awake with an almost painful erection and that a firm but soft mouth is trying, with aggressive tongue strokes, to suck from you the seed from ten years back and ten years hence. All that seed with which you have not fathered a child (and never will). Imagine that this mouth belongs to someone who is trying, by sucking your seed, to cure an acute illness and is in a great hurry to do so since every minute's delay could mean that the seed might lose its healing effect. And imagine that your hands reach of their own accord for the head that contains the sucking lips and, judging by the smooth black hair, you decide that it belongs to Maria Mindoro.

What would you do?

I doubt you would do anything different from what I did. I stroked the black hair, felt and gently rubbed two small ears, moved my hands forward and kneaded two firm, nineteen-year-old breasts, which made Maria Mindoro moan with pleasure, and moved my right hand towards her navel, caressed it slightly and enticed another moan, deeper and duller than the first, but when I continued towards her groin, to take possession of it with a suitable movement, the greedily sucking girl jumped up, pushed the blanket off the bed, leaving me naked, and in the semi-darkness rushed to the door and slammed it behind her as if she was being pursued by the Devil himself.

And she did not reappear until lunchtime.

During lunch, I was the one who stared at her as devoutly as she had stared at me before. She, meanwhile, stared enigmatically at her plate and did not bless me with even the slightest glance. I judged that she was trying to tell me: *fellatio yes, coitus no.*

69

6.

Dear Dr. Krauthaker, have you ever looked at your hands? I mean, really looked at them and been amazed that you even have them?

A few days ago I was watching a cat in the garden trying to catch a bird on a branch. It climbed the tree without difficulty, but when after its failed attempt it had to return to the ground it was awkward, frightened and clumsy. And I thought: what a privilege to have hands instead of claws. Although there are quite a few occasions when claws would come in handy and I'm surprised that evolution did not ensure that we have both. But never mind, it ensured we have hands, but also that we do not see this as a miracle and their value only becomes clear to us when we lose one or both of them.

I, Dr. Krauthaker, became aware of what it is not possible to do without hands during one of the rituals with which Maria tried to ease my imprisonment. Each time, she first seizes my member with her right hand and then stuffs it in her mouth, where it grows so much she can hardly breathe and then she sucks as if attached to her mother's breast.

Yesterday, at the height of my pleasure the sun shone through the window straight onto her ring. The flash of light compelled me to direct my eyes, which at such moments are normally closed, towards its source. And I saw that the flash was repeated each time the hand with which she held my member moved towards her mouth, for suddenly, just before the hand was illuminated by the ray of sunlight, she had decided, as well as sucking, to offer a few masturbatory movements.

And I watched this hand, this beautiful hand, moving up and down, up and down in slow, rhythmic movements, together with the rings on four of her fingers, and the sunlight flashing now on this now on the other jewel.

And I thought, Dr. Krauthaker: millions of years ago we lived in trees. At that time we must have had claws and what Maria Mindoro was now doing to me would not have been possible. Moreover, our brains were too small to think up something like this. How we sexually satisfied ourselves in trees is a question in itself; more important is the fact that in other regards claws did not serve us as well as they should. Even today, monkeys fall from trees far too often; according to some research, every fourth monkey in South Asia has at least one broken bone. Some have as many as seven healed breaks.

It's no surprise that evolution drove us down from the trees and from the jungle to the savannah, where a host of different animals were grazing. We fancied meat. But how to get it? On all fours and equipped with claws we would sooner or later have died of hunger, and so we stood on our hind legs. The front ones, suddenly free, began to develop into hands and the claws into fingers.

This had undreamed of consequences. Can you imagine, Dr. Krauthaker? The animals on the savannah were very fleet of foot and so our ancestors had to plan their hunting, to develop tactics and strategies, to think ahead, hypothetically. The five hundred cubic centimetres of brain that Australopithecus had available was not enough; a mere two million years later Homo erectus had twice as much. People and our civilisation came into existence because our front paws lifted off the ground and developed into hands. The use of our hands triggered a parallel growth in our brains – hands and brain became a team that began to manipulate the immediate environment; the two-footed creature became creative.

Throughout history, Dr. Krauthaker, the human hand should have had a least one deity exclusively its own. But it doesn't, as far as I know. The hand is the original tool that made all the other tools (and weapons). The human body has five million sensory nerves and a good third of these are found in the fingertips and palms. Can you imagine, Dr. Krauthaker? It's no surprise that for a portrait without

71

hands Salvador Dali charged 15,000 dollars, but for a portrait with hands 25,000.

Look at your hands closely, very carefully, and you'll understand why.

Think what you can do with your fingers! I'm not thinking of the fact that we can click our fingers, crack our knuckles, clap (imagine concerts, performances and important speeches without applause). No, I'm thinking that we can use our fingers to first make and then skilfully make use of instruments such as the piano, the clarinet and the guitar, as well as such devices as the telegraph, typewriter, calculator, computer, smart phone, to mention but a few. And that we can grip in our hand a million things, from the smallest grain to an apple.

In the dark, hands are antennae and when we are attacked they are our first line of defence. We fight with our hands; we stroke with them. And, lest I forget, we shake hands with them. How many hands have you shaken in your life? I know you've shaken mine quite a few times. I read somewhere that on New Year's Day in 1907, US President Theodore Roosevelt shook hands with 8513 people.

Without hands there'd be no Mozart, no Beethoven, no Rubinstein, no Tartini, no Leonardo, no Michelangelo, no Cervantes, no Dostoyevsky, no Pantheon and no pyramids, no radio, no remote control, no comb, no razor, no mobile phone and no clothes. We'd still be walking around as barefoot hairy monsters, communicating with "grrr-grrr" and similar unrefined noises.

And of course, we wouldn't have rings, Maria Mindoro has eight (all different), on all her fingers but not her thumbs, although without thumbs she would not be able to put them on.

All of this ran through my mind as I watched the flash of sunlight in the jewels of her rings, moving rhythmically up and down, up and down, almost in harmony with the rhythm of the melody that she perhaps felt deep in her soul.

And when the sun went behind a cloud, Maria Mindoro suddenly opened her eyes (she always had them closed while sucking) and looked straight at me. And she started slightly when she saw me watching her. In fact, she started enough to give me a gentle bite. Then her eyes closed again and she continued, as if in apology, emphatically gentle, less mechanical, with more feeling. This of course brought things to a head and when she began to swallow my semen, again with a look of salvation on her face, I raised my hands before my eyes and, perhaps for the first time in my life, looked at them as if staring at the face of a deity.

And I suddenly knew that only this deity would help me escape from this sweet prison in which I had begun to get bored. I knew that I had to use my hands. As a tool.

And, if necessary, as a weapon.

When I realised that Maria Mindoro, by constantly sucking out my semen (and she was becoming increasingly greedy) was robbing me of my physical strength and jeopardising my health (mainly because of an increasing lack of zinc which, as you know, we lose most of through ejecting semen), my resolution to withdraw from Villa Kirka was so strong that nothing in the world could shake it. I just wanted to find a way of doing so that would not cause Maria and her father too much hurt.

If my semen really was an effective cure for the girl's possession, she would probably do all in her power to keep me by her. Not only for a month or so, but for the rest of my days. She could lock me in a room, chain me to the bed. In idle moments my head filled with frightening scenarios. Of course, I gave no sign that I was troubled by doubts and fears; I strove to convey the impression that my stay in the Villa Kirka was one of endless enjoyment.

But in spite of this, my pretence was insufficiently convincing. The house was host to ever more whispered and furtive conversations, which included the servants; there were more and more looks that were redirected as soon as I noticed them. Perhaps one of my casual remarks during lunch on the terrace one day was at fault; I said that this idyllic holiday, probably the best of my life, had lasted quite some time and that sooner or later I would have to return to the world of work, which would be difficult, it was true, but unavoidable.

That's when, it seemed to me, the mysterious whispering began. Evidently they were discussing how to detain me. That I expected.

The only thing that surprised me was the realisation that even the servants were involved and that as the "guest of honour" I was the only one who did not know what was happening behind the façade of politeness and Maria's sexual favours (which were, hand on heart, increasingly more my favour to her).

Perhaps it could be seen from my face that I had begun to contemplate fleeing under cover of darkness. And perhaps that was why a new guard appeared at the entrance to the villa, less friendly than the previous one, distrustful by nature, who rushed from his hut whenever he saw me anywhere near the courtyard gates.

I was thus not surprised when shortly after this (the first time in a while) Father Romero came for lunch. Once again, he invited me to take a walk through the palm plantation above the house to the grave of Maria's mother. And this time, too, I knew he had something to say to me.

"Can I be frank?" he asked, as if I might expect him to be anything else. "Mr. Mindoro has noticed that feelings have developed between you and Maria that could be the basis of a lasting relationship."

He paused and looked at me. I hung my head.

"It's true she is very young and that there is quite an age difference between you, but these days that means nothing. Among Muslims, as you probably know, seventy-year-olds take twelve-year-old girls as their wives."

I still did not know what to say, so I remained silent. And then Padre Romero came to the main item on the agenda.

"In the event of your marriage, Mr. Mindoro is prepared to sign over to you ownership of the whole estate and villa, as well as ten properties scattered across the islands. Two are in Manila, in the most exclusive part of the city. He is prepared to increase the number of servants if you wished and maintain them until his death. If you wanted to travel the world with Maria – wherever and as often as you liked – he is ready to cover all the costs. If you should have children, he is prepared to guarantee them the best care and later, when the time comes, education at the best private schools. And finally: if you have debts anywhere in the world, he is prepared to settle them immediately. However great they are."

"He would like to have your answer today," he added.

Had you expected something like that, Dr. Krauthaker?

I had not. It's true there are a great many millionaires in the world and quite a few on the Philippines, but why would an apparently reasonable man give up everything to suit the whims of his adolescent daughter, who had decided that she had been possessed by a demon and then begun to think that I was the only one who could rid her of this curse.

"Father Romero," I said. "As much as I would like to please Mr. Mindoro, sadly it will not be possible. I have commitments to people that I cannot easily get out of. I have a past which is not accessible due to memory loss, but it may be full of atrocities. Even in the last few years, for which I do have data, I have bloodied my hands on a number of occasions. I am the kind of man for whom it would be necessary to create hell, if it did not already exist. Tell Mr. Mindoro that he cannot entrust his daughter's life to someone who could destroy it unwittingly. There are forces in the world that would not permit this marriage to take place."

At these words Father Romero thought for some time. He was evidently touched by them and I got the impression that deep inside he agreed with me and approved of my rejection of the offer. He was probably thinking: how many fifty-five year-olds are there who would pass up the chance of marriage to an angelically beautiful nine-teen year old, especially if this would make them exceedingly rich?

But I knew that my rejection of the offer was the consequence of *my* own obsession (the obsession that I must find out who I was before I forgot who I was). I am not deluding myself that this was not an obsession, but a normal wish that no-one would be able to forego. There were many who would do so; particularly when it became clear that stubbornly searching for my no longer current self was condemned to failure and that my wandering around the world in the hope that a miracle might happen was a pitiful waste of time.

Do you really need to know who you were and what you were doing thirty years ago? Where you grew up, who your parents were? Who you were married to (if you were) and who your children were (if you had any)? There are quite a number of people in the world who do not know these things.

It's more than obvious that I am also possessed by a demon.

"I understand your reservations," said Father Romero. "But notwithstanding, I appeal to you, not only in the interests of my ward, but also in your own interests, to thoroughly think the matter over. What would you lose if you accepted the offer? What will you gain if you reject it? There are moments in life when you have to weigh everything up. There are decisions that are not of the moment, but long-term. They can determine one's fate. At least do me this favour and think it over. I will ask Mr. Mindoro to wait a little."

"Thank you," I said. "You are the only person to see into my soul."

"God sees into your soul. I merely surmise what he sees. Like you, I see nothing. And know nothing. For me as well most things are a mystery."

Dr. Krauthaker, yet another of your ploys that I will never understand! I cannot imagine that anyone else was behind what happened today. Really, Dr. Krauthaker, you carry on as if you were a god, but all your actions bear the fingerprints of the Devil. And the moment will come when you, too, are punished for your audacity – particularly for what you allowed yourself today. I must admit that I was not expecting anything like this. In fact, it did not seem possible.

For God's sake, Dr. Krauthaker, how could you…

But let's take everything in order. After my talk with Father Romero the general feeling in the villa was transformed into something that I could not describe as optimism, but even less as pessimism. It was as if all the questions, all the hope, all the fears, all the uncertainties, all the desires, all the plans were suspended. I ate dinner on my own, in the kitchen, and there was no sign of either Maria or Mr. Mindoro. The maid who served me wore an expression suggesting that she would prefer to throw all the food, especially the hottest, in my face.

After dinner I escaped to my room to follow Father Romero's advice and thoroughly think things over. I shall not bore you with the winding corridors through which my thoughts meandered, nor with how often they came to a dead end. Suffice to say, just before midnight I fell asleep without arriving at a solution. It's hard to say how long I slept, but I don't think it was for long – perhaps an hour – when I was awoken by a strange sensation.

Actually, at first I thought I was having one of those sexual dreams that are well known to you, Dr. Krauthaker: that a beautiful young woman is riding you, has impaled herself upon you and is making harmonious, rhythmic movements, neither too fast nor too slow, while at the same time her firm mouth is attached to yours and she is licking your tongue, while her hands (perhaps even with sharp nails) grip your shoulders. And she is totally silent, as if she feared that even the most suppressed sound might be heard by someone who may have doubts about what she was doing.

Regardless of the dreamlike qualities of the event, I quickly realised that what was happening was that which I had wished for from my first encounter with Maria Mindoro. I did not delude myself that Maria had decided to step up our contact because I had suddenly become more attractive or because the demon that resided within her demanded this of her. I knew all too well that she had decided to take this step because she wanted me to stay. Perhaps she even wanted me to accept her father's offer and marry her.

What would you have done, Dr. Krauthaker?

I did not need to decide; the decision arose within me as spontaneously as the sea rises at high tide. Even before my passionate lover made me come (and that took quite some time, since I wanted to float in the sea of bliss for as long as possible), I already knew that I would stay at the Villa Kirka. Not because of the riches promised me, nor because of the pleasures that no healthy man would forego.

A more important role in my decision was played by something else. Villa Kirka offered me an ideal opportunity to escape from your manipulation. And control. And all the atrocities that I still had to commit in the false hope that they would lead me home. I had ceased believing that this was going to happen, Dr. Krauthaker. And if it does, it won't be thanks to you.

As soon as Maria Mindoro, perspiring and weary, crawled off me, made herself comfortable beside me and laid her head on my shoulder as if it were the only pillow she would ever wish to rest on, I knew that it was the end for you and for me the beginning of a new life. Far from what I had imagined, but for all that no less pleasant.

How did you know of my decision before I knew of it myself? Have you planted a chip in my brain that enables you to track my thoughts? Can you discern which direction they are taking before I have thought them to the end? For what happened next morning is your handiwork, of that there is no doubt. How did you know that I had killed the leader of the Abu Sayyaf group? I did not even notify you about this; I described the event only to an unknown and perhaps non-existent person with the email address kleinebilly@yahoo.com. I cannot believe there could be any kind of connection between you. Unless the person to whom I entrusted your name and my doubts about your good intentions searched for your address (which is not difficult) and from that time on has been informing you regularly about my correspondence.

The other possibility is that you read about the rescue of the hostages in the newspapers (I'm sure it was a major news item). And since you sent me to talk with the leader of the Muslim bandits (don't pretend that it was someone acting without your knowledge) you simply put two and two together and got four. And like a fool, I informed you about the goings on at Villa Kirka myself.

But why did it seem necessary to you to send members of the Abu Sayyaf group against me just before dawn? And only a few hours after I had decided to make my home there? How did you know you were going to lose me? I can imagine that you did not want to accept this (you have too much benefit from me), but why didn't you order the killers you sent to Villa Kirka simply to kidnap me? And to deliver me to a specific place and then collect the payment elsewhere?

Why did your executioners kill the guard and all the maids, take Maria and her father hostage and go off with them to who knows where? Can you imagine how shocking were the screams of the unhappy girl when we were torn apart? And how did Mr. Mindoro feel – a distinguished, grey-haired gentleman, whom they treated like a rabid dog? Of course, none of this interests you; while I have lost my memory, you long ago lost your heart.

78

And what will you do with me now, Dr. Krauthaker? Now that I am waiting for the departure of the plane that will carry me from Manila to Kuala Lumpur, where according to your text message a new assignment awaits me? In fact, I have come up with my new assignment all on my own. I'm going to kill you, Dr. Krauthaker. Following the terrorist attack on Villa Kirka, I can simply find no excuse for your actions. In your shoes I would begin asking myself where on God's earth you might be safe from me.

Nowhere, Dr. Krauthaker.

Nowhere.

7.

Hello, cassandra@yahoo.com. I found your address by chance on-line. You are being written to by an unusual person who because of brain damage has lost contact with his essence and his past. There are, of course, quite a number of such people around and amnesia is a subject that endless scientists deal with (and make a comfortable living from). My uniqueness is limited to the fact that I am probably the only amnesiac whose path back to himself has been offered, given or ordered via a labyrinth of events for which it is impossible to say whether they are planned or coincidental.

I need your advice, cassandra@yahoo.com. Not long ago in a market in Cairo I came across a potter who made not only pots and dishes from fresh clay but also stunningly accurate portraits of customers. I'm telling you, the modelled heads were such good likenesses that his customers could barely believe it. Not only that, they were made in ten minutes. I couldn't resist having one made myself.

When an hour later I looked in the mirror in the hotel, what stunned me most was that the clay head was like the one I carry on my shoulders (and think with) down to the *tiniest* detail. Of course, it was only one colour – a greyish brown – and did not blink, nor did its expression change, but nevertheless it seemed almost alive. And I thought: if it is possible to model the external appearance, is it also possible to model that which is inside – that which we call, for want of a better expression, one's *self*? In my case this self was a past to which I had no access. But why seek access to something that is only a memory, something that no longer exists? Why not model a new self?

Why not become Someone, if I believe that I am No-one.

What do you think?

Is it possible to artificially create what we carry inside us and for which we have invented various names? Mentality, the soul, reason, memory, psychological structure, personality, self-awareness? Certainly it is easier to shape something that is already within us. It is easier to create a new, different, more beautiful, more interesting face in clay based on one that already exists, that is made up of fragments of memory that link it to the past. Any of us could do that, though few do.

But I, dear Miss/Madam, have nothing inside me that can be reshaped. The only thing floating inside me is melancholy. That melancholy – a longing for something that remains unclear, inaccessible – is the only thing that could be called an emotion. Everything else is automatised; I do what other people do – I eat, sleep, go to the toilet, wash, comb my hair, shave, get dressed. In fact, what I am most aware of is my body and its specifities. If a piece of steak gets stuck between my teeth and I cannot shift it without a toothpick, that fills me with a satisfaction that I can barely describe; the feeling of discomfort proves to me that I *am,* that I am alive, that there is a *me* of some kind, although made up only of responses to minor irritants.

There is something else inside me that might be called a feeling, although it seems more a form of stubbornness. Besides living automatically, I also more or less automatically carry out instructions I get from unknown people. I get them via email, text messages, letters that strangers leave for me in hotel receptions or other locations – even, believe it or not, beneath stones beside roads. I'm not exaggerating when I write that I carry out these instructions conscientiously and precisely, to the best of my abilities, without weighing up whether I am doing right or wrong, whether I am bringing joy or unhappiness; I don't even think about that, it does not interest me in the slightest. I am like a retriever that goes after every stick thrown, regardless of which direction it is thrown in. And like a dog, too, in the desire for a reward from its master.

My master is the world renowned expert on rare forms of amnesia, Dr. Krauthaker (more about him some other time). The reward (only promised, since up till now there has been no sign of it) is the hope that each assignment I complete in line with the instructions is a step on the path that will, in the end (what kind of end? whose?), bring me back "home", to myself, to That Which I Was. I see that I have written "hope" – is hope not also an emotion?

To conclude: I carry that clay face made in record time by a potter in a Cairo market (I don't know why I call him a potter, when I should say Artist) with me in a cardboard box. In each new hotel room I put it on the bedside cabinet and every night before sleep I look at it until I sink into slumber. Often, believe it or not, it appears before me in my dreams and only last night, the day before I found your email address, it came towards me completely alive. Not only the face, but my whole body!

Just before the collision (or fusion) I felt that I (and that which was approaching) was consumed by flames and that we were both burnt to a cinder, into darkness, Nothing. But the dream that stays in my mind longer than any other has led me to the thought that even in a waking state we are two: the real, former Who I Was and the clay double. The first is inaccessible, but the other I can shape, being my own potter, sculptor, painter, smith, craftsman; I can shape it out of the clay that I do not carry within, but which surrounds me – in people, events, beliefs and above all (perhaps you agree with me) in philosophy.

Although our correspondence is for now one-sided, I am convinced that you understand me better than anyone in the world. Or at least better than most. Perhaps we even know each other! Perhaps we were friends, schoolmates, colleagues; maybe you were my student (or I your pupil) – I exclude nothing. From the clay of wisdom and knowledge that is currently available to mankind (available to all, although 99% take no notice and would not know what I was talking about), I decided to shape a substitute self. A man who is convinced that he knows something, believes in something, who follows an internal guide, who has a good, although imperfect insight into himself and his inclinations. Who is not an automaton for fulfilling orders and instructions. A Man Who Decides.

This I intend to do. If I receive a reply from you of any kind, even if it is only "fuck off", then I shall feel indescribably happy. At this moment I need nothing other than someone who is prepared to talk to me.

You have not replied, cassandra@yahoo.com.

And why should you? After all, my mail, looked at from a common sense point of view, is really an inexcusable intrusion into your world. But in spite of that, I cannot help but continue my conversation with you, since it might happen that my verbal bombarding will sooner or later force you to respond. And then, Cassandra, with our combined strength we shall resolve many things, perhaps even some problem of yours. Although not necessarily the problem I am now bothering you with.

I would like to tell you that, following the example of the potter in the Cairo market, I have begun to shape a new self or – to put it another way – a replacement *me,* which I hope will serve me until I find my way back to the real one. It may happen (the greatest fear) that the real one, if I ever do make contact with it, might seem inferior and incomplete in comparison with that which I intend to create and I will be faced with the question of which to accept, which to hold onto and which to reject. I at least allow for the possibility that this dilemma will not arise: that my former and my future, created self will combine to form a third and that I will be able to say that I am home again, although in a new house with extensions that were not there before.

Recently I spend all my free time (and that is not inconsiderable) in bookshops and libraries. I also surf the internet a lot, increasing the mass of clay from which I wish to form my new "face". And it is ever clearer to me that I need to train myself in the art of self-creation, otherwise it will be hard to avoid creating something that will be reminiscent of what Dr. Frankenstein produced. Even what I am now, the product of Dr. Krauthaker, is miserable enough; God forbid that in all the efforts that await me I jump from the frying pan into the fire. I need what might be called self-training; I need to learn self-control.

I doubt you have ever heard of the celebrated marshmallow experiment carried out forty years ago by some American psychologist. Allow me to describe it in brief (if you have heard of it, you can skip this description). A psychologist whose name I cannot recall closed a group of children in a room with a tray of marshmallows and told them they had a choice: they could eat one marshmallow immediately, but if they waited fifteen minutes they could eat two.

Only a third of children were capable of waiting fifteen minutes.

Twenty years later the psychologist checked the academic success of the children in question and ascertained the following: those who were capable of waiting fifteen minutes in order to get two marshmallows rather than one had, as teenagers, fewer behavioural problems and enjoyed considerably more academic success then those who sacrificed the second marshmallow in order to eat the first. The psychologist showed that self-control is a more reliable indicator of success in life than IQ; and not only in professional life, but also in terms of financial, work and marital stability.

The ability to wait for a marshmallow is a condition for firmness of character, Cassandra. And so I shall try to improve that capacity through self-training.

Perhaps you will say that this is all stuff and nonsense, but in emails from a year ago I find the information that Dr. Krauthaker, who only time will tell whether he is my benefactor or tormentor, had made a device with which he can scan the brain and determine when, for example, a person successfully resists the temptation to light a cigarette. The device clearly shows when the cognitive part of the brain intervenes and prevents the gratification of an automatic inborn desire. This device has been sold to a number of prisons around the world, where it helps the inmates develop self-control and the ability to resist impulses.

Self-control functions like a muscle; with exercise, repetition, it is possible to strengthen it. If, for example, you use your left hand intensively for three weeks (assuming you are right-handed), then consequently your self-control will increase as a result of using your conscious will against your automated habits. And greater self-control, believe it or not, will have an influence on other areas of your life: your self-discipline will be greater in everything you do.

Following the decision to model a new self, I became a member of an internet group Quantified Self, which uses the slogan: "Get to know yourself through numbers". We are constantly quantifying ourselves, regularly measuring our calories and alcohol intake, heartbeat, blood pressure, number of squats and other exercises, social and sex life, feeling in general, decline in body weight, financial state and much else.

Why?

In order to monitor what is happening because of imparted habits that we do not see as part of our self and, at the appropriate moment, to intervene, overrule habits and replace them with conscious decisions. One of the members of the movement stated online that we break into our lives in a similar way that hackers break into computer systems; we plant a Trojan horse in our brain through which we can monitor our thoughts and actions.

Did you know, cassandra@yahoo.com, that two thousand years ago Marcus Aurelius wrote his famous diary primarily to regulate his emotions? And that the first part of his *Meditations* was almost entirely devoted to the enumeration of things for which he had to be grateful to others? So as not to succumb to dark thoughts about how unfair life was towards him, he kept reminding himself that it was necessary to keep focusing on the good that it brought. He also was a master hacker, who dared to break into his thoughts and feelings, to intervene and to correct – he dared to be his own physician.

Among other things he wrote: "When you wake up in the morning, tell yourself: the people I deal with today will be meddling, ungrateful, arrogant, dishonest, jealous and surly. They are like this because they cannot tell good from evil." And such people, Cassandra, need to be accepted for what they are. If they knew how to be different, they would be, don't you think? Getting angry with them, resenting what they do, won't make the slightest difference to their behaviour.

So why the anger, why the resentment?

In the depths of my sorrow I find precisely this: intolerance regarding everything Dr. Krauthaker has done with me. At times this anger comes to the surface and takes me over so completely that I start thinking of revenge. If at that moment Dr. Krauthaker appeared before me, I would be capable of killing him, although I have no evidence that he wishes me anything other than what in his (expert) opinion will benefit me. That he has disappeared and left me hanging in the void (although the instructions I receive are undoubtedly his) is perhaps part of his strategy to facilitate my return "home".

But the moments when I am able to believe that are few and far between. Ever fewer. The anger I experience when I think of him is gradually turning into hatred.

But hatred cannot and may not be part of the replacement self with which I wish to fill the hollowness inside me. On the contrary. So part of my self-training is the practice of forgiveness, stoic assent to the manoeuvres of hostile fate. The anger inside me is a kind of smouldering cinder, the remains of a fire that cannot be extinguished, but which cannot be fanned in the hope that it will flare up and burn itself out. This constant smouldering that I feel in every fibre of my body is most reminiscent of sorrow, although in reality it is anger with hints of despair, disappointment, a sense of injustice.

At times I think that this anger, this sorrow with hints of despair, has always been inside me. That it is perhaps a remnant of That Which I Was: the only, albeit tenuous connection with my former, blocked self. Perhaps this is the smouldering, that painful glow of what is left of the wild, explosive fire that was the central character-istic of the former *me*. Perhaps my eruptions of anger were so violent that they destroyed my friendships, loves, business ventures – even the lives of my loved ones.

I'm sure that I never had the opportunity to murder in an outburst of wrath my nearest and dearest (like Nero), including my own moth-er, or (like Caligula) to force part of the audience at the Colosseum into the arena, where for the entertainment of others they were eaten by beasts. It is even less likely that, because of my violent anger and sense of outrage, I have triggered a war of revenge, attacked a foreign country, even though that which we call history is primarily a chronicle of such events.

But it is more than likely that excessive anger was a constant in my response to events in my life. Perhaps my hopes and expectations were too high – always higher than what I was allotted by fate (or what I was able to achieve in line with my talents). Perhaps I valued myself so highly that I was unable to limit my expectations and so disappointment was inevitable. Perhaps the "king" inside me was offended even if the waiter did not hurry over to my table as soon as I sat down. Perhaps I was overcome with a sense of injustice if I was soaked by the rain before I found shelter. All of that is possible.

All of us think primarily of what the world owes us and few of us how fortunate we are to have what we have. We value too highly that which we have to pay for and too little that which is paid for by others.

Are you any different, cassandra@yahoo.com?

Once again, you did not think it worth replying to my email. Although I had an inkling this would happen, I'm still extremely disappointed and I should really stick to my promise and not write again. To be honest, that was my intention, but the desire to tell someone about the progress of my shaping a replacement self proved too strong.

And so one more mail – this time the last.

I have abandoned the hope that I might be happy again in this life. I say again because I cannot believe that I never was. In the life to which I have no access, I must have had at least moments of this elusive emotion. But the replacement self, which I am cautiously and gradually shaping, cannot risk emotions that can be overturned by the slightest change of wind. The feeling of happiness, as you have no doubt ascertained yourself, is like an orange inside which a silent time bomb is ticking, that explodes the moment you experience its sweetness.

That bomb is the bitter awareness that sweetness is fleeting, it is something to which none of us is entitled and it is merely a slide down which we always – and always too quickly – roll into the cold darkness that is the basis of life. If I was ever happy in love, it certainly didn't last. Otherwise, why would I have been on a Bali beach alone?

87

I would have been with a woman, or more likely with my family; men of my age are rarely childless.

Of course, it is equally possible that I was on a business trip and I allowed myself a few days' break between flights, while my family remained where I would like to return to – the place that was once and still is my home. The speculations, which alternate between wishes, hopes and fears, are attached to my stream of thought like the jaws of a poisonous insect; they never leave me.

Actually, I am realising that the path to a replacement *me* is not all that long; that all the ingredients – or at least most of them – have been inside me for quite some time and only require harmonising, classifying, connecting. And above all, the acknowledgement that this is really the *me* that will pass the remainder of my days on this earth. Perhaps I am not too pleased with the qualities of this *me,* but they are a fact that, out of fear of the emptiness inside me, I have to come to terms with.

If you are interested which of these qualities I do not like, I will willingly enumerate them: after all, I am not writing to you in order to conceal anything. On the contrary, I would like to reveal myself to you, to show myself in all my wretchedness, all my unhappiness, all my wandering, to reveal all the bad things I have done to others, even though you shall condemn me.

But before you begin to condemn me, please consider that I have never done anything bad for *my own* reasons or for *my* benefit. Everything I have done, I have done simply because I believed that they were necessary stages on my journey home. When you are so lost that you can no longer believe even yourself, you must believe the one who wishes to help you. And if you believe him, you cannot at the same time judge his motives. On my journey "home" I have, following instructions or in self-defence, committed acts that in many places would justifiably lead to life imprisonment. I have caused so much misery and pain that my former self (who I expect was to all appearances normal) would be horrified, repent, take to drink. Perhaps commit suicide.

If I do some time make contact with that self, my suffering (or worse) can be cured by only one thing: that I forget everything that

I did on my way "home", all that I am doing and will have to do. Otherwise my conscience (I believe that at home, in addition to a wife and child, I also have a conscience) will force me to relinquish the home that I seek so persistently, for my conscience will show that I am a stranger there and do not belong.

On my way through my inner emptiness (for the external world is in reality just a stage where I put on an ordered show for the satisfaction of an invisible director) I am shielded from feelings of guilt only by a cold soullessness that accompanies me from dawn to dusk like a shadow. I cling to this soullessness like a gift from God. Only by acting like a professionally trained soldier for whom pain, either his own or caused to others, seems inevitable and almost natural, will I be able to pass through the danger and over the barriers on the way to "myself".

Am I wrong, dear Cassandra?

You must certainly have noticed by now certain contradictions in the messages I tirelessly send you. On the one hand I cling to cold soullessness, because I fear that even the mildest intrusion of conscience will halt my journey home, while on the other hand I wish to model from my experiences a replacement self that would as far as possible be reminiscent of a normal person – in case the journey home should fail and I am compelled to spend the rest of my days as a self-created subject, a man who bears at least an approximate resemblance to Someone.

I am confused, dear friend. And I really would like to get some kind of response from you. I fear that I am becoming my own enemy, my worst adversary, and that I expect too much, not just from myself, but from others. My thoughts are different every day. I too quickly fall under the influence of what I read (online, in books and newspapers). There are moments when I fear that in shaping a replacement self I am creating a neurotic who will end up in an asylum. And that my chronic apathy, my sadness is the only thing saving my brain from dissolving in bile.

Thus yesterday, I threw the clay likeness that the Cairo market potter made through the twelfth storey hotel window. And said goodbye to shaping a replacement self that may become all that I most fear.

89

Dear cassandra@yahoo.com, I know that again you will not reply, but for some unknown reason I still prefer to write to you. Perhaps because your email address is ten years old and you haven't used it for a long time. The possibility that my words fall into a void enables me to speak more frankly. Thus, without hesitation, I can tell you that (some time ago) I opened a Facebook profile under the name Niemand Nobody. Here is my description:

"Born roughly 55 years ago somewhere on Earth. Probably in a town, most probably in Europe (or Australia, Canada, USA). Education: higher, of that there can be no doubt. Maybe an MA, or even a PhD. Harvard? Oxford? Not excluded. Field of study: unknown. Profession: unknown. Journalist, economist, travelling salesman, banker, pilot, army officer? None of these are impossible. Height: 179 cm in stocking feet; weight: 86 kg; waist: 94 cm. Relatively regularly built, developed musculature, but not too much; obviously someone who has exercised regularly, maybe cycled, but not a professional sportsman. Moderately hairy. Shoe size: 43. Distinguishing features: dark birthmark near left nipple; navel slightly protruding and twisted in a small spiral; appendix scar; a noticeable diastema between two incisors; four lower teeth missing, two on the extreme right, two on the extreme left. No signs of parodontosis. Mole just behind the left ear, visible from the back; a similar one on the lower part of the left testicle. Hands larger than average, wide palms, on the lower finger joints signs of swelling characteristic of Heberden osteoarthritis. Occasionally painful. Perhaps something else, but nothing important. Employed as the implementer of instructions from unknown people. Victim of amnesia. Main interest: that someone will recognise me and let me know who I am. Reward: eternal gratitude. Perhaps even, regarding the circumstances, a small wad of cash."

I added some photographs that are nothing special: a middle aged man of moderately satisfactory appearance – but far from the kind of looks that turn women's heads. Because after joining the network I did not receive any requests for a long time, I decided to take action myself. I sent out (as can be seen from my history) "friendship requests" left, right and centre, first to people in the section "People you may know" (surprisingly they all accepted me immediately,

90

even though I knew none of them), then to all their friends (who also accepted me, a complete stranger, as if my request had brightened up their life) and so on, until I had collected hundreds of friends!

Soon after, the day came when I finally began to receive requests for friendship myself, probably from friends of friends, whose main goal was to increase their number of friends. And to show in this way they are popular? Or important? That they are something? Someone? For the first time I thought that perhaps even those who have always been what they are, who have not lost their memory, do not know too well who and what they are; that they do not believe firmly enough in their own existence, but try to affirm it with a quantity of virtual "friends". And, of course, "likes" for which some almost beg. So each day I reserved at least half an hour, even in the middle of the night if that was the only possibility, for liking everything and everyone I found on Facebook. I liked (and I'm still doing so) changed profile photos, photos in the albums of "friends", photos of cute puppies and kittens and beautiful scenery taken who-knows-where, links to newspaper articles, petitions, quotes of the most stupid statements by stupid people, even news that someone has finally, *finally* gone on holiday, bought a new car, read a new book, just returned from the Caribbean, found a room in London etc. I am undoubtedly the biggest liker on Facebook.

Soon my "friends" began to like almost everything that I put on my page: all the photos, all the links to my articles, all the more or less stupid statements that I made for a wider public, all the quotations that I copied from a dictionary of quotations, while the most likes came for the statement "I still don't know who I am – help me!" (an unbelievable 2340!). Among the comments, the most interesting was: "I don't know who I am either – shall we help each other?"

And some others: "Your self-portrait is the most original I've come across on Facebook, but I can't believe it. If you'd really lost your memory you'd be in a psychiatric institution, where you wouldn't have access to the internet." And: "I fear that you are making fun of us all and enjoying it. You know very well who you are, but you're hiding behind a made-up identity." It's true that 15% of Facebook profiles are fabricated, but I'm not pleased that some of my "friends" think that I would stoop to that, so I'm thinking of saying goodbye to Facebook.

8.

Thank you, Dr. Krauthaker, a thousand thanks! For some time I thought it was a trick, of which there are plenty on Facebook, since it's not difficult to create a false identity, borrow a photo from a film actress or model, use a false name to connect with friends and neighbours, encourage them to reveal secrets that they would not entrust to you personally – on Facebook all sorts of things go on behind the scenes.

But now, Dr. Krauhaker, now it is finally clear that through the gloomy corridors without a light at the end and through the diversions that confused me (and even filled me with hatred towards you) and through the labyrinths often with the same entrance and exit, you have finally brought me to my goal. Home. To myself. To the missing *me*. To That Which I Was. To that which I really am because it is all I can be.

On Facebook I found (miracle of miracles) the following message:

"My dear husband, how sad that I have to find you in such a banal way. Since you disappeared, a day hasn't gone by, even an hour, without me trying to find out what happened to you, where you vanished to, why there had been no word from you. Now I know, although I can only guess at the details. From your emails I could not make out that it was you. Why didn't you tell me before what name you were using on Facebook? Return to your family, please. Return to me. Whatever you've done, whatever happened, all is forgiven. I am waiting for you. Your Cassandra."

You kept your promise, Dr. Krauthaker. How can I thank you?

Especially since you severed contact with me. Perhaps it was part of the plan and I'm increasingly convinced that you did nothing just like that – the whole time you knew what might facilitate the next step on my journey home. And now, even quicker than I expected – perhaps even quicker than you expected yourself – I am on the doorstep.

In fact, I still experience it all as a dream. My wife has found me through Facebook and made contact! I know I must be cautious, for there's nothing to say that through overenthusiasm I may fall into a trap from which there's no escape; that some witch may lure me into a cave and change me into a pig; that I may be lured into some laboratory where they'll test new drugs on me.

Maybe this isn't caution, but paranoia But you said yourself when you were giving me directions to look three times before I leap; I have it all written down on a slip of paper that I carry folded in my wallet.

But in spite of my caution, Mr. Krauthaker, I have no choice but to take this step. For ever since we met I have wanted nothing other than to return to my life. To my family. To my friends.

Although some things slightly confuse me.

First of all, it seems odd that the woman who is inviting me "home" as her lost husband is considerably younger than me – perhaps twenty years or even twenty-five. Of course, it's possible that she isn't that young; many people, especially women, use for their Facebook profile a picture from their younger years. I don't begrudge her this, perhaps after my years of absence she was looking for a new partner. But perhaps she wasn't looking through Facebook – there are other, more effective channels. Where have I suddenly got the idea that everyone has a hidden agenda?

Something else seems strange. She did not want to reply to questions such as what my name is, how long we've been married, what I did before I disappeared, whether we have children, whether we lived in a normal, happy family, whether she missed me at all, whether I have friends and colleagues who miss me. "Come home and you'll find out everything. It's not seemly for a husband and wife to talk on Facebook." Then she added: "If I tell you everything in advance you may not want to return. And if you don't come, you'll never know whether or not I told you the truth – I could simply be making everything up. If you want to return to your old life, come and look for the evidence yourself. How else will your memory return? Through words that could be lies?"

"What about Morris," I wrote back, "your profile is under the name Cassandra Morris. Is that my surname?"

She didn't answer, but expressed amazement that I did not recognise her from her photograph; it didn't seem possible to her that amnesia could be so complete. But it is, as you well know. Faces from the time before the accident have been erased from my brain like everything else. So I cannot say that the picture of my (alleged) wife on Facebook is even vaguely familiar. If I passed her on the street I wouldn't even turn round, I would simply take her for one of the mass of moderately attractive women who walk the pavements of European towns.

And now, Dr. Krauthaker, the most troubling thing.

I was convinced that Cassandra Morris, when she recognised me as her lost husband, would send her address, phone number and so on, so that we could make contact. But she did none of this. She said only: "Come to London. Just let me know the day and time of arrival and flight number. I'll pick you up at the airport." She didn't want to tell me how to get to her, to the house where we must have lived for some years and where she is probably still living, with or without the children, which she does not even want to tell me whether we have or not.

As if she was also afraid. Of what?

That my Facebook profile is fake? That my whole story is fake? That behind me is concealed someone who would like to worm his way into her life as a supposed husband after having killed him, stolen his photos, used them as his own? And perhaps there is a sufficient resemblance that she would not even suspect he isn't her husband? After all, that possibility, although unlikely, is not impossible – these things happen. Maybe she's right to be cautious.

Why shouldn't she be, if I am?

This is what I'm thinking: if my wife sent me her mobile phone number we could be talking already, exchanging text messages, keeping track of my journey home, exchanging some emotional message (not at all unusual for a couple that hasn't seen each other for six years).

Am I wrong?

Perhaps after six years emotions are frozen and it will take some time for us to thaw them out and suffuse them once more with new trust. What do I know about what she was doing in the years we did not see each other; what does she know about what I was doing? For both of us there is an underlying fear that the other was unfaithful. That needs to be accepted, understood and forgiven before we can become close again.

But her mobile phone number, if she entrusted me with it, could be the *beginning* of a new closeness; we could at least speak, so she can hear my voice and I hers. The sound of a voice does more to establish trust than a thousand words by email.

But no, she didn't send me the number.

Perhaps because I didn't ask her to. Perhaps because I didn't send her mine, although I could have done. I had been about to send it when I thought that perhaps it wasn't a good idea; after all, she hadn't asked me to. Maybe it seemed impolite (outrageous how far apart two people can grow in six years!). Maybe she was afraid that I would ask her on the phone for the explanations that she had made clear on Facebook I would have to wait for.

And why didn't I offer her my number? At least for easier coordination in London?

I don't know, Dr. Krauthaker. Something about this unexpected development does not seem quite right. Something is filling me with anxiety, with the fear that I might be disappointed. Even with an underlying feeling that maybe I shouldn't return home. Because there (who's to know) something awaits me that is worse than what my replacement self is experiencing.

So I have made a plan, Dr. Krauthaker. As my plane circled Heathrow in the company of others, waiting for permission to land, in the aisle seat in the twelfth row of the Boeing 777 sat a middle aged man with a thick moustache and a light coloured wig that was somewhat longer than one would expect considering his age and tidy appearance, but which gave him a slightly artistic look, with which he had extracted from the female cabin crew on the nine hour flight from Singapore quite a few friendly smiles. Because I knew that Cassandra was expecting clean shaven, dark haired Trevor Morris, there wasn't the slightest chance that she would recognise the Swede Sven Lindgren, who was coming to London on "business".

I saw her as soon as I emerged from the green customs channel into the arrivals hall at Heathrow; she was standing among the crowd right next to the barrier that separated those waiting from those arriving. She was clutching a clumsily cut out piece of cardboard on which was written TREVOR MORRIS. As if she was afraid I wouldn't recognise her; as if she was afraid that she wouldn't recognise me. And it's true that if it wasn't for the sign I wouldn't have found her in the sea of faces that seemed unusually alike (for a long time now all faces seem alike to me: indistinct).

Above all, I wouldn't have recognised her because she was quite a bit older than her Facebook photo – perhaps ten years older, around forty-five. This did not make her any less attractive, quite the opposite. I don't mean that she was a beauty, but some women radiate an attractiveness that has no connection with stereotypical notions of feminine beauty. I'll be completely frank: Cassandra had average looks, but her features – tired in a particular way, weary, but her eyes sharp as if looking for prey that she could toy with – attracted, even demanded attention and evoked the feeling that you owed her something. I didn't want to stare, but I nevertheless noticed that she was dressed in tight black trousers with which she wanted to emphasise her best feature: good legs.

The passengers behind me were bumping into me, and so I speeded up and went into the main part of the hall to implement the second part of my plan. I stopped near the exchange office and began to go through my wallet as if I was counting the banknotes that I wished to change. Cassandra was doggedly waiting for Trevor Morris to appear.

What surprised me most was that I didn't recognise her even in the flesh. Basically, I had never seen the woman before in my life.

I don't know why I had expected that my lost memory would miraculously return as soon as I met someone who had been part of my life *before* the accident. I had expected that at least a part of what was lost would return and then one by one, as if awakening from a deep drug-induced sleep, other forgotten parts, until the whole of my lost life would reassemble itself.

But nothing; Cassandra was a complete stranger to me. There was still a possibility that my memory would return gradually, one piece at a time, each in a suitable context, and perhaps I would more easily recognise my wife at home, in the house where we had lived together. I would recognise the furniture, the pictures on the walls, things of mine, a computer, slippers.

Cassandra Morris grew tired of waiting; after an hour and a half it was clear to her that Trevor Morris was not on the flight from Singapore. Frowning slightly, she made her way out of the press of people; she wondered for a while how to get rid of the piece of cardboard bearing my name (thanks to the threat of terrorist attacks, for quite some time there had been no litter bins at British airports), and then she simply laid it on the ground and headed for the exit labelled Underground.

Imagine that, Mr. Krauhthaker: she didn't come by car but by the Underground.

As a matter of fact, that suited me better.

Sven Lindgren, with a suitcase in his right hand and a map of London in his left, followed her.

I will skip some things, Dr. Krauthaker, the details wouldn't interest you, particularly not my doubts, ruminations and the diversionary tactics I used to avoid possible traps. So in brief: I followed Cassandra to a house in a respectable part of West London (Stamford Brook) and made a mental note of the number (10 Pleydell Avenue), for all the houses in the street were the same, and then two streets away found a room in a bed-and-breakfast, but before that I removed my moustache and wig so that I was once more Trevor Morris (or rather the one whose photo I had put on Facebook).

At two in the morning I made my way back to Cassandra's house. After the short walk I went up the short path up to the door and shone a torch at the nameplate.

MORRIS was engraved on the silvery metal.

She had not lied!

I looked up and down the street, which the streetlights were bathing in soft light, and tried to work out if I remembered anything – perhaps the unusually tall chimney on the house opposite, or the tasteless statue of a mermaid in the front garden of another house, or even one of the cars parked near Cassandra's house. I might be able to remember my own car, at least, if of course she had not changed it, which was more than likely.

Everything looked somehow familiar. But things look familiar to me everywhere (I always have the feeling that I've seen them before, and I'm sure I have, since today everything looks pretty much the same all over the world). But at the same time, nothing was familiar in the way it would have been if it had been part of my forgotten life. Of course, I did not exclude the possibility that Cassandra and I had not lived on Pleydell Avenue, but elsewhere in London, and she had sold that house and moved here when I disappeared; that was not impossible, was it?

But something is bothering me more than anything else, Dr. Krauthaker, and for quite some time. How did I become Trevor Morris? I have it written down that I *took part* in selecting fake identities; you asked me to suggest names for the forged passports (as well as camouflage for each of the false identities).

So why did I suggest the name Trevor Morris?

Did I *know* somewhere deep inside that I was Trevor Morris?

And the other names: did I pluck them from the air? Did I suggest the names of friends from my forgotten life? Why did I have to think up different appearances just for them? Just because I couldn't have the same photo in five different passports? Was that the only reason? Why the moustache and light hair for Sven Lindgren, why the full beard for the Greek Asimakopulos, why the glasses and goatee but no moustache for Alfred Haidacher, why the wig with a bald patch and the fake scar on the left cheek for your compatriot Youngson? Why

98

did I want to remain unchanged as Trevor Morris – like I am? And why do I go around the world most of the time (really all the time) as Trevor Morris, whereas I transform myself into others only when trying to evade the police or a pursuer, or when I have to carry out one of the riskier assignments that you suggest to me?

Could that mean that I *am* Trevor Morris? And that Cassandra really recognised me as her husband? And I am doing her an injustice in not trusting her? Have I taken my automatic mistrust of everything and everyone to absurd lengths?

That night I came to the realisation that I had nothing to lose, so after breakfast I paid the bill, threw my things in my suitcase, went around two corners to 10 Pleydell Avenue and rang the bell. For a long time there was silence and since it was already ten o'clock I thought that Cassandra was probably at work.

But then there was the noise of a key turning, the door opened and there stood Cassandra. Although I forget most things within a few days I shall never forget the look on her face.

"You?" she said, barely audibly. "You weren't there! I was at the airport!"

I lied that I had missed my flight and had to wait for the next one. I couldn't let her know because I didn't have her number. "But I'm here now."

"How did you find me?" she asked in surprise. (Was it my imagination, or was there a shadow of doubt in her eyes?)

"How could I not," I said. "This is our home, isn't it?"

"This is my home," she replied, "but we lived in Hampstead. Did you go there first?"

"No, I didn't," I admitted, so as not to dig myself into an even deeper hole. "I came straight here."

"But how did you know you'd find me here?" she persisted.

"Let that remain a mystery for the time being," I said. "And since I see that we are going to stand outside the door forever, I'll go back to the airport."

I bent down and picked up my suitcase.

"Don't be childish," she said. "Come in."

And I went inside.

The house was not a big one, with only two floors and at the back a neglected designer garden, as is usual in the better parts of London. But it was tastefully furnished, tidy, clean, with a full bookcase in the living room and framed theatre posters on the walls – everything indicated that an educated woman lived here, perhaps one employed in the arts, or at least someone with a penchant for reading and theatre.

Did this ring any bells?

I'm afraid not. I put down my case and said that first, if she had nothing against the idea, I'd like to look round the house; I'm sure I would find something that would remind me of my previous life.

"But you've never lived here!"

"Whatever," I replied. "Some object, photograph…"

And I went upstairs. Cassandra followed me. I opened the bedroom door, but there were no photos on the walls or the bedside cabinets next to the double bed. I opened the door to the neighbouring, slightly smaller room, which obviously served as a storage room, as it was full of all sorts of items, from cases and bags to old irons and some exercise equipment that had probably been used and then forgotten about.

"Did I ever use the exercise bike?" I asked.

"Never," she said. "I didn't bring any of your things here."

And even in the largest upstairs room I found nothing to remind me of anything that might have been "mine" in the past. The room was most reminiscent of a child's room, although more of a student than a younger child, with a large bookcase, a desk with computer, a sofa that might turn into a bed, a wardrobe, shelves full of CDs, a stereo system discreetly placed in the lower part of the desk and speakers almost hidden among the books on the shelves.

"Our son's room?" I asked. She shook her head. "Daughter's?"

"Let that remain a mystery for now. Come to the kitchen for a coffee and a chat."

We sat at the table for some time, sipping nicely sweet instant coffee without saying a word. I noticed that Cassandra looked quite jaded and had bags under her eyes; she looked like someone who wasn't quite healthy, or not getting enough sleep, or suffering a great deal.

100

"When you moved why didn't you bring anything of mine with you?" I asked.

"You went off, you left me without a single word of goodbye, you simply vanished. The police treated you as a missing person for a year. Then they said you were probably dead. But of course, I didn't believe that. I knew you hadn't disappeared off the face of the earth. You had run off with another woman, maybe to Brazil, to start a new life. I threw everything that was yours away."

Although I still didn't trust her, her explanation seemed plausible.

"Perhaps you know," I asked, "how I found myself with no documents on a beach in Bali, where a clumsy surfer bashed into me and damaged my brain so that I lost my memory, and I no longer knew who I was – and I still don't."

"You should ask the one you left your family for, rather than me – she must have been with you."

"There was no-one else," I assured her.

"How do you know if you've lost your memory," she teased. "Perhaps you forgot."

"It's possible" I admitted, stunned by the truth of what she said.

"But you don't remember me," she said, as if that was self-evident.

"No," I said. "I don't remember ever seeing you before."

At these words, Dr. Krauthaker, Cassandra began to sob. She was shaking and then she leapt from her chair and ran into the bathroom, locking the door behind her. I heard her whimpering like an upset child, although that is not the best metaphor – it was more like the whining of a beaten animal.

"Cassandra," I said, knocking on the door. "Stop it and come on out."

"Leave me alone," she sobbed. "Just go away."

I knew I had to give her some time, so I returned to the kitchen, sat down and waited. If this was put on, I thought, perhaps Cassandra was a professional actress. The only other possibility was that she really was my wife, that I was her husband and that I had *really* left her in the way she described.

After a few minutes she returned to the kitchen, mouthed a barely audible "sorry" and sat down again.

"Can you tell me what I did in the life I no longer remember?"

"Nothing," she replied, with a hint of bitterness. "You studied languages at Oxford, all sorts of languages, even some outside the regular programme. But you never graduated, even though everyone said you were extremely talented. Then you wandered around the world for some time, teaching English as a foreign language. You said you wanted to get to know the world. We were already together and I, in love with you, waited patiently. You would come, stay for some time and then leave again. When I decided that nothing lasting would come of our relationship, you retuned and said the world had begun to bore you. You said we should get married and we did."

"Do we have any kids?"

"A twenty-year-old son, who said after you vanished from our lives that he wanted nothing more to do with you."

"And where can I find him?"

"He's studying languages at Oxford," she replied with an ironic undertone. "It's possible that he'll follow his father's footsteps and eventually lose his memory!"

She gave a nervous laugh that she immediately controlled.

"And what did I do when I returned from my wanderings?"

"You wanted to be a journalist. You wrote travel articles, sent them to hundreds of addresses and some were even published, but no-one wanted to employ you."

"So what did we…?"

"I supported us, who else? And our son. I inherited the house in Hampstead when a prosperous but childless uncle died. Otherwise, life wasn't easy. Your occasional earnings didn't even pay the bills."

"And what did you do?" I asked.

"I'm an actress," she said. "Thankfully, in my younger years I got a lot of parts. On television as well, usually in cheap soaps. But with a small child and a husband who preferred drinking with friends than looking for a job, I didn't care."

"Do you still act?"

"Not much. Now and then, some minor part, usually a disappointed housewife. I somehow get by, I live very modestly. Luckily, Jacob got a grant."

"Jacob is our son?"

She nodded.

"Will you show me his photo?"

"That can wait," she said so firmly that I didn't insist.

"Can you show me the house in Hampstead, where we lived?" I asked after a while.

"Why?"

"I might remember something. Some small detail that will set off an avalanche. There's nothing I want more than my memory back and to be once more what I was."

"But you are you, you just don't know it."

"Do the following names mean anything to you? Alfred Haidacher, Sven Lindgren, Kevin Youngson, Kostas Asimakopulos. Have you ever heard of them?"

"Those are the friends you drank with every day."

"Where can I find them?"

"I never met them. You just talked about them, repeated their stupid jokes."

We were silent for a good minute, each thinking our own thoughts.

"More coffee?" she asked eventually.

I shook my head.

"There may be only one thing that can bring your memory back," she said, "if it's possible at all."

She looked me right in the eye. She might even have blushed, almost imperceptibly.

9.

Dear Dr. Krauthaker, it never occurred to me that sex, such an ordinary thing, can change into a deadly game and I really don't understand why we can't multiply as we did at the very beginning, through cells dividing and the odd mutation to ensure the appropriate evolutionary development. Of course, mutations during cell division were very rare and became more frequent only when blue green algae started to multiply, more than a thousand million years ago.

And look how far we've come since then! To cloning, which is once again a kind of cell division (though more complicated), a reproduction of identical living creatures. And in between... well, so we don't stray too far into biology, I'll limit myself to the energy that forces all living creatures, particularly the human kind, into the hilarious and at the same time deadly serious activity that is reproduction in the form of (almost) bare fist fighting. At moments merciless and hostile.

Without lust, life on earth would have disappeared long ago, but the Great Regulator who guides our instincts could be satisfied with moderation, not only in the case of people, but also the animal world, where excesses are more brutal and it seems that animals are really slaves to sexual energy. Among the animals there are no examples of individuals who decide for a life of celibacy and withdraw to a monastery. You'd be least likely to find one among frogs, who after the long winter return to the scene literally bloated with hormones. You'd think they'd be most interested in food, but no; male frogs are most obsessed with the need to grab hold of something. And they grab anything that is roughly the same size and shape as a frog – even a piece of wood, a human hand and (of course) another male frog. He will immediately be aware of the mistake and will protest loudly, which will compel his attacker to go in search of a lady frog who will quietly submit to his attentions. Once he finds one he finishes quickly and goes in search of the next. Of course, Mr. Krauthaker, the noise that frogs make when mating is well known to you – croak, croak, croak.

But the noise that frogs make cannot be compared to the sounds made by my Cassandra during love making.

What will the neighbours say?

I could probably cope with the noise somehow, it might even encourage me at moments to give her more than is good from a health point of view. But I'm much more concerned by the biting that my wife has got into recently; evidently her greed is increasing and perhaps she's aware of that but can't control it. It started with her digging her nails into my back (and her nails are claws!). But that will be familiar to you, Dr. Krauthaker, since your delectable Milly does that when she climaxes (by the way, give her my regards). But it didn't end with scars on the back, she soon progressed to biting my neck, shoulder, chest, ear (she almost drew blood from my left ear), plus all the other body parts she can reach during her spasmodic twisting and turning beneath or above me.

Biting has become a kind of overture to our sexual encounters, a kind of invitation, a kind of warning that an enemy has appeared on the horizon that needs, through our combined efforts, to be defeated. When it begins (usually when watching TV on the sofa, or at six in the morning when one would like to be asleep) it is completely clear that there is no hope of retreat, except for a foolhardy leap through a closed window (which I have already thought of a number of times). Men actually have no choice if they want to retain the reputation of a Great Lover (which is how Cassandra buys my willingness to sacrifice myself for her pleasure).

You can imagine that my anxiety is increasing, is actually turning into fear, for I know all too well (as do you) that some animals die

105

during the sex act; and if not during the act, soon after. Allow me to mention only the black widow spider, the mayfly and the octopus (female, but not male). You are no doubt much better informed about this than I am, since you studied medicine, whereas it began to interest me only when it became clear that what was happening with my Cassandra could hardly be a mere consequence of a six-year wait for me.

What do you think, Dr. Krauthaker, about the grasshopper that, just before it lays eggs, eats as much of its partner as it can get into its stomach? Or of the female of the innocent sounding cricket, which pulls off its dear one's wings as soon as he has rubbed its evening serenade, destroys his musical instrument and as a reward almost devours him whole?

I had not expected that upon returning home, instead of peace and slipping back into the furrow of life, I would be faced with a life and death struggle, a mixture of sadism and masochism, which is not (or shouldn't be) a rule in the marriage relationship. A number of times I wanted to suggest to Cassandra that we go and seek help from marriage counsellor or even a psychiatrist, as I can barely control myself and it won't be long before I start to insult and threaten her; it might even happen that I strangle her in self-defence.

I can't understand why God, in his infinite wisdom, did not make man a hermaphrodite; then he could satisfy his sexual needs himself and decide for offspring without having to negotiate with the opposite sex. It might all be a bit less exciting, but we would be spared a lot of suffering and suicides, the Greeks would never have attacked Troy, even prostitution would remain within the boundaries of self-negotiation. We would avoid sexual diseases and the abbreviation HIV would not exist. Think, Dr. Krauthaker, what God would have saved mankind from.

Or not.

I remember (since I lost contact with the past, certain things that followed the event I remember pretty accurately), that you like going to French restaurants (you invited me on a few occasions). And that your favourite dish is that well known French speciality, snails. *Escargots*. Did you know that these snails are hermaphrodite and not all that unusual in the animal world? And that (how ridiculous!) they don't impregnate themselves, but look for other hermaphrodite snails to procreate with?

Escargots are equipped with such a large penis (relative to their size) – a gigantic erectile tube – that no other creature on earth can compete with them, not even, sadly, your Australian koala, which is also famous for being unusually well endowed. What's more, snails have sadistic leanings. Two hermaphrodite snails become embroiled in a wild dance, they stick together with their feet, frantically swaying and exchanging noisy kisses. Then one of them, the most aroused, suddenly fires into the body of his fellow dancer chalk like arrows and with only one purpose: to harm him. The wounded snail partner visibly twitches with pain and it's hard not to get the impression that you are witnessing a crime of passion. In fact, these arrows sometimes pierce the stomach or lung cavity and kill the partner *before* sexual union.

This cannot be at all pleasant, for a wounded partner behaves no better. As soon as the arrows strike, the snail becomes extremely disturbed and immediately begins to respond with arrows and darts. And with them, of course, an enormous penis, no smaller than the sexual organ of his hermaphroditic partner. After strenuous efforts and wrestling the partners finally succeed in shoving their penises, side by side, into each other's sexual orifices. This mutual copulation lasts several minutes. The male sex organ must penetrate the female sex channel deep enough to eject semen into a special bladder in which several minutes later it will inseminate the eggs that have just appeared. Don't forget, Dr. Krauthaker, that both snail partners are hermaphrodite, at the same time both male and female, but they need each other to produce offspring, so they must ejaculate more or less simultaneously.

When their goal has been achieved they roll away from each other and lie there exhausted for more than half an hour. Then they each go their own way without any goodbye, without any sign of friendship.

Let alone love. That is, God helps us, a human invention.

Before I returned to Cassandra I had a very naïve perception of sex. Even the copulations I paid for involved, at least on the surface, some gentleness, some signs of consideration. And when my blocked libido expressed itself in aggressive, even violent forms, I never forgot that there was a woman with me who was letting me use her body and so I exerted myself to enable her to derive at least some pleasure from the experience (although in most cases she could hardly wait for it all to be over).

With Cassandra the engagement of our bodies is like the pairing of hermaphrodite snails. For her sex is more connected with sadism, torture and death than with the pleasure that an orgasm is supposed to bring. In fact, I doubt she experiences orgasm; it seems to me more that Cassandra is fighting all out and that I am merely a handy weapon in her fight, for want of a better one. Although after two weeks of our bedroom battles I cannot shake off the feeling that she could find a better one only on Mars.

"Trust me," she keeps repeating.

But something isn't right. This feeling is ever stronger. Cassandra's assurance that she is only trying to make up for what she missed in the long years of my absence is increasingly unconvincing. After all, we have in front of us enough years to be able make up for what we missed a thousand times – but not in a few weeks, for heaven's sake! It might happen that these excesses drive a wedge between us, rather than bringing us together once more.

But no, even if she agrees with me to some extent, she cannot escape the claws of her passion. Although passion, we both know, Dr. Krauthaker, can be satiated. Hers is insatiable, infinite.

If this is the home I was longing for, I would rather take refuge again in amnesia.

Dr. Krauthaker, instigator of the winter of my discontent!

I have found out that in the life that, thanks to you, I returned to I was nothing, no-one; a drunk, a dreamer, a shirker, maybe even a con man, perhaps unfaithful to the wife who looked after me and our child, as if this was her only source of happiness in life; she cared for us so much that she prostituted her talent in the most worthless TV serials, sacrificing her career for someone who did not deserve it.

I can't believe this. Since the accident on Bali (that perhaps never took place) and since meeting you, I have done nothing to suggest that I am lacking in seriousness, unreliable, unworthy of trust, lazy, full of excuses, under-educated; that I am, in short, in any way like the man described to me by Cassandra.

Who perhaps isn't my wife. And who has, cunningly, given me the role of her sexual lackey in her very own soap opera. Until she grows tired of me and kicks me out onto the street. Perhaps saying (because she likes to take an eye for an eye): "I don't remember ever setting eyes on you before."

She did take me to Hampstead and showed me the luxurious house where we supposedly lived before my disappearance, but nothing about the house or its surroundings gave me even the hint of a feeling that this might be true. But I only began to doubt seriously when she was reluctant to show me photos of our son, who was supposed to be studying in Oxford. She claimed that she had none because she had stopped keeping photos some time ago – they reminded her only of how quickly time was passing and how rapidly the moment was approaching when her body was shoved into the crematorium.

When I said I'd like to visit him, she looked uncomfortable and tried to hide it, but only partly succeeded. "Not right now," she said, "he has exams and a sudden encounter with the father that he thinks is no longer with us would completely throw him. Can't you wait a while, why are you so impatient? I waited six years for you!"

And once again her words sounded like an accusation, as if it was *my* fault that I had been absent for six years, as if I had *made up* the accident and the amnesia. And let's be honest, Dr. Krauthaker: I really was impatient. I accused her of impatience in bed, which after the six years of my absence would after all be understandable (I don't know why men resent it when women show an exaggerated desire even more than when they show a complete lack of interest), but I was unable to convince myself that I had no right to make demands of her and expect her to fulfil them immediately. After all, it was me who had disappeared from her life, not she from mine. Why didn't I ask myself how I would feel if it was the other way round?

Well, I eventually did ask myself that question and immediately my view of her behaviour changed. I felt that her more or less concealed criticisms were a kind of defence; that they concealed great fragility, great fears. That this really was the case became obvious when her sexual energy was pretty much exhausted and we drifted into a normal life. To spend more time with me she cancelled a minor role in some serial (for which she would have been rather well paid), explaining that she preferred to look after me. Until we become close once more, forgive each other all the real or imagined sins, get to know each other again (we cannot deny the distance between us) she would like to spend as much time with me as possible: she would like to cook for me, care for me and my wellbeing, get used to me, allow me to get used to her, for she's aware that she is alien to me, perhaps even more than I am to her, and only in this way, step by step, with extreme caution, can our life together regain its meaning. Of course that didn't mean, she emphasised, that we had to keep talking, that she had to immediately answer all my questions, which at times are too impatient, even violent. Why was I in such a hurry when I said that I had finally come home and achieved my goal? Why not allow time to sort things out? We had plenty of time, hadn't we? If I had doubts and felt this was not my real home, that she was not my wife, that I was the victim of some kind of conspiracy, I could leave, she could not stop me. She would not crawl at my feet in order to hold onto me. Without *me* deciding that I wanted to stay, without *me* accepting this was really my home, we had no future together.

She was right, of course. Although it took quite some time to shake off the feeling of mistrust with which I came to the house, I nevertheless found enough courage to realise how incredible must seem the story of my accident and amnesia (uncannily similar to the "story" told by a cheating husband), so that she too could not immediately trust someone who might have returned home with a serious desire to stay, or simply to see whether it was worth staying. Or even worse, he intended to stay just long enough to forget about the lover that had probably left him and find another. Trust, Dr. Krauthaker: the only thing that can guarantee us a future is that there is once more trust between us. But trust does not appear on its own, you need to work at it. To be patient, to understand, to take a risk.

Thank you, Dr. Krauthaker, for continuing to make transfers to my bank account. (I checked and everything is as it should be: the payments are regular and satisfactory, especially considering that Cassandra is well into the red.) I expected that now you have fulfilled you side of the bargain and brought me home, you would start to turn off the tap (you and your associates, whoever they are) and leave me to rely on Cassandra's resourcefulness and particularly my own. You probably understand that I cannot immediately get a well-paid job (as who? as what?) and want to help me for some time. It is probably also clear to you that although I am "home" with the woman I once lived with, nothing has changed as far as my amnesia goes; I still do not remember the past, I still forget ongoing events within five or six days. In short, it *seems* to me that I have come home, but my absent memory cannot confirm that I have. Cassandra does not like to talk about her overdraft, nor does she like to accept any contribution from me to the household expenses; she wants to know where my money is coming from and of course I cannot tell her. Nor do I want to, not until she tells me at least some of what I expect her to.

And so we live more or less from day to day; she cooks, usually Indian (unbelievably tasty), sometimes we go to one of the res- taurants on King Street in Hammersmith, ten minutes' walk from her (our?) house, and a few times I've insisted that I cook (I won't describe the results), but she still doesn't want to invite any friends from our shared past for a cup of tea (let alone dinner). It's too early, she insists; too early to face them with the husband who has been absent for six years and who on top of everything else remembers nothing. Could I imagine what embarrassment there would be at the table? We must wait, she says. Wait until my memory returns. My polite observations that my memory might (perhaps) return that much sooner if she was willing to be open with me about our (former) life together make no impression on her; things have to unfold naturally

111

she replies to my entreaties that one way or another we try to speed things up. Where are you rushing off to? she asks. Who's waiting for you and where?

It increasingly seems to me that she is most afraid of loneliness. She fears that one day I shall simply disappear, as I did six years ago. It's not surprising that she has hidden all five of my passports; I don't remember how many times I have searched every corner of the house without finding them. Maybe she's taken them to the bank, locked them in a safe. She wants to hold onto me, of that there's no doubt. In fact, I feel sorry for her in a way (more than I feel sorry for myself). For some people life consists only of work and saving for something, with no interest paid; the lives of others are merely the consequence of trusting in the benevolence of fate and the absence of any kind of strategy. Both apply to Cassandra: she saved and ended up with an overdraft (me); she trusted in fate and it turned out that fate passed her by without a glance. It seems, Dr. Krauthaker, that I could slowly become accustomed to this fragile and confused woman and with time, believe it or not, I could even love her. She tries so hard to do nothing wrong; she strives so carefully, strategically to build on the ruins of the old a new, fresh relationship, unconnected with the past.

Aren't you going to commend me, Dr. Krauthaker, for trying to help her?

But increasingly, Dr. Krauthaker, I have the feeling that she doesn't want to help me. That this admittedly pleasant companion (even in bed we have, would you believe, reached an agreement that satisfies us both) will not allow me to cross certain boundaries. That she is hiding something. That although she wants to keep me by her and in her life, there are things she doesn't want to disclose that may threaten this. A good month after she said that I shouldn't disturb our son in Oxford because he had exams, she came up with a new excuse: that my son, who thinks I left them both for another woman, does not want to see me and he must be prepared for the encounter gradually, since first he must get used to the idea that his father has returned.

Like most of her excuses, I could not quarrel with this one. But when after six weeks she didn't want to show me his photograph (she said that, amnesiac as I am, I probably wouldn't recognise him, which is probably true) curiosity arose in me. The mistrust had evaporated some time before, but was replaced by *curiosity*. I have a son? I'd like to see him. Was there anything unnatural about that? But she stubbornly stuck by her guns: if I wanted everything to sort itself out, I had to curb my impatience. For it was my *impatience,* she said, that most threatened our future together.

A number of times she allowed me to use her computer (I couldn't get a connection on my iPad) and when she wasn't in the room I clicked on My Pictures. She didn't have many photos and there were certainly none of me. Nor any showing us together, which was understandable. I found a number of her with other men, but not necessarily lovers, they were more reminiscent of colleagues, fellow actors, TV people.

But I did find two of a young man who was the spitting image of Cassandra. One was labelled Jacob 1, the other Jacob 2. On the first he was serious, on the other he wore a faint smile.

Our son?

I decided to look for him in Oxford, make his acquaintance, ask about his father; of course, not as Trevor Morris, but as Kostas Asimakopulos, expert in Ancient Greek literature. I wanted to get to the bottom of the matter particularly because Cassandra persistently rejected my requests to introduce me to one of our common friends. She kept replying that we had few friends in common and that she had stopped seeing them soon after I disappeared, since she was convinced that they knew where I was and with whom.

And why was I so concerned to get in touch with friends from a life that no longer existed? Hadn't I made any new ones in the last six years? And, come to think of it, wasn't she enough for me? My attempt to find in the phone book the names of the friends I had supposedly gone drinking with and later unconsciously chosen as my alternative identities was also unsuccessful. Not one of the four names was in the London directory.

Nor was Trevor Morris.

And so to Oxford. Of course, I didn't tell Cassandra what I was planning; I lied that I wanted to spend the whole day driving and walking around London; maybe I'd recognise something somewhere, remember something – often restoration of the memory only required a small spark, that's what the experts had assured me, I said

I saw that she was not happy to lose sight of me for the whole day, but she could not object because she knew that she would then only strengthen my ever clearer discomfort at her insistence that we were once an ideal couple and could be again. It had not escaped her that her excuses struck me as increasingly suspicious; and it had not escaped me that she was increasingly concerned about this.

On arriving in Oxford, Kostas Asimakopulos first asked himself where he could find a student called Jacob Morris who was studying at one of the colleges. Which? He couldn't ask Cassandra because she would immediately suspect that he intended to visit his alleged son, so he did what anyone in his place who was sufficiently au fait with the workings of the modern world would do. He ordered a coffee in the first café he came across, went online with his iPad, googled Oxford Classical and Modern Languages Best College, and discovered that among the best offering this programme was Merton College.

Had Trevor Morris also studied at this college, if he had really studied at Oxford? Trevor Morris, failed student, peripatetic teacher of English as a foreign language (you can get that kind of work even if you've only finished secondary school, as long as you're English), failed journalist, failed married man, failed father, a failure in every regard, a total loser? Dr. Kostas Asimakopulos, Associate Professor of Ancient Greek at Harvard, could not believe this as he *knew* the all-round capabilities of Trevor Morris and his other identities.

Merton College is one of the oldest in Oxford and certainly among the most attractive: it occupies a collection of medieval and seventeenth century buildings that look out on a meadow that gently runs down to the Thames, although the entrance is on High Street, close to the university libraries and lecture halls, and with the possibility of living and eating in the college or in your own house not far away.

But all this is known to you, Dr. Krauthaker, since you probably studied at Oxford, too. Well, perhaps in Cambridge, or somewhere in the States, but you must certainly have at least visited Oxford.

And so Dr. Asimakopulos turned up at the porter's, showed him his business card and asked if there was a Jacob Morris on the list of students. The porter checked and confirmed that there was, at which the bearded lecturer in Ancient Greek asked him to give the card to the young man in question with a request that he go to Le Grand Cafe, two hundred metres from the college entrance, because he wished to speak to him in connection with an important matter.

And that it was urgent, because the professor was returning to New York the next day.

So simple, Dr. Krauthaker.

And I waited.

Amidst the noisy students I drank four coffees, looked at my watch, wondered whether the boy would come (he might have lectures, he might be ill, he might have gone on a trip, perhaps the porter can't reach him); all sorts went through my head as I watched the behaviour of his peers who occupied almost every chair in the café. He's probably like them, I thought, since he was also a member of the millennial generation born after 1980 that had grown up with computers and mobile phones and were obsessed with fame, three times more narcissistic than the previous generation, convinced they were entitled to everything they wanted and once they graduated hoped immediately to become managing director of an international corporation.

I couldn't imagine that my supposed son would be any different, as most youngsters bow to the habits and dictates of their time, particularly to peer pressure; nobody wants to be excluded, everyone wants to belong. I'm no exception: why else would I be so tirelessly searching for the memory of a life where I had been part of something bigger than my personal ambitions?

When he came through the door I recognised him immediately, since he was the spit and image of Cassandra and just like in the photograph. He was gangly, slightly bent at the shoulders and, of course, submerged in a conversation on the mobile phone he was holding to his left ear and nodding without actually saying anything. He headed straight for my table without even looking around – at least, I didn't notice him do so; he sat down as if the only empty chair in the place was reserved for him, still on the phone, and felt no need to check whether he was at the right table.

"Listen, I've got to talk to this prof from the States, I'll call you back," he suddenly said and put the mobile away. Only then did he look at me and smiled politely, as naturally as if we'd known each other for ten years. "I hope you haven't been waiting for too long, the porter only just got me, I came as quick as I could."

A polite lad, there's no denying. Calm, relaxed, with just the right degree of confidence, no sign of nerves, concealed traumas, mistrust, adolescent uncertainty. If he really was my son, I wouldn't want him to be any different. But there was nothing of me in his appearance and that somewhat diminished my pleasure in the awareness that my own flesh and blood was sitting opposite me. However, it wasn't unusual or grounds for suspicion that perhaps he wasn't my son, since children are often very like one parent and completely unlike the other.

"Can I get you something?" I asked.

"Yes, please," he replied and confidently gestured to the waiter. "Guinness."

At eleven in the morning.

The blessed student life.

The next moment he looked at his watch and said, considerately and politely, as would any well brought up young man: "Actually, I don't have all that much time, my lectures begin in half an hour."

The hint that I should get on with it was obvious enough and so I dropped the idea of chatting about the weather and similar things.

"Your father and I studied together," I said "At Oxford, Merton, classical and modern languages. We were good friends but after

116

graduation we each went our own way. We kept in touch for a while, but you know how it is… families, obligations. I'd like to get in touch with him again and I thought you could tell me where he is. Is he even in England? I can't find him in the phone directory."

He looked down, sipped the Guinness the waiter had brought him.

"You'd like to get in touch with my father?" he then asked, with slight surprise. "How did you find me? Who told you I was at Oxford?"

"Intuition," I said without hesitation. "Sons often decide to study at the same place as their father."

"And how do you know I am the son of your friend?"

"It seems highly unlikely that Jacob Morris wouldn't be the son of Trevor Morris."

"Trevor Morris isn't my father," he said.

I got a lump in my throat that stopped me from replying and so he continued.

"My father never studied at Oxford. And certainly not classical and modern languages. My dad was a theatre director."

"Then I am mistaken," I said, trying to find the quickest way out of the mess. "There are lots of Morrises and I don't know why it didn't occur to me that the Morris I studied with might not be your father."

"My father isn't even called Morris," he replied. "His name is Alfred Haidacher."

"Oh," I breathed, barely audibly. "Then why is your surname Morris?"

"After my mother, Cassandra Morris. When my father disappeared off the face of the earth, she wanted to erase him from her life so she gave me her surname. At that time I was too young to object. Now I probably would."

"Your father's name was Alfred Haidacher?" I asked as if I still couldn't believe it. "And he was a theatre director? When did he disappear?"

"Six years ago," he replied.

"Would you recognise him if he suddenly reappeared?" I asked.

"I doubt I'll ever see him again. Mum's convinced that he ran off with another woman, changed his name and is living a new life somewhere. Maybe Brazil or Australia, that's where husbands usually run off to. But I think he died in mysterious circumstances."

"No!"

"Maybe I'm wrong, but that's my favourite explanation."

"Is there any possibility that Trevor Morris was related to your mother? A cousin or uncle or something?"

"Mum was an only child, so am I. She has relatives but we don't have any contact. And none of them are called Morris."

"I vaguely remember," I said, trying to salvage something, "that the Trevor Morris I studied with mentioned an Alfred Haidacher a couple of times. I think they were friends. What did your father look like?"

"Oh," he shrugged, "perfectly ordinary, he had a goatee, wore glasses, was a nervous type, he liked to get angry but before he disappeared we were a happy family. I have fond memories of him. My mum got rid of absolutely everything of his, even all the photos showing us together, which seems a bit sick to me, but I put three photos aside and held onto them. On one we're all together in front of the Hampstead house where we lived, in the second my father and I are at the top of the Eiffel Tower. He often took me with him when he was directing abroad – he worked all over Europe and even in America."

"Do you have one of these photographs with you, perhaps in your wallet?" I asked, which was a mistake.

"Why are you interested?" he asked in surprise. "I thought you said you were looking for Trevor Morris, who you studied with."

He emptied his glass, pushed the chair back and got up.

"The beer's on you," he said.

And he left.

On the train back to London I was tormented by speculation, rumination, suppositions, hypotheses and feverish attempts to connect things that refused to form a pattern, other than one which I knew the next minute was more the result of wishful thinking than fact.

Was it possible that in the life I had forgotten I was Alfred Haidacher and not Trevor Morris? Had I been a theatre director and not the all-round failure described by Cassandra? Then I really was her husband. And Jacob Morris really was my son. But in that case Cassandra would *know* that I was Alfred Haidacher. It was impossible that after six years a woman would not recognise the man she had a child with.

So why did she see me as Trevor Morris? Why did she insist that she had been (and still was) married to me and that Jacob Morris was our son? None of it makes any sense, Dr. Krauthaker! Help me! Where can I turn, what can I do to unravel this Gordian knot? And one other thing: do I even have real identity? Was I once someone who could with certainty say that he was this person and no-one else? Someone who others acknowledged he was who he said he was? I know that way madness lies and perhaps soon you will be visiting me in one of the endless number of psychiatric wards in the world, but my torment, Dr. Krauthaker, has intensified to the extent that I feel at any moment my head will explode.

Allow me to come and see you, Dr. Krauthaker. I'm begging you on my knees. Allow me to talk to you face to face. After six years of wandering the world (and carrying out your orders) hasn't the time come to conclude you neurological experiment? And to allow me for some years, at least some years, to lead a normal life.

Are you really completely heartless?

Of course, now I had been deprived of the last good reason to stay with Cassandra any longer than strictly necessary and it was time to throw my things in a suitcase and call a taxi. Sooner or later (if he hadn't already) her son would call her and he would tell her that some Greek called Asimakopulos had been asking about his father, who was supposed to be called Trevor Morris, and then God knows what would happen. I knew I had to disappear as quickly and irrevocably as I had (allegedly) six years earlier. And never return. And erase all traces of Trevor Morris, as well as of my other personas.

But without the passports she had hidden, I couldn't go anywhere. Since I couldn't ask her to hand them over (which she wouldn't) I decided once more to search the whole house. Although we'd gone food shopping a number of times together (me paying with one or other of my credit cards), two days after my return from Oxford I said I didn't feel so good and could she go to the shop on her own. As soon as her rusting Fiesta disappeared round the corner I locked the door and got down to business. I was in luck. And how! I found all five passports wrapped in cellophane in the vegetable drawer at the bottom of the fridge, from where I took a nectarine that I fancied when I opened the fridge door. I had done so by chance, looking for something to eat before Cassandra got back from the shop.

Ten minutes later I was already packed and waiting for the taxi I had called. It appeared in three minutes – someone in heaven must like me. And I vanished. How did you know, Dr. Krauthaker? For in the taxi I got a text message: "Where are you going?" Sorry for not replying. At that moment my answer could only have been: "Wherever."

10.

Dear millymolly@gmail.com. I'm writing to you for two reasons: first, because it occurred to me that there must be at least one expert in the world who would know how to help me and, second, because I know that you will inform Dr. Krauthaker. I doubt he will find the time and the motivation to open my message (one of the thousands to which I received no reply), I'm sure he simply erases them without even taking a look.

Tell him that I've decided to seek a second opinion. I no longer trust your (ex-)husband's diagnosis. Perhaps he really did send me on a "voyage home", as he said, and in the interests of successful treatment has given me obligations that so far I have not been able (nor dared) to refuse. But to be honest, I am no nearer home than I was five years ago, when he sent me forth from his clinic.

Tell him I've found another amnesia expert, as well known or even better known than he is, and that his examinations have filled me with the hope that my problem might be solved by an operation. Your husband did not even consider that possibility!

My new doctor, let's call him Dr. X so that there won't be any sense of competition or envy, accepted my case simply because it reminded him of that of another patient in his care and he hopes that comparing our conditions will lead to new findings. (Another self-centred taker of the Hippocratic oath, but what can you do – better that than being treated by tribal shamans, even though they may be more successful.)

121

I cannot reveal to you where Dr. X is based, because Dr. Krauthaker would quickly track him down (he'd be knocking on his door in less than a week).

I'll tell you only what Dr. X told me and what he promised.

He told me that the memory and *only* the memory creates that which we call identity. At the same time it uncovers the illusion of the complete self, for memory is not a thing, an entity, but a process that changes and rearranges the memories that we collect from the warehouse of the mind. It is wrong to think that the memory of the same event is always the same. It might be approximately so or it might be different – so different that it seems not to relate to the same event. Although we can train the memory process to be surprisingly sharp, it unfolds in complete autonomy beyond the reach of consciousness.

As we get older mistakes arise (like the engine of an old car): new events do not impress themselves in our memory as faultlessly as in our youth. But, surprisingly, the long forgotten past comes close and within reach: it becomes easier for us to remember what happened in school, but harder to recall what we came downstairs for.

But if we were to freeze our memory at, say, twenty we wouldn't retain the optimal image of ourselves. We would retain a draft, almost, you could say – jumbled memories of childhood and all the trivia we learn at school. We would preserve something that in thirty years would be in complete disharmony with time.

That was exactly what happened to my comrade in the care of Dr. X. His name is Harry. At the age of twenty-seven a clumsy operation destroyed his brain's ability to form new memories. For fifty years he has lived in a constant present. He knows only what is happening to him and only *while* it is happening. Over the years he has been the object of more than a thousand scientific tests (without remembering anything about them); he has supplied material for more than a hundred doctoral theses and thousands of articles that have appeared everywhere from academic journals to the sensationalist press.

And what's more, he has also been the subject of two books. Twenty years ago digital images of his badly damaged hippocampus began to appear in prestigious neurological journals; he has become a world famous case, a warning of what can go wrong with a brain operation. He has become one of the rare patients that have done more for neurology than the experts!

Recently, MillyMolly, in each new hotel room I first go into the bathroom and stare into the mirror for several minutes. I don't examine my features – in fact, I don't even see them as they quickly go out of focus and become a blurred stain. I examine my brain. I don't really think I see it, it's probably a projection of a picture from memory: a photograph from a medical book seen *since* the accident, not *before it*.

Through staring at my brain like this am I trying to find traces of the "scar" – that part in which my memory met its end? Or am I doing so in the hope that I will find something, some spot, perhaps barely visible, that will show in which of the endless twists of grey matter my problem resides?

This grey mass, if you didn't know, is made up of a hundred billion nerve cells. These cells or neurons are 85 per cent water, while the rest is made up of proteins, amino acids and inorganic salts. Neurons act as messengers, not only between different parts of the brain, but also between the brain and the rest of the body. The messages are transmitted via electrochemical impulses, which means there is electricity in our brains. That is why an electroencephalogram (EEG) tells us what's happening there; during an epileptic attack, for instance, the line goes crazy like a seismograph during an earthquake. It also behaves oddly when we are dreaming or when we are in the throes of ecstasy.

Our lives, dear MillyMolly, take place in our brain, primarily or even *exclusively* in our brain. There is enough electricity there to power a ten watt bulb and one impulse requires only a thousand-millionth of a watt, so there is no danger of getting a shock if you touch the brain with a finger (especially in your case). But there is a strong possibility of causing a short circuit in the brain, even a large number of them.

That is what happened to me.

Why am I telling you all this?

Because Dr. X said that close examination of my brain had revealed a stunning particularity, something hitherto unknown in neurology. According to Dr. X, I should be experiencing about three epileptic attacks per day – and not mild ones, but brain storms at tornado level. In my brain, more or less the whole time (with breaks that last no longer than three hours per day), all four kinds of waves are happening simultaneously – actually, not simultaneously, but woven into a strange chord so disharmonious that, if it could be heard, would sound like a combination of a locomotive whistle, loud drumming, the convulsive crying of a frightened baby and the whirring of a drill.

I do not of course hear these sounds, he only offered them by way of illustration. It's not surprising, he said, that the connections between the neurons are broken and I don't remember my past, while also forgetting what is happening in the present.

As to what could cause such a catastrophe in my brain, he had no answer. He said only that even a sharp blow to the head would be insufficient for such serious consequences and that clearly something, perhaps an operation, had gone seriously wrong. He could not exclude this because he had noticed on the crown of my head something that could be the healed wound from a hole that someone had drilled in my skull, which was now covered by hair and too undefined to be confirmed without further examination.

Did your husband, MillyMolly, carry out an operation on my brain? Did he implant an electronic chip through which he is controlling my thoughts, feelings, actions? Maybe you've no idea what he did. And if you do know you won't tell me because, I've no doubt, you're both involved in this dirty business.

Dr. X's examinations revealed something else. Particular areas of my grey cells sometimes work independently and without the awareness of the other parts, so I am not even aware of many of my thoughts, and above all my actions and events, since they are not accessible to those parts of the brain that are capable of judging them. How, when or why this fragmentation came about he could not say.

He also warned me of the possibility that something I thought was real might never have happened; and in the same way, many things that had happened I would not remember. Many things that I took to be real events would actually be hallucinations.

Are many of the things I think I've done really just hallucinations?

Is *everything* that happens to me a hallucination?

Dr. X is certain this is not the case – after all, he is also happening to me and he *is* real. Much of what I've told him about myself must have happened and is not only the product of a sick mind. It did not necessarily happen exactly how I remember it as I don't remember things for long, but they don't disappear from my memory instantaneously, instead they fade gradually so that the picture I record in the form of an email is already modified and interpreted on the basis of insufficient data.

What's more, even an intact memory hides within itself a slapdash editor for whom everything is not of equal importance. From randomly selected fragments it assembles a picture that is far from what happened in reality. So don't be surprised, my dear MillyMolly, if I put a question to you: are you real or are you one of my hallucinations?

Dr. X is equally amazed by the *combination* of injuries suffered by my brain. As you may know, amnesia is not a single, uniform illness; it encompasses many different kinds of memory loss. With anterograde amnesia you lose the capacity to form new memories; you cannot remember what happened the previous day, but your past remains accessible to you. This kind of memory loss occurs due to head injury, but is also characteristic of alcoholics and in their case almost always leads to dementia.

With retrograde amnesia, which is equally often caused by a strong blow to the head, you lose your memory of everything that happened before the blow occurred. Some or even all of the lost memories may gradually return (in days, weeks, months). Or not. In rare cases they return suddenly and completely. If that is the case it is because it has been triggered by something, but it is hard to ascertain what. And it is impossible to foretell what might trigger it.

With a third kind, transglobal amnesia, the victim forgets why he finds himself in a particular place. He finds himself, for instance, in the centre of town, but cannot remember the sequence of events that brought him there. This kind of memory loss usually passes in a few hours without any consequences, but it can recur and often. A fourth kind of amnesia is Wernicke-Korsakoff syndrome, which is caused by thiamine deficiency resulting from alcohol abuse. The patient's short-term memory is intact, but he has problems retaining new information and remembering things that preceded the illness. The condition is incurable and develops into a range of neurological problems, uncontrolled trembling, the loss of sensation in the fingers and toes, and worse. Hysterical amnesia, the only one unconnected with brain damage, is caused by a traumatic event that the victim cannot come to terms with and thus does not let it be imprinted on the memory. Here the cause is psychological and the memory usually returns within a few days, although the victim does not remember the incident that triggered the loss in the first place.

As you can imagine (and Dr. X emphasised this), in treating amnesia the victims are best helped by those nearest to them – their partner, children, parents, siblings, close friends – who can play them their favourite music, show them photographs, describe past events. Thanks to your husband, as you well know, I am deprived of all this. Before my nearest and dearest (I must have some, most people do) can help me, I have to find them.

But how can I find them if no-one helps me?

Your husband least of all, even though he managed to convince me that he sent me round the world with precisely that purpose.

I'm convinced that Dr. X is my best shot and so I'm going to stay in his clinic and allow him to carry out the procedures which he thinks are reasonable or necessary. Regardless of the consequences. I have no other choice. In fact, he gave me some hope with the first tests he carried out. He stuck electrodes to my head, attached them to a computer and in that way measured all sorts of things going on inside my skull. That was how he discovered that the different waves were present in my brain at the same time, or at least in rapid – too rapid – sequence. During the tests it happened that one of the electrodes came unstuck and slid down from the top of my head to my neck. At that moment there appeared before me a clear picture of a five-year-old girl running naked across soft sand towards the sea and from the other side appeared a dark-haired woman in a bikini who was trying to catch her before she got there. I even heard a voice that seemed slightly familiar: "No, Sandra, no!"

And the whole time I had the feeling that I was there, watching. And that some force also sent me after the girl.

Then the vision vanished

When I described it in detail to Dr. X he thought it over for some time. Then he removed all the electrodes and asked me to close my eyes and relax. He pressed a single electrode to my skull and moved it in different directions. All kinds of images began to flash across my mind, some lasting only a few seconds. The woman who I saw in the bikini was now standing at a cooker in a well equipped kitchen, stirring something; in a mirror on a wall I saw a reflection of myself, much younger but recognisable, at a table in a large reference library. Then I saw the same young man making his way along a crowded city street; and then a mill wheel, creaking and turning; and then the girl from the beach, sitting in my lap with a book. Then a fist flew towards my face and I even felt the force of the blow. And when the fist withdrew, I saw in front of me the face of a young man of about thirty years old with almost white hair, distorted in anger.

The next thing was a feeling that I was standing in the middle of a spacious old house, completely empty, the doors removed, the plaster crumbling from the walls and the windows without panes, through which a cold wind was blowing. I was standing in the centre of a large room, almost a hall, completely empty, with three other empty rooms visible through the doorways. And it all seemed strangely familiar to me; as if I had been in this building or that I had dreamt of it and remembered my dream.

Then Dr. X removed the electrode and the pictures in my brain vanished.

When I described them Dr. X said that the memory of my past was still evidently accessible, stored in different parts of my brain. This was also characteristic of normal people, but in my case something had torn the *connection* between these islands of memory. And since there was no connection, the fragments could not form a whole. This could perhaps be done with the right kind of electrical stimulation, by the strategic planting of mini electrodes which could, if the attempt failed, easily be removed.

He suggested I should think about an operation.

Considering that Dr. Krautkaker has already performed God knows what operation on my brain, I would rather say: no, anything but an operation! Dr. X said that it has to be my free decision, that he has no intention of pressuring me, since he can't even guarantee that it will work; it could happen that it won't and the electrodes will have to be removed. But there is a chance (he can't say how great it is) that my condition will at least slightly improve.

Not only that: there is a possibility that my memory will return completely.

Why am I telling you this? Because I know you will immediately pass the news on to your husband, who will explode with anger and jealousy. I cannot believe that he will be able to accept the loss of the tool that he used for five years to carry out his heinous schemes.

But enough of that.

I'm faced with a big decision and there's no-one to advise me.

Except for Harry, who can't advise me.

Fifty years ago, when he had an operation, he was unfortunate to have a neurosurgeon who, out of professional zeal, wanted to try something new. Besides which, in those days it was believed that the memory was like a sequence of photographs of sensory perceptions like the frames of a film. Over the following decades the academic field of memory was colonised by information theory and the computer, and memory was divided into coding, storing and recall. Scanning of Harry's brain showed that this was all nonsense; the human brain is so complex that no computer can get to the bottom of it.

Besides which, MillyMolly, I would like to emphasise that my fellow sufferer was not operated on because he lost his memory, but rather he lost his memory because he was operated on. From the age of ten onwards he had been the victim of epileptic attacks that over the years became increasingly unmanageable. A neurosurgeon (let's call him Dr. Y, so that an international professional muddle does not arise) decided to carry out an experimental procedure. With a drill he made himself from car parts he drilled two holes into the epileptic's skull the size of a fifty cents coin, a "double door into the patient's brain" he called it. Then through these holes he vacuumed out most of his central temporal lobe, the front half of the hippocampus and almost the whole amygdala.

When the patient came round, the intrepid surgeon ascertained that the number of epileptic attacks greatly diminished. But at the same time it became clear that the patient remembered no details of his time in hospital. Nor any important event from recent years. The operation had caused general anterograde amnesia: he had lost the capacity to form any new memories!

I know what you're going to say. Like everything else in this world, medicine progresses over the bodies of its victims. Why shouldn't one victim enable the treatment and cure of dozens, thousands of patients? I don't doubt that's how your dear husband thinks, too. Anything for science! Anything for fame! Even at the price of the suffering of chance individuals. Even at the price of the end of the world.

At this point I won't tell you any details of my treatment with Dr. X. Let Dr. Krauthaker be on tenterhooks for some time. Let him occupy himself with the painful possibility that a hitherto unknown neurologist (and neurosurgeon!) somewhere in the world has overtaken and surpassed him. If his surgical intervention returns to me the memory of everything or at least most of what happened before the accident in Bali, then I shall recommend him for the Nobel Prize.

Dr. Krauthaker can go hang.

Harry is something special, even in comparison with me. I'm sure your husband will have heard of him, since in 1990 the digital images of his damaged hippocampus became an integral part of every textbook of neurology, especially those which deal in detail with the issue of memory. Your husband probably, considering his relative youth, studied Harry's amnesia – he might even have been one of those who devoted his degree dissertation to it. I don't remember us talking about it; if we did, I didn't make a note of it (although that applies to many things).

After the death of his mother Harry passed into the care of Dr. X, who wanted to protect him from the role of circus clown (which he played for some time without being aware of it), so he cared for him at his clinic in conditions of complete anonymity. The clinic staff had to sign a statement that they would reveal the patient's identity to no-one and that they would not take his photograph. Of course, Dr. X did not usurp him; over the years more than a hundred neurologists and students of neurology were allowed to scan Harry's brain and carry out cognitive tests. But none of them knew Harry's name.

Even I don't know, although we have neighbouring rooms in the clinic. Dr. X knows who Harry is, but he doesn't know who I really am (because I cannot tell him). I've shown him the five passports I was given by the Great Manipulator and I've told him everything I think about Dr. Krauthaker's actions and hidden agenda.

I don't think Dr. X believed everything, or at least has reservations about a number of things. Above all, he seems to find it hard to accept that Dr. Krauthaker has malicious intentions towards me. Perhaps he has reasons for his doubt or maybe it's just collegial loyalty. Maybe they even know each other, although he never either confirmed or denied that.

Anyway, he recommended that I stay in his clinic for a time and after he has carried out the tests he is planning, I can decide for or against an operation.

My colleague Harry is fortunate that he doesn't even know his own story. The most he can tell about himself is the occasional statement that he has "problems with his memory". If I keep questioning him, he is at first confused and then he waves his hand and says: "Maybe I had an operation or something." And he repeats that ten or twenty times, convinced that he's telling me for the first time. Because his capacity for remembering things is minimal, he keeps repeating himself, even to the extent that he forgets he has had lunch and eats it twice.

Conversations with him are like the dialogues of a dramatist who has himself suffered memory loss and who lives in the constant present; he is obsessed with crosswords and if you say to him that he is a real crossword master, he will wink at you and say "a crucified master". And he is not aware of just how precisely he has described the actual nature of his condition. At moments he is overwhelmed by frustration, anger or panic, but never too seriously and generally he is a calm, naturally placid, cheerful sort, unaffected and withdrawn, with no regrets about the past or fears for the future, completely without anchor in an age that causes many people unbearable torment.

So, he never complains about the tests and examinations that Dr. X and visiting neurologists carry out on him, from EEG to CT to MRI, as well as cognitive tests relating to his memory, his attention span and reaction time, his IQ, ability to identify shapes and images, his ability to find the fastest way out of a maze, perceptual learning, language skills and tolerance for pain. He goes through each test as if for the first time, although sometimes he gets the feeling that something is happening that has happened before – a feeling reminiscent of *deja vu*.

One big question is whether he can remember his dreams. Often when he wakes he describes what he dreamed, but Dr. X is convinced that it's all made up and in truth he does not dream, but rather collects unconnected scraps of memories from marginal parts of his brain – memories of events at which he has been present since the operation, which although it saved him from epilepsy (and possibly saved his life) condemned him to an eternal present. Not long after his father died a slip of paper was found in Harry's wallet on which was written "Father is dead", as if he knew that he would forget this. And as if he wanted to ensure that he would every now and then remember the loss of his father.

During our next conversation Dr. X put some questions to me.

Did I really want an operation to return my memory and my full awareness of myself? This would not bring a state of bliss, far from it. To be *me,* the real *me* with no side tunnels of forgetfulness to flee down when life takes an unpleasant turn, also means suffering. Was I ready for it? Did I wish once more to become Tantalus, threatened by the rocks above my head while also suffering from hunger and thirst? Did I want to be once again someone tormented by jealousy and eaten by fear? Did I want once more to become a person whose life was devoted to the fruitless pursuit of pleasure, like the Danaides who had to fill a bottomless vessel with water?

"Bliss is reserved for the poor in spirit," said Dr. X.

Then he read Harry and me an extract from the *Encyclopaedia of Stupidity:* "Fear is the only hell. Moreover, it is an inextricable part of our existence. Fear mars our enjoyment, but makes the world go round. Through fear of death we submit to life. Fear of death leads to a blind and insatiable desire for sex, power and fame, which lead to fear of punishment, pain and death. We are caught in a vicious circle."

Is that what I wanted back? Did I want to be scooping up water with a sieve again? Did I want to be dragging logs that I'd already carried down back to the top of the mountain in order to roll them down, because I'd realised that was easier than carrying them? Did I want to tie myself to the mast again so that the ship would go faster? Did I want once more to put my head through the hole in a millstone so as not to lose it before I rolled it down the hill?

That was the kind of life that awaited me if my memory returned completely. I couldn't avoid it, I couldn't arrange things differently. Why then *me* at any price? What I am now is also *me,* although different from the previous one. But the self is never constant; when I was twenty I was different from when I was forty. And what will it be like when I'm eighty-five and a fading memory becomes part of the natural order of things?

Why am I so keen to be where I have never been and never shall be?

You can imagine, MillyMolly, that I was somewhat confused after our conversation.

Was Dr. X raising Harry's mental state into an ideal way of life? Was he trying to warn me against a possible unfavourable outcome of the operation? I thought about this for a long time (in between tests, I had plenty of it) but I did not find an answer that I could accept wholeheartedly. He emphasised that the decision was mine. I would have to sign a statement that in the case of failure I would not take legal action or demand damages. That's how these things work.

But at least Dr. X was open about it. Your husband was not.

While staying at Dr. X's clinic I got two text messages – I don't know whether they were from your husband or one of his associates. The first demanded that I travel to Taipei and collect from the reception at the Hotel Riviera an envelope addressed to Sven Lindgren (containing instructions for my next action). I received this text ten days ago. Because I did not reply straight away (I always had before) and the letter to Sven Lindgren lay there uncollected, today I received a new message: "You have failed to fulfil the agreed assignment. There will be consequences!"

Okay, I said to myself, bring it on. Let's see what actually happens. Let it finally be confirmed that your husband is exploiting me. Let me finally have it in black and white that I am being wronged. Then, perhaps, I will be able to persuade the police somewhere in the world to start an investigation into his doings. Tell him that. And tell him that this isn't a threat, but self-defence. If he would prefer it to be a threat, then he can take it as such.

Once the investigation begins, he'll find it difficult to wriggle out of it. Be prepared to be visiting him in jail for twenty years.

Anyway, now I am receiving the "You have failed to fulfil the agreed assignment…" message twice a day. I've got used to it and am not the slightest bit afraid. I have decided that the operation – even if the outcome is not what Dr. X and I wish it to be – is the least worst option I have.

What's the worst that can happen? That I become a prisoner of the moment, like Harry? If I am as calm and content as he is then I have nothing to fear. I should be more afraid that the operation is a success and that I am suddenly, like a bolt out of the blue, confronted by what I have been most of my life.

What if Dr. Krauthaker, for scientific purposes, borrowed me from prison where I was serving a life sentence for the murder of my wife

133

and three children? Dr. X has warned me that such possibilities cannot be excluded.

We are sailing into the unknown, he said.

Greetings, kleinebilly@yahoo.com. It's a long time since we heard from each other. That's primarily your fault, since I've never received a reply from you. The other reason is that I've been very busy, a lot has been happening. I am right now getting ready for an operation in a neurological clinic in a city in a developed part of the world (I cannot reveal the location, because I don't know who you are connected with) which is intended to return my memory. Actually, my memory is not lost (I am assured by Dr. X, one of the greatest authorities on amnesia), but rather fragmented, scattered around my brain as if blown there by the wind. And the reason I cannot remember my past is because these scattered fragments are not neurologically connected.

Dr. X intends to plant mini electrodes at key points in my brain, which will use electrical stimulation to extend the reach of my brain waves. These waves from different ends of the brain should then reach far enough to meet and merge, thus creating the possibility that the scattered fragments of memory will identify each other and combine into a whole.

I haven't the slightest doubt that Dr. X is a genius; who else would be capable of coming up with something like this? Of course, the operation is risky and this could easily be the last email you receive from me. My condition might worsen and the centres that enable the ongoing formation of memories might also be destroyed – those that are retained for five to six days.

To be honest with you, I wavered for a long time. But in the end Dr. X convinced me that I have nothing to lose; even if something goes wrong and I am stuck in the present, at least I won't be unhappy any more. I'll no longer need to roam aimlessly from one place to the next, carrying out assignments ordered by God knows who, which I feel are at odds with my true nature. In recent days, even at the clinic where I am awaiting the operation, I have been bombarded with text messages about such assignments.

This time, I am going to dig my heels in and I won't leave here until the thing is completed. If my memory returns, I will know *who* and *what* I really am, and my "employers" will no longer be able to get to me. If the thing goes wrong and I can't even remember that I ate lunch a few minutes ago, then I will have become useless to them.

Either way, I'll finally shake them off.

Above all Dr. Krauthaker.

But wait, kleinebilly@yahoo.com. I'm talking as if I'm still preparing for the operation, as if it's going to take place tomorrow or the day after!

As if I hadn't already laid on the operating table; as if Dr. X hadn't already arranged his surgical equipment on the trolley – alongside scalpels and various hooked instruments, an electric drill with which he intended to drill holes at different locations in my skull (six or seven, he said). As if I hadn't already been surrounded by five assistants in white gowns, including an anaesthetist who was waiting for the order to inject me with something that would put me to sleep. As if I hadn't yet signed a statement that in case of failure or an insufficiently successful operation I waived my right to take legal action. As if I hadn't signed this statement with my five aliases, as Trevor Morris, Neil Youngson, Sven Lindgren, Alfred Haidacher and Kostas Asimakopulos. As if I hadn't written the relevant passport number next to each one.

Had I forgotten that I am no longer at the clinic and that I am writing to you from a hotel room?

In truth, it's behind me already.

I don't mean that the operation is behind me, for Dr. X never got an opportunity to carry it out. At the moment when the anaesthetist raised the syringe to inject the anaesthetic into my arm, my mobile phone beeped. I had it in the pocket of my trousers, which in the case of a brain operation there is no need to remove; that also was agreed with Dr. X.

I pulled it out and pressed the button. A message.

"Carry on!"

I put my mobile phone in my right pocket and from the left pulled out my folding knife. I had that with me, although that was not by agreement with Dr. X. As far as possible, I have it with me at all times. I jumped from the operating table and stabbed Dr. X in the heart. Will I ever forget the look of surprise in his eyes? When he crumpled to the floor I stepped across him and stabbed the anaesthetist in the stomach. I thought: they'll save him, but I didn't want to finish the business. Let him live.

The other assistants fled.

In no great hurry, I went to my room at the end of the corridor. I threw some things into my case and travel bag, went along the empty corridor of the clinic, where an alarm was ringing, to the main entrance, hailed a taxi which conveniently came round the corner, calmly got in it and drove off.

And thus, kleinebilly@yahoo.com, ended yet another episode in my life. Dr. Krauthaker won again, as so often before.

11.

Dear whoever@gmail.com, I'm writing to you because you might be bored and interested in a short description of my emotional state. I am increasingly convinced that what I am experiencing most of the time is not chronic grieving for the lost person but clinical depression. Cast into a world populated by masses, I feel most separate from the world in the midst of the greatest noise, the midst of life, which others celebrate with singing and dancing. As if I was dwelling inside a transparent balloon, where I can stretch out my arms, but I cannot touch anyone. And no-one can touch me.

In fact, people usually fail to even notice me, except when I decide to make contact with them. Because I have been instructed to do so. But even in those cases I am separated from them by an invisible wall and whatever kind of transaction I have with them, it always remains half real in a way, something that I participate in conditionally. Often I feel like a prisoner in solitary, watching his life like a film on the television screen.

I fear this solitude and would like to avoid it, but the fear I feel in company is worse, so I prefer to be alone, locked in this or that hotel room. In company, even if my interlocutors are quite witty, after a short conversation (in which I never participate with more than ten per cent of my energy) I am overcome by extreme weariness. I stop listening, I sink into my own thoughts, I float away.

There are things that fill me with more fear than others. Some only trigger a feeling of anxiety, others literally paralyse me.

Sometimes it is the view from a train that is travelling across an endless plain of green fields, with not a single house in sight and not even a single tree as far as the horizon. Another time – and how strange these contrasts are – it is the view from a hotel window on the twentieth floor in the midst of an urban desert of skyscrapers in the middle of Tokyo or some other mega metropolis, of the limitless sterility of the strivings that create such concrete ant heaps. The thought that behind each of the hundreds of thousands of windows lives someone who does not fundamentally differ from any of the other millions of human ants, causes such pain in my chest that I think I am having a heart attack.

The pain of emptiness.

If I think it through thoroughly, it is emptiness that fills me with the greatest fear.

The emptiness of ideas, theories, striving, ambition, wishes. Also feelings and emotions. The emptiness of everything we carry inside us. The emptiness of all that surrounds us, in every micro particle, in space. But above all in people. Other people. Hell is other people, wrote Sartre. And for me they are. Their emptiness is a mirror image of my own. Inside me, too, everything that happens to (and through) me is in a way devoid of content, without real foundation. As if I was dreaming it all and that the external world was made up only of leaping shadows that appear and disappear at random, aimlessly, just like that. Which are because they just are. Without reason.

I often watch them. Other people.

I sit on a bench in some park or square, sip beer at a pavement café, stare through a restaurant window onto the street and observe the human ants as if trying to find a place for myself among them. As if trying to see myself among the mass of others hurrying, hoping, laughing, frowning, committed to goals that are perhaps around the next corner or far in the future, wrapped up in their intentions, their schemes, obsessed with problems that are *less than dust* in the context of eternity and the universe.

Although the worst pain is caused by the awareness that we are all just bits of the emptiness, I cannot find myself in the mass of Others. There is nothing within me that is not temporary, a moment at a particular point on the way to nowhere. With what can I win the favour of those with whom my contacts are merely conditional? From some of the exceptional Others in my life there remain only shadows which the inaudible wind drives past me. Why would I want it to be any different?

Only the real *me* could wish that.

Actually, my life is simple in a special way. Nothing touches me sufficiently to become a cause for concern. I know we live at a time that is approaching the end of days; I know that the political elites around the world are dripping with hypocrisy, lies, selfishness; I know that the greed of the few (a minority because the majority never get the opportunity to behave in the same way) is remorselessly driving mankind towards the abyss where (and rightly so) those who are pushing us towards the abyss will also find themselves (I'll never understand how they can close their eyes to the fact that the same fate awaits them). I know that poverty, stupid wars, human cruelty, indifference and treachery have passed the point at which the train hurtling towards ruin can be stopped.

I know all that.

And much else besides.

And I am indifferent to it all. Not indifferent like the majority of people who are not even aware of these threats (only a minority is aware), but indifferent because they do not even concern the (conditional, hollow) person I have been for the past six years. As far as I am concerned (I-at-this-moment), the world can plunge into the abyss tomorrow, together with the emptiness inside me, and I would not miss it (I am not someone who *could* miss it). The only reason I don't really wish for this to happen is the stubborn hope that, by the will of God (or rather, happy coincidence), I will finally reach home and connect with the One That I Was.

And perhaps even find out why I am here.

Why I came to this world.

Dear whoever@hotmail.com, living in the present (but not in the past and the future, between which the present is a bridge) also has its good side. It seems to me that the majority of "normal" (brain undamaged) people live in a kind of fog, a cloud of memories, rumination, regret, resentment, reliving events flattering to the ego, plotting revenge against those who have wittingly or unwittingly caused them offence, and that because of being trapped in this cloud certain moments do not even exist for them.

Moments of which I am all too aware. For I am aware primarily (if not exclusively) of moments, which unfortunately fade into oblivion.

Maybe it is precisely because of this that the moments when I am aware that I *am,* that I am *in this world,* that I *live* are all the more intense. Because I am not shrouded in a cloud of memories or obsessed with planning the future, the only thing that I perceive without restriction is the here and now: the sound of my shoes on the pavement; the tremor of leaves in a gentle breeze, the swaying of the treetops in a storm, the splash of waves at a distance or close by; the colour, shape and smoothness (or roughness) of the reception desk in the all too many hotels in which I have passed the nightly part of my existence in recent years; the smell of food in the restaurants where I eat (since I have no opportunity to cook); the intimidating silence that permeates the sky on a clear night; the infinitude of space, which lies far beyond the visible stars; the pain in my heart because I cannot connect it with events in the past; the boredom of people in the airport lounges where I spend so much of my time; those constantly evasive eyes, as if they wished to conceal God knows what secret; the roar of aeroplane engines and the sudden changes in their sound that always makes me afraid we are going to start falling from the sky; and the strangers who speak to me with their head tilted slightly back as if they were looking at a menu. Not to mention the dripping taps in the bathrooms of the innumerable hotel rooms that have been my home in recent years and the stubborn inaccessibility of what I was and experienced before my accident. An inaccessibility which is like a tattoo that has become such a part of me that I do not even think about it. And the inaccessible ambitions I must once have had, although they have been left behind me like invisible and scattered ash from a burnt out fire.

Thanks to the narrowing of my perceptions life has long been more poetry than prose, more the simultaneity of flickering moments than

140

a sequence of episodes. Here I am thinking above all of the content of my perceptions, which are focused (ever more, it seems) on the visual, audial and olfactory incursions of the environment into my consciousness of myself in time, space and the world. For instance, the intrusive noise of crickets that doesn't let me sleep in one of the innumerable hotels; or the rattle of the air-conditioning unit, which is never silent, even in the best hotel; or the bed cover that I know will outlive me; or the sickly sweet music that pollutes the lifts and corridors and restaurants of the better hotels; or the toothpaste ads that cannot be avoided even on a plane twelve kilometres in the air.

And of course, the books I cart with me.

What am I reading? *War and Peace, Ana Karenina, Lolita, Heart of Darkness?* I have read all of those and so my luggage contains books that cannot be read at one go and which I find on book shelves under the heading of "philosophy". I know that among the arrogant intellectual elite that category has been long overlooked, even devalued, but for me it is precious because even the name (love of wisdom) leads me to the thought that in such books I might find the way to myself. That is my main goal (as well, it seems, of most other people, including those that have not suffered memory loss).

Finding the true self that lies beneath or behind everything that has been inculcated within us should be the goal of everyone who has enough depth not to shrug off such a question. We must not forget, dear lady, that publishing philosophy books is not an industry that brings the publishers villas and yachts and gold jewellery. They can only compete with self-help books by pretending they belong among them. Literature is also wasting away, dying. But if they could convince people that novels are a survival tool and not just "stories about other people", then people may start reading them again.

Would they learn more from them than from self-help books? I don't know. I read novels quickly because I want to find out what happens. I cart philosophy books around the world in the hope that I may one day read them to the end. And ascertain if there is anything useful in them, advice on how to solve a problem that is exclusively

141

mine. I'm still convinced that no-one reads novels to admire the verbal exhibitionism of the narcissistic authors, but in the hope that in the midst of the story, among the words of an aesthetic nature, they may find something that alleviates their anxiety.

Unfortunately, in contemporary novels I can hardly find anything to give me more than a slight satisfaction that I have persisted to the end of a made-up story about made-up people. Perhaps the fault lies with the novels that have flooded the market in recent years from the tireless publishing production line. Perhaps they are all written too formulaically; perhaps they contain too little that is new, different, too little formal risk. When I've read a few, I get the feeling that I've read two thousand and I don't feel inclined to start the two-thousand-and-first.

There is a difference between reading books and directly experiencing my environment (whichever it is, for it is constantly changing, although remaining similar) which many are unaware of. In novels, whoever@hotmail.com, life follows (more or less hidden) literary rules, perhaps prescribed by literocrats who, like doctors, claim the exclusive right to diagnose (literary) health or sickness. And who, just like doctors, reject any kind of shift towards alternatives.

Life runs its course with mistakes that a novel would not tolerate. At times it drags, it lacks dynamism, it lacks dramaturgy, there are too many complications and not enough resolutions, it is unconvincing, static, the story barely gets anywhere. Everything roughly turns in a vicious circle of endless repetition, of experiencing one's own life like leftovers that we forget to put in the fridge.

And something else: we can give up on a novel by closing it or giving it away, we can throw it in the bin, take it to a second-hand bookshop or return it to the library; we can get rid of it without a second thought or feeling of guilt. The story of the life we are really living (if we are not fortunate enough to have Fate end it for us) can only be ended by suicide.

Of course, we only have one life, however monotonous, while a novel is supposed to be literature and in literature there are supposed to be certain rules that few authors dare to break, since they don't want to risk losing the reader's interest or the wrath (not to say arrogant scorn) of the literocrats. Even novelists have to make a living and cannot afford to ignore the latest trends. The life that we really live (as much as we do, as much as we are even aware of what is happening to us) goes its own way, regardless of how stubbornly we try to insert into it more "artistic" twists and turns, a more convincing tone, a more significant sub-text.

Who do you think, whoever@hotmail.com, is the author of the life we live? Did he ever learn the rules of good narrative? Did he ever go to a creative writing school? Has he ever read a book? But above all: who is the author of the life that I am being forced to live? Is it some messed-up writer of detective stories who has never managed to create anything worthwhile and who has decided, out of revenge, to write something that is a mockery of life?

How else am I to interpret what is happening to me?

If I knew what the meaning was of the path I am being compelled to follow; if I knew that it served a purpose that could at least be guessed at, if not defined, then I would experience everything that happens (and happens to me) differently. The story of my journey would not be so foreign to me, so pointless, and I would move forward in a committed, dedicated way. The knowledge that I was sacrificing myself for something worthwhile would give my life direction and then the path would at least be bearable, if not pleasant.

The hope that my years of wandering from one end of the world to another represent a journey back to what I was (and which is no longer accessible) has evaporated. If I haven't returned home after five years, then it's highly unlikely that I will in the next five. I shall remain forever a stranger in my own life, for the rest of my days a puppet in the hands of a perfidious manipulator who knows precisely what he is doing with me and the purpose of the performance that is being staged.

Dear whoever@gmail.com, colours, sounds and smells are the main ingredients of life that enter my awareness as I move through the world. Through a world that knows no limits, since all the continents are at my disposal and I've visited them all (except Antarctica), and all the endless seas that I have flown over, from the smallest to the largest, or sailed across on passenger or cargo ships.

I'm on the road, always on the road – my middle name is Movement. Not only through space (and spaces), but also through time, which is squeezed into a few hours, perhaps a day, sometimes two, before I once more have the feeling that my life is starting anew, although not a new life.

I truly live each day as if it were my last and in a sense it *is* my last, since I don't remember the previous one well enough, unless I take a peek at my electronic records. But then it is no longer *my* day, for what I read is already so alien, so distant, that it's like a story – not necessarily mine, but one which anyone could be experiencing.

Although consciousness, which is awareness of every sequential moment, is made up primarily of feelings, don't you think? And because my memory is restricted to ongoing events, my experiencing of what I am, what I do and what in certain moments surrounds me, is that much more intense. My image of the world and my presence in it is so heightened that even the most sophisticated TV screen could not compete. I am literally floating in a world of colours, smells and sounds, which paradoxically, thanks to their almost intrusive presence, I sometimes stop perceiving, perhaps because I am too accustomed to them. Whereupon, they once again assault me so suddenly that I am startled – as if thrown from a deep sleep.

This, I imagine, is how Robinson Crusoe got accustomed to the colours, smells and sounds of his desert island, which at the beginning so agitated and disconcerted him because they were unknown. Then he, too, was suddenly aware of them once more, as if the wind had changed and they were forcing their way into his eyes, ears and nose.

Actually, our fates are similar.

He was living on and had to cope with a desert island. I am living on and have to cope with an island of time, which is cut off from the world by a sea of oblivion.

However, do not most people live on such a desert island of time? Is not the content of their thoughts like a scrap of isolated land with ancient plants, trees and fruits, and where animals and particularly the birds in the treetops call with always the same voices or with voices that contain little variation?

For the thoughts of most people, even the most educated, and perhaps them most of all, are so encoded in acquired patterns that it is hard, if not impossible, to include anything new or different – anything that is not in tune with the established, traditional melodies. Even though each bird is convinced that his song is his alone – original and best.

And if that really is the case, then I'm deprived considerably less than I thought. And perhaps the wrong I experienced is not so bad that I need to suffer too much. There are moments when I think that I could accept my fate, that I could end my (supposed) journey to my (supposed) home.

For what awaits me at my goal other than the chance of finding out who I was in the past? And even that will have to be told to me and described by someone else, since my memory, when (if) someone recognises me, won't miraculously start to work again. And whoever is prepared to describe my past runs the risk (after the Cassandra episode) of not being believed.

Colours, sounds, smells. Is there anything else that makes up our life? Is all the rest not just a fog of dreams, a flickering of outlines from which it is difficult to create a lasting image? A fabrication, a fiction that most people "adopt", just like infertile couples adopt a child so as not to be left without offspring?

For me, what is most real (perhaps the only thing) is what I perceive with my senses. Not what I simply perceive, but what *attacks* and *occupies* my senses. The smell of a hotel room carpet, the stains on it left behind by who knows which guest before me, and the dirty buttons on the remote control, which every time I enter a new hotel room I spray with Spitaderm (destroys even HIV, it says on the bottle). And not only the remote, but all the switches (the most notorious breeding ground of viruses and bacteria), as well as everything else that I will touch during my stay (not to mention the toilet seat).

And of course the smell of sweaty socks when I take my shoes off in the room, as well as the smell of leather, soles, laces, which with every kilometre walked is slightly different. The smell of freshly washed (or crumpled) bedding when I lie down to rest; the smell of toothpaste when I bend over slightly in front of the bathroom mirror, brushing my already decaying teeth. The smell of cleaning fluid in hotel lifts; sometimes a whiff of perfume when I have been preceded by a lady who at any price wishes to conceal her natural odours.

The smell of red hot pavements in tropical and subtropical towns along which my slightly worn shoes gently creak or rhythmically squeak. I have three pairs for different occasions. Although I could buy new ones, I don't want to change them; they represent in my life the most visible evidence of the continuity of *me* (although the *me* of only the last six years).

And thus I travel through space and time, while there build up inside me the colours, smells and sounds that are my only life; the only thing I really perceive; the only thing that confirms in my mind that I am, that the world surrounds me. I can recognise more than sixty different drinks by colour and odour, from mescal to Malibu, from vodka to cognac, and more than thirty wines, with my eyes closed, by smell alone, I can differentiate between Australian Shiraz from the Barossa Valley and Malbec from the vineyards of Chile. There is no doubt that I am a freak, although no-one would know that from my exterior, which suggests a boring, trustworthy, middle-aged businessman. There is nothing about me that suggests I don't know who I really am, that I am a marionette in the hands of unseen puppeteers. No-one sees the suffering that I carry with me through this strange, unfriendly world.

And who would be at all interested in my suffering? We all carry through life our *own* burden, our *own* losses, our *own* unanswered questions. Although we are accompanied by the same smells, colours, sounds. Sounds from the street at night, traffic during the day, silence in the desert, voices on television, in restaurants, pubs, the sounds of thunder, the wind, storms, a laptop keyboard; sounds from the stomach, the circulation of blood through the carotid arteries; the irritating sound of car alarms, mobile phones ringing, sounds from neighbouring hotel rooms, the sounds of lifts going up or down, the sound of car horns in traffic jams, the sound of laughter in bars I wander past on the way to work or home (or nowhere).

And colours: the colours of walls, items in hotel rooms, other people's shoes, clothes, faces on buses, on pavements, behind car wheels, at tables; the colours of sunsets, desert sand, flowers in botanical gardens, keyboards; the colour of paper in books. Trees by the roadside and the melancholy colours of falling leaves in parks and gardens. Colours, smells and sounds.

And, of course, hotels, the only home of the wanderer who is not allowed to stay more than a few days – in rare cases, a week or two. Not only hotels, but accommodation of all kinds, including rooms more reminiscent of cupboards, even tents and quite a few park benches, but also grass or sand beneath the stars or in a violent storm. I am accustomed to the best and the worst. I am accustomed to the kind of luxury that should be banned since it mocks the platitude that we are all born equal. I am accustomed to poverty, which fills me with anger and hatred towards those who are responsible for it; to the one per cent of greedy hypocrites at the top who would allow their grandmothers to forego a hot meal in order to improve their bank balance.

I am accustomed to war and bloody slaughter, broken skulls, charred remains of children, severed heads and bodies hanging from a tree in more than a dozen pieces; I am accustomed to the hypocritical expressions of politicians and other "important" figures, who are not ashamed to lie to my face or to the camera, and are not the slightest bit embarrassed although they know that I know they are lying. As Terence said: I am human, nothing human is alien to me.

All the more because I am not innocent myself. Only God knows how many people I have deprived of life, injured, tortured, harmed; how many children I have deprived of a father or mother, or both; how much blood I have spilt because ordered to, because I received instructions through a chip planted in my brain. The details of such acts I do not (other than exceptionally) include in the emails I send around (or to myself), as I don't want to remember them (if I could read about these events after I have forgotten about them a few days later they would burden my whole life and it's possible that sooner

147

or later I would kill myself). It's bad enough that horrendous scenes appear in my dreams, where they have evidently not been subject to forgetting; it's a rare night when I do not awake soaked in sweat from a terrible nightmare. At moments I also consider the possibility that the deceased Dr. X mentioned: that these are hallucinations connected with the damage to my brain and that I've never actually killed anyone. Maybe I've just imagined it all.

Maybe I'm imagining most of what I think I'm experiencing.

How much of what we think is happening is really happening? I cannot find an answer to that question in any of the philosophical books I cart with me around the world (and which, after reading, I leave behind in hotel rooms and replace with new ones). Of course, there is also a lot of philosophy and useful data about many things online. But although I am almost obsessed with Googling, it seems to me that the internet is nothing more than a vast rubbish dump, full of stupidities, half-truths, disinformation, falsehoods, big headedness; full of the excreta of average minds, which stifles (and almost completely smothers) what is of value online.

Who to believe? *What* to believe?

It's true that I'm not just a directed human robot doing dirty work around the world – I am also a known and acknowledged journalist who has brought to public attention many things that would otherwise have remained hidden. I know you won't hold it against me if I praise myself a little.

Among my most obvious achievements are reports on the "me me me generation" (which includes the boy who I thought was my son and who perhaps is, as I have no evidence to the contrary); and on poverty in the USA, where evidently no one gives a damn that some people are forced to live like animals; and on the fall of the Mubarak regime in Egypt, where I was the only one to accurately predict the consequences (which are now unfolding); also, on how deluded mankind is digging its own grave through accelerated climate change, which it is not prepared to halt (and is even less capable of doing so); and on how the international corporations that rule the world are

148

transforming peripheral European countries into colonies; and how the concluding phase of capitalism is becoming a new kind of slavery where thanks to the latest technological developments we shall be completely monitored without even being aware of it.

About the big lie that is democracy (camouflage for dirty business even where they are most proud of it), as well as less concrete things that are nevertheless of vital importance to the future of mankind: the influence of new technology on our ability to concentrate; the general trivialisation of all human activities, from art to media reporting to (sadly) philosophy; global and national conspiracies that are supposedly believed by semi-educated gullible types, but which are in reality highly likely (there is enough evidence for some); and…

I'll stop enumerating, whoever@gmail.com. I don't want to deter you from reading about other things I wish to inform you about.

Unfortunately, I can't reveal more about myself as it could jeopardise my journey "home" (which is still the primary goal of everything I do). I could say that I have two expensive leather suitcases, a small canvas travelling bag, a shoulder bag with a number of compartments, three pairs of shoes (in the left sole of all of them is a space cut out for a sharp foldable knife, my only weapon) and a wallet in which I keep, in addition to as much cash as I need, five credit cards (Amex, Diners, Mastercard, Visa, MBNA), each with the name of one of the false identities that were supplied by my doctor, master and manipulator, the world-renowned neurologist Dr. Krauthaker.

And that is all that I carry with me from country to country, from city to city. I am (probably) the most mobile person in the world: I might be in Taiwan in the morning and Ecuador in the evening. There are moments when I get the feeling that I spend most of my time above the clouds. Literally. Business class – I always fly business class. (Of course, I don't carry my knife with me on the plane: I put it into an antique pencil case that I put among the other odds and ends in one of the suitcases.)

I carry with me clothes for three situations: jeans and pullover or t-shirt for tropical places; a dark grey suit with a white shirt and a tie for meetings with various important people and bureaucrats; tight leather trousers with a loud red jacket for times when I most easily avoid pursuers by pretending that I am gay. Naturally, I replace, change or add to my wardrobe as required. But basically, the three described outfits are the ones in which you would most easily recognise me if we were to meet.

Of course, we never shall. Because I don't know who you are. And because you don't know who I am.

And above all, *I* don't know who I am.

12.

Dear Dr. Krauthaker, it's me again, with no hope of getting a reply. Again with news at which you'll probably shrug. If you open my email at all. But if you do, then you will certainly be delighted by the news. I am ill. I am the victim of bacteria currently unknown to science, or at least to the staff of the hospital where I am being kept. This, believe it or not, is in the coastal town of Palu on the west coast of the Indonesian island of Sulawesi (formerly Celebes), from where I had intended to travel by boat to the much bigger island of Borneo in order to carry out an assignment entrusted to me by your colleagues (if not you personally).

A bacterial infection is not a trivial matter and it can be fatal long before medical science ascertains whether or not it is a case of over consumption of beans. Of course, I first tried to convince the doctor that I had malaria, which is not unusual in Indonesia, and if not malaria then perhaps Dengue fever, which is also not unknown on the archipelago of 17,000 islands. And if not Dengue, then certainly typhoid, which you can catch in a roadside restaurant on a remote island *before* it occurs to you that maybe you should forego the food covered in flies that has been on display for five days.

They checked my blood and found none of the above, though they did find what they at first thought was cholera. However, since I had no characteristic cholera symptoms they shrugged helplessly and said they would send a blood sample to an American laboratory in Jakarta, where they may know more. But they warned me that it would take quite a while before the results came back. In the meantime, they would treat me with three different antibiotics: ciprofloxacin, amoxycillin, azithromycin.

When they asked me whether I was allergic to any of these I could not of course answer. I said I could not remember and ascribed my memory loss to my current feverish state. I had registered as Trevor Morris, an Englishman; I had stuffed my four other passports, wrapped in an old creased envelope, in the leather bag where I kept other documents I did not want to let go of. I put them under my pillow and now live in fear that someone will remove them while I'm asleep. If that happens, there's a risk that, in addition to unknown bacteria, I will also have the police on my back

And what then, Dr. Krauthaker?

I would have no choice but to tell them everything! They would make contact with their colleagues in Australia and sooner or later – perhaps very soon – they would be knocking on your door. So pray (if you know how to) that my bag with documents remains beneath my pillow and my laptop, which I also don't want to lose sight of, beneath the bed.

Fortunately, the three locals sharing my stuffy hospital room are, at first glance, nearer to death than I am. So it is unlikely that one of them would want to appropriate something of mine.

But I'm worried about the hospital staff. All of them, from the doctors to the cleaners, are too friendly for their smiles not to conceal at least dishonest thoughts, if not devilish cunning.

And so I am now swallowing antibiotics, antipyretics and analgesics, vomiting into a metal dish beside my bed, sweating (the ceiling fan is so high up it does little more than stir the warm air around it) and thinking how pathetically my life might end. Instead of dying with dignity surrounded by the loved ones that I must certainly at one time have had. It's true that no-one is master of his fate, but it is not written down anywhere that this fate cannot be an unjust one. Nor that responsibility for this cannot be ascribed to anyone.

Thus be informed, Dr. Krauthaker: for everything that is currently happening to me, you are to blame. If you hadn't and if you hadn't and if you hadn't and so on, I would be elsewhere and something different would be happening to me. It's hard to believe I will survive this invasion of bacteria that no-one knows. And even if they identify it in the American lab in Jakarta, the news will come too late: by that time, I'll already be buried or cut into pieces for research purposes. It might even be that one of my organs is transplanted into someone else's body and my heart is pumping blood round the body of a stranger who *does* remember his past.

As a neurologist you certainly know the basics of microbiology, so I don't need to emphasise how tenacious some microbes can be. You well know that a cholera bacterium in a test tube, given the right nutrition, can divide within thirty minutes, creating two identical, independent bacteria, and each of these two more within thirty minutes, and each of the four two new ones, each of the eight two, and each of the sixteen two, and so on, exponentially. That means that after twelve hours the test tube (or bloodstream) contains more than 16 million bacteria! And if there is enough food and space this process can continue *ad infinitum.*

Of course, since we've had antibiotics in most cases we can successfully deal with this frightening multiplication of deadly enemies. But not in every case. There is a possibility that a small colony of bacteria – perhaps even a solitary one – might survive the destructive antibiotic attack. How is that possible? It is possible, Dr. Krauthaker, because of metabolism. During division, every so often a mistake occurs. In one in a million bacteria the amino acid chain is created in the wrong order. A colony of millions of bacteria with billions of metabolic reactions involves a vast number of different individuals, some of which may, due to their specific features, be resistant to all known antibiotics. It doesn't even have to be two – just one incorrectly formed bacterium is enough. It isn't aware that an antibiotic massacre of all its relatives is taking place around it. On the basis of the already mentioned principle of division, within twelve hours it will have multiplied into more than sixteen million identical individuals.

If I have such a defective bacterium in my bloodstream then I shall die.

Considering that the doctors don't even know *which* bacteria I have, my journey into eternal darkness is only a matter of time.

Whenever I'm not asleep (thanks to the insufferable heat and the unbearable pain in my joints I sleep little more then five hours a day), I think about things that have often (I can see from my notes) bothered me, but have not (as I wasn't faced with death) demanded immediate answers.

I ask myself why, for instance.

Why this infinite universe (with the possibility of infinite numbers of parallel universes); why (and to what end) the Big Bang, which was supposedly the birth of everything; and why the predicted demise of the universe, which in a million million years will be replaced by Nothing? That which was (or was not) before the universe was born – why did it not remain Nothing?

And why me, why not someone else? Although I am (I couldn't give a reason) grateful that I am, that I'm aware, that I suffer, that I have enjoyed a number of things (and suffered because of it, most often in parallel with the pleasure, because I knew it was ephemeral) I cannot help marvelling at the fact that the universe and time and growth and passing have actually taken place. For there must be an equal chance that they would not have happened.

That's what I think about, Dr. Krauthaker.

Many would say I was thinking about God.

But on the threshold of death, who wouldn't, Dr. Krauthaker?

If the Bible is not just a literary text (a kind of *Collected Works of Unknown Authors*) and the Last Judgement is not just a fabrication by clerics who wish to frighten believers and widen their economic base, but somewhere – who knows where – there really are forces that punish and reward on the basis of ethical laws (it is not clear whether these are a divine or a human construct), then I ask myself: will the judge I face after death, in passing sentence, take account of the extenuating circumstances?

Will he take account of the fact that I am the victim of your manipulation, Dr. Krauthaker? Will he take into account that what you demanded of me (alone, or through your associates) I carried out because you (as an expert) assured me that this was the only way to break through the blockade in my memory? What if the judge on the other side, in that darkness (or light, who knows), is not wise enough to take all that into account when deciding whether my place is in heaven or hell?

At times I think that heaven is that which was (or was not) before I was born; that purgatory is what I am living through; and that hell is what awaits me after death. I cannot believe in a hell where fires burn and sinners are roasted on a spit; even as a metaphor the idea is the half-witted product of a worse than average author.

But I can conceive of worse versions of hell. I can imagine time standing still and everything coming to a halt: growth, decline, death, awakening, renewal, birth, change, continuing the journey towards the death of the sun, the death of the universe, of everything that is. I can imagine not being robbed of memory, but of the feeling that I have a body and being compelled to live seventy years as a tetraplegic, only in my head, with all my memories untouched, in an endless whirlwind of repetition: *that* for me would be hell.

Perhaps there is no other heaven than the possibility that we can at any moment blow life out like a candle.

Actually, Dr. Krauthaker, I can't imagine any other heavens. Except as a fairy tale. The Christian heaven seems to me so boring that I'd almost rather be sent to hell (even suffering is better than eternal boredom). And there is one other reason why I'd rather go to hell than to heaven. It's colder in hell. That has been proved by science on the basis of no lesser authority than the Holy Bible: "Moreover the light of the moon shall be as the light of the sun and the light of the sun shall be sevenfold, as the light of seven days."

That means that heaven receives from the moon as much radiation as the earth receives from the sun, plus seven times seven as much, which together means more than fifty times more than the earth. On the basis of this we can calculate the temperature in heaven: by applying the Stefan-Boltzmann law of radiation we get 526 degrees Celsius.

The exact temperature of hell cannot be calculated, but it must be less than 444.6 degrees Celsius. Why? Because in the Bible it says:

"But the fearful, and unbelieving ... will be cast into a lake of fire and sulphur." A lake of sulphur means that the temperature must be below the boiling point of sulphur, which is 444.6 degrees Celsius, for above that temperature the lake would evaporate.

Interesting, don't you think?

We won't meet, Dr. Krauthaker.

You'll go to heaven, I to hell.

But not necessarily immediately.

For thanks to an anonymous benefactor (was it you?) I have been brought by private plane to a hospital in England (as Trevor Morris, who is English and therefore not subject to special scrutiny on the border). At the same time this fabricated person has Coris insurance and assistance. Thank you that in your selfish wish to have me at your disposal as long as possible you thought of this!

Although I must say, the place I'm in does not fill me with confidence.

I don't know by what logic I ended up in hospital in Basildon, which just over a week ago was named as the worst in Britain. The scandalous state of the British public health system is currently the main topic in the media; the newspapers are full of outrage at the negligence of those in charge and at their offensive selfishness. For example, the former director of the hospital which became the worst in the country received a more than seventy thousand pound bonus for his responsible and committed work. The world really does seem to be out of joint and values of any kind are now mere folklore (and will soon be on display in museums), while the immoral behaviour of those responsible for the catastrophe in public health care of this once model country no longer verges on farce – it is farce.

And since farce is the only truth of our expiring times, we won't get excited about the fact that the hospital director received his bonus on top of his annual salary of *a hundred and fifty thousand pounds*, plus a guaranteed pension fund of approaching *two million pounds.*

And what was his great achievement? Something magnificent, Dr. Krauthaker: his achievement was that during the time of his leadership of the hospital 1,600 patients died unnecessarily due to errors.

It seems highly likely that I will be the next. And I'm increasingly convinced, Dr. Krauthaker, that I was not sent here by accident, but intentionally. I know that Basildon is no particular exception, since it has been established that in fourteen health districts more than 13,000 patients have died due to staff errors. But Basildon was declared to be the place that people should avoid.

I was examined, they took my temperature, which was excessively high (41.6 Celsius), my blood found its way to the laboratory and I am waiting for the results. I was examined by Dr. Okugwi Bokambo, from one of the sub-Saharan countries, and Dr. Swarnendu Sen, a specialist in infectious diseases from Bangladesh. In British hospitals there are now hardly any doctors trained in Britain or Europe and it's quite possible that some of the unnecessary deaths were the result of linguistic misunderstanding.

"You have bacteria?" asked Dr. Bokambo.

"That's right," I nodded. "But no-one knows which one!"

"No problem," commented Dr. Swarnendu Sen, "send me the bacteria to the lab."

"With pleasure," I replied, "and I hope it will stay there."

"No, no," they both said, "the bacteria in your blood. If not discovered you will die!"

"Like the other 1,600 patients?"

It turned out that they didn't read the newspapers. Even though they were perhaps at least partly responsible for some of the unnecessary deaths, they didn't know what I was talking about.

By the next day my condition had deteriorated. I thought I would doze off from tiredness, but I lost consciousness. It's hard to say how long I was out, but when I came round the breakfast tray, which the dour, overweight orderly brought at eight on a small trolley, was still by the bed, although it was dark outside.

I pressed the buzzer to call someone.

I discovered that while unconscious I had wet myself. Someone should come and change me. I had to press the button for a good half hour before the door opened and a fat black nurse stomped aggressively into the room with the words: "What now?"

My feeling that they hadn't liked me here from the very beginning was reinforced. But why? After all, I was just a patient, one of many, I hadn't done anything to harm them. When I told her I'd been unconscious all day, which didn't seem normal, she frowned and said that wasn't her problem and why hadn't I called the doctor.

How could I when I was unconscious! So I said: "I insist that you call him."

"You're in no position to insist on anything," she replied tetchily. "It's up to me to decide what needs to be done."

When she found out that I (and the bed) was soaked with urine, she got agitated:

"For heaven's sake, the toilet is just around the corner!"

At this point, Dr. Krauthaker, I'd had enough.

"Listen to me!" I raised my voice. "If you don't bring me some clean pyjamas this minute I'm going to start yelling at the top of my voice. And if you don't call the doctor straight away I'm going to phone the hospital administrator. Tomorrow you'll be standing in line outside the job centre."

I hoped this would intimidate her a little.

But it didn't."

"How dare you talk to me like that?" she shouted. "Who do you think you are, threatening those who are looking after you? I could be sitting quietly in the nurses' room reading a fashion magazine. But I'm here. Am I not here?"

She looked as if she was almost ready to hit me.

And perhaps she would have done if at that moment Dr. Swarnendu Sen and Dr. Okugwi Bokambo had not appeared. In less than a second the nurse shrank by five centimetres. She muttered something, she grabbed the trolley with the untouched, already dried up breakfast and disappeared.

I thought I ought to file a complaint about her. But I didn't. I realised in time that she might add poison to my supper.

My death would be ascribed to infection with still unidentified bacteria.

"Sorry, sorry," said Dr. Bokambo.

"Sorry," added Dr. Sen. "Unusual bacteria. The lab doesn't know."

"But," said Dr. Bokambo, "we prescribe two new antibiotics."

"I'm already taking three!" I protested.

"Five together kill bacteria!" Dr. Sen assured me.

Dear Dr. Krauthaker, do you know that you will die, too? Are you aware of it each moment? Or is the thought of death, as it is for most people, just a stain on the periphery of your mind?

Maybe you'll say I'm becoming morbid. But considering I don't know who I am (beyond the fragment that I am) and thus I don't know *who* will die when my heart stops beating, I'm interested to know what you think about your demise.

You, who are so at home with all the elements of your identity that you never even think about it, let alone search for it across the world, as I am compelled to do.

Perhaps I am wrong and you are just as much a puzzle to yourself as I am to me, for there is no rule to say that a neurologist, however recognised and well known around the world, has any more insight into himself than a five-year old child. I don't want to insult you, that's the last thing I'd wish to do, but the fact is (isn't it?) that we who belong to western civilisation have somehow pushed death from our minds.

In every hotel room where I have to stay I have at my disposal a television with an LCD screen and an endless number of channels, with most of them offering an endless number of bodies – shot, hung, run over, crushed, poisoned, beheaded (I'll stop, since you watch the same channels).

But all these bodies remain part of the scenery – no more significant, disturbing or shocking than the rubbish bins in which many of the bodies are stashed by criminals. Even on television, where we see broken jaws, fractured skulls and bloody insides from a distance of two metres, death is still somehow remote, unreal. Acted, choreographed.

Don't you think so, Mr. Krauthaker?

Television and cinema offer us death as if it isn't real. As if bodies are just props in a not too convincing performance. And how many people, Mr. Krauthaker, see death in a similar way – as something that happens (how could it not, we all read death notices and obituaries), but does not concern them directly?

Even on the news (that seems to us, assailed by fiction on all sides, itself ever more fictional) bodies remain considerately concealed behind hospital curtains or in coffins. And in news reports of earthquakes that led to many thousands of deaths the emphasis is always on the child that was miraculously pulled from the rubble without any serious injuries, maybe a couple of scratches, while the thousands of corpses are not shown. To look death straight in the eye, Dr. Krauthaker, is more than we can bear.

Life with the thought that death is merely theoretical – something that certainly awaits us in the future (but not now, not now, not now ad infinitum) – is of course more tolerable, but is it not the greatest of all deceptions? Would we not be capable of living more fully, more genuinely, if awareness of the inevitability of the end perched on our shoulder like a fluttering dove that every few minutes shat in our ear and reminded us that at the end we would be nothing more, nothing nobler than the abomination that it squeezed into our orifice?

You'll say that it's a matter of consideration, of respect for the dead. As if those who are no more deserve more respect than they did when alive! I cannot accept such hypocrisy, Dr. Krauthaker. Respect for the dead can be expressed in different ways; thanks to you, I've seen enough of the world to make that more than clear.

I was in the Toraja region of the Indonesian island of Sulawesi, where the dead are embalmed and stay with the family in the house until they collect enough money for the purchase and slaughter of a large enough number of buffaloes. The dead must be sent to the land of spirits in a way that will preserve or even increase the level of social respect enjoyed by the grieving. The worth of the deceased is measured by the number of slaughtered buffaloes and the quality (and size) of his likeness carved from wood (tau tau), which will guard his grave in a rockface.

Of course, even in our culture the size of the gravestone is an important indicator of the status of the family from which the deceased departed. But we bury the body straight away, get rid of it, replace it with photos of the deceased when alive, with a forgery of life which is nothing unusual in a world where forgeries of forgeries are the only thing we are capable of seeing as original. We Westerners do not share our home with an embalmed member of our family for a year or two. We don't dine with them as if they were still with us. We don't sleep in the same room, we don't wait (a year or two) for a skilled craftsman to carve their likeness from a piece of wood.

Why am I telling you this? And why in an aggressive tone, as if it was your fault that we are no longer able to accept death as a fact? Because, Dr. Krauthaker, one day, perhaps soon, I too will meet my end. And because that end, partly thanks to you, will not be that which a normal person would wish for. Here I don't have in mind my manner of departing from this world. Perhaps we shall both, you and I, have a heart attack, perhaps the same day, the same hour; perhaps we shall get stabbed in the back or the stomach – you by your wife, me by a passing stranger.

I think about what will happen to us when we breathe our last breath.

Here you have a big advantage. When you die you will know *who* is dying. Everyone around you will know who's dying, the newspapers will be full of obituaries, there will be a funeral procession, at the open grave your best friend (or perhaps the head of the neurological department at the best Australian university) will speak of your personal virtues and career successes (lying terribly, as is the custom). There might be the odd tear shed, albeit a crocodile tear (perhaps even a genuine one – I don't know you well enough to exclude the possibility). And then there will be a party with good wine and canapés (for what is a wake other than a party at which the widow begins to flirt surreptitiously with friends who have survived the deceased?).

There will then follow flattering obituaries in prestigious publications. At this and this age the world famous neurologist Dr. Krauthaker has departed from us. And so on. Your death will be evident and recorded – no less than the dissertation of one of your students.

161

What about me?

Not only will I not know myself *who* is dying when the final hour comes and to *whom* I am bidding farewell, but it won't be clear to anyone else whose remains must be interred one way or another or transported to the nearest crematorium. I'll be no more than a corpse, the rigid body of an unknown man that will have to be disposed of within the prescribed timescale by the still living who will be paid to perform the task. There will be no-one to shed tears, to lay a rose on my coffin, to speak of what I achieved in life.

And whose death will be officially recorded in whichever part of the world it takes place? If they find on my person a passport in the name of Alfred Haidacher, then it will be his death; if the passport says Kevin Youngson, then my demise will be recorded under that name. And if they find all five fictitious passports what will they do? Which one will they decide has died and on what basis?

Of course, the passports also contain addresses, but they are also made up – the streets and the numbers, even the places (although there must be some places with the same or similar names). They will try to contact relatives at these addresses. They will find none. They won't even find the addresses! I will die and be buried as No-one.

The more I think about it, the more I'm sure that I would like to die in other times. In days when people still knew how to live with death; when the dead were seen as a severed piece of their own being and by grieving for the deceased they were grieving for their own *reduced* essence.

Recently (thank you, Mr. Krauthaker, that you haven't been giving me assignments every blessed day!) I have been spending long hours in libraries and on Google; I am looking for information about death as a concept, as the physical end, as a symbol of eternal renewal, of eternal spring, and about what might await me on the other side. Also, the possibility of life after death, of reincarnation – everything that should also interest you, Mr. Krauthaker, since you are no further from the judgement day than I am. You could easily slip in the bath today, or tomorrow be run over by a bus.

In the Middle Ages, Dr. Krauthaker, in case you don't know, graveyards were somewhat similar to today's public squares. People

162

didn't only walk on graves, they danced, ate, drank, traded, enjoyed themselves on them. Isn't joy the highest form of respect towards the dead? Isn't joy basically the same thing as grieving?

Did you know, Dr. Krauthaker, that Alexander the Great's mummy was one of the most respected objects in the Antique world and that a visit to his grave won political points even for the Roman Emperor? Caesar Augustus even went so far as to kiss the body of the liberator who died too young (and in doing so through clumsiness knocked off his mummified nose). Soon after this, the early Christians began to build their churches above the graves of martyrs, while at the same time showing absurd levels of respect for parts of their corpses – fingers, toes, tongue, eyes and other body parts.

Why? Because they believed they could perform miracles. An unsigned letter from AD 156 ascribes more value to the bones of Saint Polycarp than precious stones and pure gold. Of course, worshipping religious relics is not unheard of; but the question is whether you knew that this tradition also influenced the worship of "secular saints", such as (to mention only two) Galileo in Descartes.

Do you know what happened, Mr. Krauthaker, in Florence in 1737, when Galileo's bones were exhumed for transfer to a more impressive grave? On the way there, collectors of relics removed from his skeleton a number of fingers, a tooth and several vertebrae. And in Sweden in 1666, when the remains of Rene Descartes were dug up so as to remove them to his native France, the guard stole his skull and the French ambassador expropriated his right index finger. During the French Revolution a conservator admitted that he had made a number of Descartes' bones into rings, which he then gave to "friends of good philosophy".

Please don't think that I have finished. In this feverish state when I have become obsessed with the thought of death, I won't spare you until a number of things are clear between us. Changing bodily remains into jewellery seems to me such an original idea that I would realise it myself, if the Romantics hadn't beaten me to it long ago. In

Victorian times, rings, bracelets and pendants made from the remains of dearly departed loved ones was something quite normal.

Did you know, Mr. Krauthaker, that Mary Shelley, the author of *Frankenstein*, kept the heart of her husband, Percy Shelley, who drowned in the Gulf of Spezia, in the drawer of her writing desk until the day she died? Extremely morbid, you will say. But is it really? Voltaire's heart is still kept in the National Library in Paris. Chopin's heart is preserved in alcohol in the Church of the Holy Cross in Warsaw. And if we go back a little further in time: when Thomas More was beheaded in 1535 and his head put on a pike on London Bridge, his daughter Margaret took it down in the middle of the night, anointed it with herbs to prevent its decay and before her death ordered that she be buried with her father's head in her hands.

I'd like such a daughter, Mr. Krauthaker.

And a small P.S. We are both aware that the question of death is connected with God. Scientists keep repeating that God is not necessary to explain the workings of the world and the universe. Perhaps not. After all, the mass of water in the Pacific Ocean is not required in my hotel bathroom: what runs from the tap is adequate. But the Pacific still exists.

If scientists were somewhat less addicted to the empirical, if they had a slightly greater gift for metaphor, then they might comprehend that the Bible does not need to be taken literally, nor the Quran, nor any other collection of holy regulations, commands and threats. They would understand that you need to make your way to God through the imagination. In drama, too, the message is not transmitted to the viewer explicitly, but as an intuition that floats between, behind and above the spoken words. Intelligent members of the audience are aware of this and take the intuition home with them, preserve it in their subconscious, and do not talk about it using stale literary theoretical phrases. They allow it to grow into their spiritual tissue, to become a part of them.

That is how art works. Why can't faith work in a similar way?

You won't believe it, Dr. Krauthaker! The mysterious bacteria that they were unable to identify in Sulawesi or even in the American

164

laboratory in Jakarta have been identified by the worst hospital in Britain! Considering their previous "successes" I still can't believe that they are right. My bacteria are completely ordinary. Ordinary in the sense that it is not actually a bacterium but a virus. A gigantic mimivirus that multiplies within the protozoa *Acanthamoeba polyphaga*. It has three times more genetic material (DNA) than any hitherto known virus and is bigger than some bacteria. It was discovered only in 2003 and I am one of the rare individuals in whose bloodstream it has been discovered.

Five years later another enormous virus, even bigger than the mimivirus, was discovered and referred to as a mamavirus. Since it can only multiply inside cells infected with a mimivirus it was named Sputnik (a virus that orbits a mimivirus and grabs other viruses).

The head of a lab not far from the worst hospital in Britain (excellence and criminal negligence are never far apart) uncovered the presence of a mimivirus and its "Sputnik" mamavirus. Both, although it happens rarely, can cause viral pneumonia. Which can be fatal. Or not. There is no medicine for viruses, so the outcome of my illness is uncertain, regardless of the fact that my temperature has fallen to 39.2 Celsius.

Which would you prefer, Dr. Krauthaker?

That I live or die?

13.

Greetings, kleinebilly@yahoo.com. I've realised that I don't write to you often enough, so I've decided to entrust you with the latest developments. In case you're interested. I still don't know who had me transported from Sulawesi, after I was infected with an unknown pathological agent, to the worst British hospital, in Basildon, or to what end (was it Dr. Krauthaker, in the hope that they would finish me off?). But I do know who saved me from that institution. Actually, the whole thing was very surprising – I didn't realise there was anyone around who really cared what happened to me. Four days ago Dr. Swarnendu Sen came to my hospital bed and told me that my relatives had come for me and would take me somewhere where I'd receive personal care; they had dealt with everything regarding payment and insurance; I should quickly shower, dress, get my things together and be ready to leave. Perhaps it was better that way, he added.

"I don't have any relatives," I objected. "I'd rather stay here."

"That's not possible," replied Dr. Sen. In a slightly lower voice he added that this "wasn't the best place for sick people"; he himself, a doctor, would rather leave, but he had nowhere to go.

Upon seeing the young man who was waiting for me in the reception area my fears at least partly abated. "Hello," he said, reaching helpfully for my suitcase. He also wanted to take my travel bag, but I held onto it; it contained my laptop, passports and other things I didn't want to be separated from.

He was of medium height, light-haired, not exactly handsome but likeable enough, at least on the surface friendly and worthy of trust. In spite of a cautious self-confidence he radiated what might be called grace. And like most of the people I meet for the first time, somehow familiar. I didn't pay this much attention, as I am used to it; probably you also, sir or madam, would seem familiar if we were to meet.

"A relative?" I asked.

He grinned and said that he had simply made that up, otherwise they wouldn't have entrusted me to his care. He'd had to sign a statement that from this point he was responsible for my health.

"But why?" I persisted.

"You'll find that out when you come home with me," he said. "We need to hurry, you ought to be back in bed as soon as possible – on the way we'll stop at a private laboratory so they can take a blood sample."

"That's not necessary," I said. "They've established that I have a mimivirus and a mamavirus."

"Not necessarily," he replied. "In this hospital they inadvertently amputated my aunt's right leg, though she had gangrene in the left one."

In the car park, at the wheel of a white Rover, sat a man of my age who my benefactor introduced as a friend. He was less friendly – he actually wore quite a hostile expression. I immediately categorised him among those people who it is wise to get to know before you trust them.

We drove toward the edge of the town; I had no idea where.

"Please don't take offence," I said from the back seat to my "relative", who was sitting beside the driver, "but who are you, actually? Were you sent by Dr. Krauthaker?"

"Who's Dr. Krauthaker?" he half turned his head. His surprise seemed genuine.

"In spite of that," I persisted politely, "I'd dearly like to know the reasons for what you are doing. Are you rescuing or kidnapping me?"

"Everything will become clear," he said.

"Do you even know who I am? Are you certain you didn't take the wrong man from the hospital?"

167

"Completely," he turned his head and gave me a friendly smile.

As you can imagine, kleinebilly@yahoo.com, my confusion was increasing inexorably. I was ill, seriously ill, totally worn out and perspiring, my temperature had started to rise and I thought I was going to pass out. But if this was a trap there was nothing I could do to avoid it; everything indicated that the hospital had wanted to get rid of me. Perhaps I should have been firmer from the start; I should have insisted that the young man tell me why he had come for me and who had sent him; and until he gave me an answer I should have dug my heels in and said I was not going anywhere. But I had to go somewhere: where else could I go – the street?

One way or another, it was now too late: I was in a car with two strange men who were taking me to an unknown destination. In fact no, for on the edge of Basildon the driver turned onto the driveway of a house where above the door I saw a sign saying "Laboratory". My abductor got out, opened the back door and asked me to follow him. I was unsteady on my feet, so he took my elbow and walked me to the door.

"Everything'll be alright," he said.

In the empty waiting room I looked him straight in the eye (and was startled to see that, although he had light hair, they were chocolate brown). "Can you at least tell me your name?"

"William," he said. "My name's William. And you are Trevor Morris."

Since there was no one in front of me I was seen straight away. A young Indian nurse took a blood sample and immediately went into the next room with it. "Ten minutes," she said. "Wait in the waiting room."

The waiting room was empty. My unknown benefactor (William? I was really curious as to whether he really was William!) had vanished! The white Rover was no longer in the car park. He had disappeared with my luggage, with my disguise props, my laptop and all my emails, and the passports I had foolishly left in my travel bag, although at the hospital I could have shoved all five of them in my jacket pocket. I was always cautious; what had happened?

168

It was clearly my illness. The next moment I sank to the floor and everything went dark.

When I came round I was lying on a trolley in a small room. The first thing I noticed was the expensive looking crystal chandelier hanging from the ceiling. Then I saw there were three people beside me: the young Indian nurse in a white uniform, my abductor William and a corpulent man with a bushy moustache, also in white and evidently a doctor.

"We were afraid you'd never wake up again," joked the nurse.

The young man named William said nothing.

I didn't know what to say, so I asked "Did I pass out?"

"We worked that out as soon as we saw you on the floor," said the moustached doctor. "And not only that. We have checked your blood and ascertained that you have Legionnaire's Disease. All the previous diagnoses were mistaken. Which doesn't surprise me," he added. "Basildon has two mortuaries and one of them is the NHS hospital."

"Legionnaire's?" I couldn't believe it. "Where could I have got it?"

"I was told you were brought to Basildon from Indonesia. It's quite possible that you ended up in hospital there because of malaria or Dengue Fever or food poisoning, and you caught Legionnaire's in the hospital, from the air conditioning. But not to worry – we'll do what needs doing."

"But Legionnaire's is…"

"Yes," agreed the doctor. "Mortality with Legionnaire's is twenty per cent, regardless of the treatment. But eighty per cent is four times twenty! We'll give you an antibiotic, Levofloxacin. You'll take it as instructed. You'll be very ill for some time, but there's no need to panic, my young friend William Youngson will take care of you. Amrita," he leaned his head towards the nurse, "will visit you regularly to see how you're getting on."

"William Youngson?" I looked at my young kidnapper.

"William Youngson," replied the doctor. "I'm also Australian, but I've lost my accent. William's lost his even more. We know each other from Sydney. We were neighbours. He was still a child when I was studying. Then he moved with his mother to Switzerland and we didn't see each other for twenty years. A few months ago we found out that we were both living in Basildon! Coincidence is our fate. Trust him. You'll be safer with him than in your mother's arms."

I looked at the young Youngson, who gave me one of his innocent smiles.

I was about to say: "I'm Kevin Youngson", but at the last moment I remembered that I had registered in the hospital as Trevor Morris. And so I said, more because of the doctor and nurse "Thanks, Mr. Youngson. I hope you'll tell me how I can pay you back."

That I would survive became a real possibility the very next day when my temperature fell by two degrees after taking two Levofloxacin tablets. The way I felt generally also improved. William Youngson had a small, tidy house on the edge of Basildon. He gave me one of the three upstairs bedrooms, where he also carried all my things: suitcase, travel bag and laptop. There was no indication that he had opened or examined anything.

In spite of that, I felt like the first man on Mars: nothing was clear, each possibility was contradicted by others, I had no idea what was happening or why or what the outcome would be, or who the young man was who had organised the correct diagnosis of my illness. Or why, at an age when he should have a wife and two children, he was living completely alone in a comfortable house. And (apart from breakfast, which was bacon and eggs) living on food delivered from various restaurants: Turkish, Chinese, Vietnamese, Indian, Italian, Mexican.

Since my arrival he had insisted that I do the choosing and so as not to disappoint him I chose something different every day. He was happy to go along with that, but I got the feeling that he would have preferred Turkish and Mexican. He said that a cleaner came three times a week to do all the housework and change the sheets, so I needn't worry that I'd be convalescing in a pigsty. Which was perhaps unusual for a single man of his age, he admitted, giving me one of his smiles to reassure me that, regardless of the mysterious circumstances, I was not threatened in any way.

But, kleinebilly@yahoo.com, it was all very odd, wouldn't you agree? That one of my fabricated names was Kevin Youngson; that

170

I had a forged passport in that name; that I had been removed from the hospital in Basildon by a young man with the same surname, who even after three days in his house did not want to tell me why he had done this and how he had known about me; that the house gave the impression it wasn't his real home, but that he had rented it in order to look after me until my health recovered; none of it added up.

Although my state of health improved day by day, I couldn't shake off the fear that my situation was dangerously complicated and that during my journey home (how I can't stand that phrase!) this was the hardest, most mysterious and most dangerous nut I'd yet had to crack. The Indian nurse from the laboratory visited me only once. When she saw I was a lot better she said they had evidently prescribed the correct medicine and that there was no need for her to keep coming. If my condition suddenly worsened, William should call the lab and a doctor would come and see me.

The first three days my saviour-host-abductor William was out most of the time (he gave work obligations as the reason), so I had plenty of time to examine all the rooms and to establish that it was a lot more likely the house was rented than a permanent residence. The telephone never rang and although William often spoke on his mobile phone in the living room, that was such a regular part of contemporary life that it would have been suspicious if he hadn't done so.

But why would someone rent a house so as to be able to offer me care and time to recover? And why someone called Youngson? And why was he so consistently avoiding the issue of who he was, how he knew me, why he was looking after me and what he planned to do with me when I felt well enough to move on?

Of course, I could shove him up against a wall and demand answers. But the more forcefully I did that the less likely I would be to get the right ones. I decided to play it cautiously.

Yesterday I received from my invisible masters the first text message since I was brought to Basildon from Sulawesi. "Where are you?" Of course, it never entered my head to reply. I connected to my bank account from my laptop and found that the regular payments to my account had not been stopped. That was what I feared most. Evidently they hadn't written me off yet. How strange that I was happy about that!

Today, in the space of ten minutes three texts arrived: "Where are you?" "Send us your coordinates" and "Independence has more serious consequences than a transparent lie".

I wrote back: "Contracted Legionnaire's disease, recovering in England, more later."

There was no reply. I concluded that they had accepted the clarification as genuine. Dr. Krauthaker and his people. Or God knows who. For now it was not remotely clear to me in whose hands my life was being manipulated.

Out of gratitude to young Youngson I didn't want to be impolite. I hoped that the facts would be revealed slowly during one of the casual conversations that normally accompanied our slow and protracted evening meals. The food was always delivered by others, but the wine was always brought by William: always red and Australian.

"Once an Australian, always an Australian," I commented yesterday, as we ate five different Sumatran curries.

"Does that also go for you?" he said, looking at me.

"I doubt it," I said. "My story, which you probably know to every last detail, is too open for me to come to any kind of conclusion."

"Actually, I don't know your story at all," he said. When he saw my sceptical expression he added: "No. Mine is too cruel to talk about at the table."

"I doubt it's any crueller than mine," I said quickly. "Which is also hardly believable. Above all it remains, at least for now, without head or tail."

"Mine, too. But precisely because of that it's true. Stories that are probable and conclude without any lack of clarity are characteristic of novels, don't you think? Reality never offers us simple answers. Often it offers us none. It's because of the frustration that life brings on a daily basis that we resort to reading fiction."

"I agree. That truth is stranger than fiction is not only a phrase, but a fact. At least as far as I am concerned."

"Maybe we should tell each other our stories," he suggested.

"Who'll go first?"

He felt in his pocket and brought out a coin. "Heads or tails?"

172

I chose tails, he tossed the coin, it was tails.

"So?" he looked at me.

And I told him everything, kleinebilly@yahoo.com, from beginning to end. Not once did I consider the possibility that my openness might have any unpleasant consequences; I was more concerned that he wouldn't believe me. I was surprised that no important detail escaped my memory. Since I had recorded what happened so many times in electronic format and I'm always reading and adding to these notes, at least the basics were lodged in my mind. That could mean that the condition of my brain is gradually normalising. Perhaps I could speed up the process by telling my story to three different people three times a day.

Of course, I also mentioned Kevin Youngson, one of my made up identities and how I arrived at the name. There is nothing to say that I am not really Kevin Youngson, an Australian from Sydney. I plucked the names right out of the air, but it's quite possible that I unwittingly included among them my real name. Which would mean, seeing that we had both lived in Sydney (if I really *am* Kevin Youngson, of course), that we might be related, regardless of the fact that I at least don't remember ever seeing him before.

"Me neither," he said after a long silence. (Evidently he needed some time to recover from my story.) "If we were related, I could even be your son. But that can't be because my father disappeared twenty years ago, not six."

"Your father disappeared?" I asked in surprise. (There was no good reason for this, since fathers are always disappearing, leaving their wives, children, vanishing from the face of the earth, changing their name and beginning a new life in South America or elsewhere; and after all, it is not unheard of for a mother to leave her children.)

"In slightly different circumstances," said William.

"Tell me."

Young William Youngson poured us both some wine and began his narrative. However, in contrast to me, who had told my story in a straightforward way so as not to get drawn into the quicksand of memory, he started at the margins and approached the central point gradually, via detours. He said that since he was a child he had wanted to travel the globe. Australia was at the end of the world and he felt cut off; at the time of his birth young Australians had just started travelling overland to Europe. But as he grew, the way in which he wanted to discover the world changed. At first he wanted to be an explorer and discover hitherto unexplored corners of the globe; then he wanted to travel from place to place, ideally on foot, as a pilgrim seeking spiritual goals; then as an ordinary tourist, safely and comfortably on package holidays; and finally, ashamed at the decline of his ambitions, as a nomad with a rucksack on his back and a small tent, moving from place to place without a plan, following the wind or intuition, aimless, going nowhere in particular.

In line with this desire (which quickly became his life's goal), he decided to study geography and philosophy. But then a conflict arose between his father (who was called Simon and *not* Kevin Youngson, he emphasised) and his mother. Their whole life together they argued. His mother (together with her son) returned to her native Switzerland. There, because of his poor German, he fell behind at school, his dreams of study faded and he became what in his younger years he had most despised – a tourist guide!

"But it is an interesting and respectable profession," I commented.

"Is it really?" He expressed his pain with a bitter smile.

For a while we sipped our wine without speaking and then William continued.

"Our fates are similar in a special way."

"Oh," I replied, "I find that hard to believe."

"Although I was disappointed that my ambitions remained at the level of tourist guide, I soon realised that the job not only made possible but even made easier my real mission in life. And that was simple: to find my father."

"Your father?" I asked. I was seized by an unusual sense of anxiety. Luckily, the next moment it proved to be unnecessary.

William told me that after a few years he and his mother, who was a pharmacist, returned to Sydney to resume life with the father. But then the husband found out that during her time in Switzerland his wife had had an affair with a German director named Haidacher. He said he could never forgive her. He was very hurt. She spent so much time lecturing him on how as a psychiatrist he should understand the female psyche that one evening during dinner he flipped and in an attack of rage stabbed her through the heart with a kitchen knife.

"Your father is not a psychiatrist, he's a psychopath," were the last words he spoke to his son. "Call the police." He hugged him, squeezing him so tight he almost suffocated him, then went out the door and disappeared.

Forever.

And since that day, twenty years ago, William had not seen him. And since then he had been searching for him. Although he did not know how or where he would find him, he travelled the world as a tourist guide in the hope that one day he would come across him by sheer coincidence. He could not abandon this hope, since he'd be left with nothing to live for. Once he had joined a club of suicides. Then he left. But now he was thinking of rejoining.

I told him I, too, had contemplated suicide. Not because I was looking for my father with no hope of finding him, but because I was looking for my lost self without *any* hope of finding it. I was weary of the irresolvable mysteries that accompanied my restricted life. I envied people who knew how to make enough out of what fate had granted them, even if it was only "something".

"What would you do if you found your father," I asked him.

"I would punish him," he replied without hesitation. "I wouldn't stab him with a kitchen knife, but I would convince him to take his own life. In full awareness of what he was doing. And why he deserved it."

He was very worked up and his hands were trembling. He emptied his wine glass and said: "Tell me: am I right? The mother I loved so much is dead. Am I right to want more than anything else that my father also die?"

"Perhaps we should talk about more concrete things. You said that your mother had an affair in Switzerland with a German director called Haidacher. Alfred Haidacher is one of my made up names. The woman in London who claims to be my wife told me that Haidacher

175

was one of my drinking companions. Her son, who is studying in Oxford and who I thought was *my* son told me that his father is Alfred Haidacher. What if that's who I am? What if, when I selected the names for my forged identities, I unconsciously chose my actual name? If I did, then your mother had an affair with me and your father killed her because of me. Is that why you removed me from Basildon Hospital?"

"To kill you?" he gave a laugh with a bitter edge. "Far from it. Nor is it really true that I want to kill my father. I'd like to find him, that's all. I'd like to find him and tell him that I forgive him for what he did. That I can understand the rage which he could not control. The French have an expression for it, *crime passionnel*. And as far as I know the perpetrators often receive a symbolic sentence. I'd like to find my father because without him my life is empty. I miss him. And I'm surprised that he's not at all interested in what happened to me. As far as I remember, he was fond of me. Very fond. I wonder if he even realises that I was raised and put through school by a friend of the family. If I had a son I'd still be interested."

"You were raised by a family friend?" I asked.

"Father's colleague. A Greek by birth, Kostas Asimakopulos."

There was a good minute's silence.

"Now I really do expect an answer to my question," I said eventually. "Who told you that I was being treated in Basildon Hospital under the name of Trevor Morris? Why did you take me away from there? And why to a rented house, when your real home is elsewhere?"

This time he did not hesitate. "I'm afraid my reply won't clarify anything. First I got a text message from an unknown number. Check your email, it said. When I did so I found an email in which an unknown sender instructed me to go and get you, to ensure you got the correct diagnosis and to stay with you until you were capable of moving on. In exchange, I would get information about where I could find my father. I had to rent a house because I don't live here, but in Switzerland."

"And did you get it?" I asked. "The information about your father?"

"No. I'll get it when you report that you are well and available again."

"Who sent you the message?"

"It came from info@media.com."

"The people who commission newspaper articles from me. How did they connect you with me?"

"I don't know."

"And what will you do?"

"It depends what you do," he replied.

"I'm not well enough to carry on," I said. "I don't even know where they'd send me. In any case, my next home would be a hotel. One of the many in which I pass my life."

"Why not break contact with them? Disappear?"

"Because I'm still hoping that in the end I'll find out who I am. Who I was. Do you think I'm wasting my time?"

"No more than I am, looking for my father."

"At least you have the possibility of finding him."

"No more chance than you have of finding yourself."

"So why do we carry on?"

"Evidently we are on a track that we don't know how to leave, other than by being derailed."

"But tell me… Doesn't it seem strange to you? All these names with which we are connected? All these coincidences?"

"Maybe they're not coincidences," he said. "Maybe we are just pieces in a game of chess that someone is playing to amuse himself, or perhaps to win."

"Do you have a photo of your father?" I asked.

"Why? Are you thinking of the possibility that you're my missing father and I your lost son? Things like that only happen in novels. Besides which, I was old enough to remember my father. He was very tall. A head taller than you. And as I said, he disappeared twenty years ago, not six."

At that moment, kleinebilly@yahoo.com, my mobile phone beeped. I received a message.

"Carry on," it said.

14.

Dear MrGod@gmail.com. Since there are too many questions connected with You and the world and life and not least me, I am turning to You, for which I apologise, as You probably have more important work than replying to emails from one of the many billions of souls in Your creation.

At first sight it may seem that You are dealing with a mental patient; who else would dare to think that he could contact You via email? But let's be logical: if everyone on earth can contact You via prayer (because what sense would prayers have if they could not be answered?), it is no less likely that You are reachable by email – not only gmail, but also Yahoo, Hotmail and all the others that are available. Because You are ubiquitous, You are everywhere at every moment, which means You have access to all my emails and not only mine: You have simultaneous access to all the world's databases – personal, business and national.

In comparison with You, the American agency that illegally collects data on people around the world is an amateur association and I really don't know why the world's data ombudsmen get worked up about such trivia. As if they didn't know that the biggest database is controlled by You. How could it not be, when even the smallest sinful thought does not remain hidden from You! So at first sight it is absurd that I am writing to You, as You know more about me than I do myself and I could simply pose the questions that are bothering me in my thoughts; I doubt they would get lost on their way to You.

The reason for the use of technology is that recently my thoughts are very badly stored in my memory. Even after a few days I would not know what I had asked You. And if You mercifully, as is in Your nature, answered me, I would not know which answer to connect with which question. In electronic format the questions are saved and I can get access to them even if a virus erases the hard disc on my laptop; I can take a peep at my past from any computer. I know that You know that; I know that You understand. I know also that You understand why it is so important for me to emphasise this. There are two involved in our communication. You are perfect, I am not. That is precisely why You made possible the invention of the internet: so that we could more easily connect.

I know that connecting with You can be dangerous, for (as it says in the ancient Hassidic text) "God is not nice, he is not your uncle. God is an earthquake." With email, there is probably no more serious danger than that You burn my computer. There is probably more danger involved in other forms of contact with You; in those that people made use of before You (as a great proponent of progress) authorised the invention of the internet. And as You well know, there are quite a few such methods.

Did not Saint Paul, on the road to Damascus, fall from his horse and go blind for three days? Did not some who made direct contact with You lose the gift of speech, while others succumbed to epileptic attacks or fell into a coma? God's ecstasy is wild and cruel, there is nothing gentle in it and many who wish to get too close to You realise this only when it is too late. Those who feel You inside them begin to speak languages that they have never learned, they foam at the mouth, try to pull out their hair, stab themselves with metal spikes, their faces take on expressions of sweet agony. Expressions that appear on our faces in moments of fury or deep sadness, pain or horror; in moments of orgasm or violent death.

But enough of that, dear and respected Friend. (Am I permitted to call You that?)

I am writing to You because I would like to accuse one of my fellow Earthlings. I know that denunciation is not nice, particularly

179

when I leave out the intermediate stages and turn directly to the highest authority. (I could, for instance, report him to the prosecution service; I could demand damages and a court would almost certainly find in my favour, while the villain would receive a life sentence.)

A suspicion has taken root in my head, Oh Great Creator, that the accident on the beach in Bali never actually took place. That it was suggested to me by Dr. Krauthaker and I swallowed his bait hook, line and sinker. I have studied quite a number of academic texts on hypnosis. You of course know, since hypnosis is one of Your gifts to man (which man, like all Your other gifts, quickly abused). As You know, hypnosis has been successfully used in surgery in place of anaesthesia. It is used during childbirth and dental treatment, it is used in psychiatry. In surgical interventions, even those as complex as a heart transplant, it works even when the hypnotist has not even suggested to the patient that he will not feel any pain. And it is possible that the patient himself suggests this, if the hypnotist has somehow turned him into an ally.

Did something like this happen in my case?

I thought about the possibility that I didn't experience brain damage quite recently, in India, when by chance I came across a performance by a travelling fakir and his son, a twelve-year-old boy. More than a hundred curious spectators had gathered on a football field in a small town, including business people (who are known for being difficult to deceive) and, judging by appearances, two doctors, perhaps even a scientist. And, of course, me.

The fakir brought a coiled rope, unwound it and threw it into the air; the boy climbed it and disappeared. There then began to fall from the air parts of his dismembered body. The fakir swept them up into a basket, climbed with it to the end of the rope and disappeared. Half a minute later the fakir and the smiling boy climbed down the rope to the ground and gave a bow. People were so stunned they didn't even clap. But not one said that he had seen anything different from what the rest of us had seen.

Of course, the event was so interesting that I took a lot of photographs. When, back at the hotel, I transferred the photos to my computer, I couldn't believe my eyes. The fakir, the coiled rope and the boy remained on the ground the whole time. At first I thought that I must have taken all eighteen photos before the magic began. But twenty minutes after the event my memory was still fresh: I took my camera out of my bag only when the rope was already in the air. And I took photos of *every* step in the procedure, including the pieces of the boy's body in the basket.

What happened?

The fakir hypnotised us. First he told us what he would do and how things would unfold, and when he said: "Now I will take hold of the rope and throw it in the air," things began to happen as he wanted us to see them. Can You imagine, Highly Respected Friend? Actually, that's the wrong question: You don't need to imagine anything, You know, so I'm wasting time when I explain to You in how many ways it is possible to use hypnosis. But immediately after looking at those photographs, a strange feeling shot through me. It was as if I had touched a live electric wire.

And I thought: there is no proof at all that an inexperienced surfer crashed into my head at the beach in Kuta and that my amnesia is a result of that event. The fact that no details were found about a missing guest at any hotel on the island led me to the thought that something else must have happened. My "new" memory began at the private clinic in Sanur, where Mr. Krauthaker was as familiar with the doctors as if they had known each other for years and they all told me the same story – but what if it was a fabrication?

I can't state with any certainty that Dr. Krauthaker and his Milly are controlling me from a distance; I don't believe in science fiction. But it's more than possible that Dr. Krauthaker hypnotised me and then suggested the story of the accident at the beach and amnesia, ordering me under hypnosis to remember nothing about myself or my life, giving me instructions that when I heard certain words or phrases I should perform certain actions, travel here, travel there, kill a prostitute in a Singapore hotel – a specific prostitute; that I should use one of my false identities for one assignment and a different one for another, and that I should forget each assignment I carry out within five days of its completion.

Of course You, who sees everything, even the movement of a fly's wings, know what really happened. You know also who and what I was before all this happened to me. Because for You the past, present and future happen at the same time, You also know the outcome (or possible outcomes) of my unhappy story. But I'm certainly not asking You to tell me, because I know that would break one of the fundamental rules of Creation: that everything must happen in its own time.

God does not break rules, particularly divine ones. God does not reveal secrets, particularly to those who have been granted free will. But my freedom of choice has been taken away from me, Respected Lord. Since those who have made contact with Satan are also free, the less cautious among us quickly fall prey to them; they plant a Trojan in our brain through which they control our thoughts, goals, actions.

I have no doubt that someone is controlling my life. Someone has possessed me and that person is Dr. Krauthaker, my supposed benefactor.

Please punish him. That's all I ask of You, nothing more. I beg You on my knees. By doing so, You will break none of your rules. I know that You are the God of love and forgiveness, but things have gone too far. Permeated by cynicism, greed and casual cruelty, and riddled with lies, the world has become a caricature of what You had in mind. If hell exists and human souls suffer there, then it is You who has sent them – who else would have done so? So send there the malicious one who has taken over my life. I am convinced that only after Dr. Krauthaker has been removed from my path can I recognise my true identity and return home.

Do this for me, revered God. Prove to me that You really are the God of love. If not love for every living thing, at least for most people. And if not for most, at least for some. What would it cost You to include me among the few fortunate ones?

I don't want to be conceited, but after all that I've been through I deserve it.

Dear MrGod@yahoo.com, you haven't sent me a reply. That probably means that You don't often open your gmail. So, just in case, I am writing to one of the other addresses that You undoubtedly have; I'm sure that sooner or later my message will reach You. It's also possible that my email angered You. And how would it not, since I went beyond every boundary of respect that an unimportant creature owes to its Creator! Undoubtedly You already know that I am sorry, so an apology would sound insulting.

On the other hand, I cannot abandon the hope that You failed to reply because You didn't believe me. It simply didn't seem possible to You that one of Your creatures could do something so underhand to a fellow being. Perhaps You thought: this person is exaggerating, telling tales – people are wicked, but for someone in God's creation to be so *basely* wicked is simply not possible.

It is hard to accept that something we have created is flawed and so I understand You. But I told You the absolute truth (at least, that which has been revealed to me). And as proof that not everything in Your creation is as it should be, I will now describe to You some events that unfolded in "God's own country", as the inhabitants of the USA like to refer to their homeland. Of course, they didn't just unfold – the authorities deliberately instigated them. I know that they were not hidden from You, but perhaps You store them in a more marginal part of Your universal awareness, so do not be angry if I bring them to the centre of attention.

The closest example to what Dr. Krauthaker did to me (and is still doing) is the experiments that Dr. Donald Cameron carried out between 1957 and 1964 at the Allan Memorial Institute in Montreal, Canada. The experiments were financed by the CIA as part of Subproject 68. There was a single goal: to find the best method of influencing the human brain – changing it, adapting it, subordinating it – and ways of extracting information from people who did not wish to divulge it. To this end Dr. Cameron admitted patients with bipolar disorder or various anxiety disorders, under the pretence of "treating" them.

He did something else. In the seven years funded by the CIA he "treated" patients with electroshocks that were thirty or even forty times above the normal level. He used drugs to send some into a coma lasting months, during which he bombarded them with recordings of repeating noises or simple statements. The victims of his experiments lost the power of speech, they forgot who their parents were, they suffered from differing degrees of amnesia.

Dr. Cameron did all this to Canadian citizens. The CIA didn't dare risk such experiments on Americans. But the CIA did instigate and finance the project. And when the money ran out Dr. Cameron, with agreement of the CIA, extended his "treatment" to children. One of these children, when semi-conscious, was offered to a high government official to be sexually abused. Afterwards, the doctor used a secret recording of the event to blackmail the official into providing additional financing.

In the mid-20th century, when scientific advance led to the danger of chemical warfare, the CIA, the American military and government did not ask whether they could use their own citizens as experimental guinea pigs. In order to ascertain what would happen in the case of a real chemical attack, a large quantity of the virus that causes whooping cough was released from boats in Tampa Bay. The epidemic spread like wildfire and twelve people died. The navy sprayed bacterial pathogens above San Francisco and many people fell ill with pneumonia. In the states of Georgia and Florida, above the towns of Savannah and Avon Park, the army released millions of specially bred mosquitoes to see how rapidly yellow fever and Dengue fever would spread. The result was years of fevers, stomach typhus, breathing problems and stillborn babies. The army returned to both places in the guise of health workers whose main role was not to help, but to identify the long term consequences of the diseases they had caused.

Allow me to direct Your attention to one more of Man's "charitable acts" in Your Creation. In the nineteen forties, when it seemed that penicillin would become an effective treatment for syphilis, the worst sexually transmitted disease of the time, the US authorities decided to check whether the medicine would have any unacceptable side effects. The project leaders chose as their guinea pigs citizens of Guatemala. They sent infected prostitutes to prisoners, patients in mental hospitals and soldiers. This strategy did not prove successful, so they decided for inoculation. The selected victims had syphilis bacteria transferred to their penis, hands and face; some had it injected through a lumbar puncture. Then the majority were given penicillin, but a third of them not. It was only in 2010 that Hillary Clinton issued a public apology for these experiments; it was only then that they looked into whether any of the victims were still alive.

Nice, isn't it?

Imagine that You are lying in a hospital with a completely curable condition, perhaps waiting to have varicose veins removed, when one of the doctors, unbeknownst to you, injects you with plutonium. This is what the Americans did as part of the Manhattan project, when they were manufacturing the bombs that destroyed Hiroshima and Nagasaki. They wanted to establish what the consequences of the atom bomb would be for those that survived. Eighteen people received plutonium injections without their knowledge (let alone their permission): fifteen soldiers and three patients in Chicago. Twenty days later only five were still alive. A Dr. William Sweet received financial support for injecting eleven of his patients with uranium. They all died. For a number of years the doctor used tissue from the deceased patients for research purposes.

I could continue, but there would be no point, for now that I have brought these and similar events to the centre of Your attention You are faced with the whole sad story of human abuse from time immemorial. I am not criticising You, I am sure You had Your reasons for creating an imperfect world and perhaps it was inevitable that giving mankind freedom of choice meant that it would be abused (which no doubt fills You with great sadness).

But my sadness, Esteemed One, is equally deep – perhaps even greater than Yours. For I am just a man, a helpless being who cannot control his feelings. In Your case sadness is part of Your nature. It must be, otherwise You would not be perfect. I mention all these things only because I want to draw Your attention to the fact that what Dr. Krauthaker and his associates have done with me is nothing unusual and is perhaps, in comparison with the crimes committed daily in every corner of the world, less important than a minor traffic offence.

185

But for me, Esteemed One, that offence is fatal. And so I ask You (if for some reason You do not want to or cannot steer me on the correct path to myself) to punish Dr. Krauthaker and all those involved in this experiment with the greatest punishment that Your boundless imagination can come up with. Not with an ordinary death: I want them to suffer. For a very, very long time. And any apology would have no effect: I shall never forgive them. You shall, I know that: it is in Your nature to forgive all those who repent from their heart. But my nature, Esteemed One, is not divine – it is human. Hatred, resentment, thoughts of revenge are part of that nature.

That is how You made me.

Actually, RespectedFriend@heavenbepraised.com, now that we're in touch I have another question. Not so much religious as philosophical. And at the same time empirical, scientific. For the more I think about my fate and that of others which in comparison with mine is quite bearable, the clearer it becomes that man is a disaster and the more I wonder why You created the world. Perhaps You couldn't foresee what a monster a creature with free will would become, but that You were unable to do so seems impossible.

So the question arises: why does Something exist instead of Nothing? For it is logically possible for there to be Nothing. Of all the possibilities that would be the simplest. Why did You choose a more complicated one: that there be Something? This endless universe about which we now know enough to make us truly afraid. Today Your will is manifested through science, through which You try (since You could not do it through goodness) to guide us back to You. When we uncover the last secrets of the universe, its origin, its laws, its fate, the only explanation for all that there is will be You, of that there is no doubt. So don't be offended if I repeat: why Something instead of Nothing? And what is Your role in this puzzle?

And one more question, perhaps a presumptuous one: who created You? If You are eternal and exist because you are absolutely perfect (the universe without absolute perfection is logically impossible), what did You do before You created the universe? We now know that

You created it with the Big Bang and that in a few seconds a grain of primordial matter expanded into infinite time and space (and is still expanding, according to those whom You have blessed with more powerful brains than me), but what did You do in the eternity of Your Being *before* that event?

Of course, God doesn't have to do anything, it is enough for him to be, so we cannot say that You were doing nothing; just by existing, you are already doing all that is expected of God. But I'm still interested why it didn't remain like that. Why did You at some point cease to be enough for Yourself? The world You created (or as it became, when it all too obviously ran out of control), cannot entertain You, for You are not a child who wants to play with broken toys. The reason there is Something rather than Nothing must be more than (or different from) what can be embraced by the human spirit. And what can be imagined by someone like me, who is not among the great thinkers. On top of which I am, through one of the coincidences which are a fundamental law of Your Creation, legally not of sound mind.

But my brain, Highly Respected Friend, is impaired in only one way. Perhaps because of my impaired memory, my capacity for logical reasoning and abstract thought is even enhanced. How otherwise would I be able to discuss with You things that the majority of Your creations (if they think about them at all) accept as something given? As something that has to be left to Your judgement, for what is a man to ask questions of his Creator?

Since You are good, since You are Goodness manifested in optimal form, You won't begrudge me my curiosity; after all, You even love those who think that You are not at all necessary for the existence of the world and its functioning.

I don't think so.

That doesn't mean I believe You created the world in six days and rested on the seventh and all the other fairy tales strung together in the Bible. Maybe such fairy tales were essential to convey important messages to people at a considerably lower level of development. Today, we can read them at best as educational allegories in support of an ethical life. I'm sure You agree with me. Today, You send us messages about Your existence and Your nature through scientific findings. It's true: today, scientists are Your ambassadors on Earth, for it is they (and only they) who can show us intimidating Nature and the Majesty of Your Creation.

As one of the many in the world who have suffered wrong (in that regard, I doubt I am any kind of exception in Your Creation), I would really like to find the answer to the question why these things happened to me in particular; why that and not something else; and why through sheer coincidence, although coincidence then determined the rules of what followed?

Of course, I don't expect a reply, for even the stars on this (un)fortunate planet cannot reply to every stupid question sent by faithful fans. And You are the Star *par excellence*, the Star among stars, in the stars and *above* the stars. Although I address You as though You are the trinity (Father, Son and Holy Ghost), I know that You are not, for then You would be so in every religion that honours You. How many times have You been named, You for whom every name is inadequate! How many times have You been described, You who are indescribable! I know that You have answered a thousand times all our questions that were not too stupid for You even to bother with. But sadly, we did not see, or hear, or recognise Your answers.

I did.

It seems to me that Your answer to all the questions men may ask is the fact that there is Something rather than Nothing. This is the way I see it: for every truth there is a reason why it is true. No truth can explain itself. There is nothing that lacks a satisfactory reason for its existence. There is nothing that is simply and only naked, brutal fact.

(Although the English philosopher Bertrand Russell, who I'm sure you are familiar with, claimed that the world was precisely that – brutal fact – and that each why in connection with its existence was a waste of time.)

Reality, which is SomethingInsteadOfNothing, can manifest itself in an endless number of ways (also, after all, as Nothing). But because it did so in only one way – the one we perceive – a choice must have been made. Who made that choice? And what are the advantages of that choice over all the others? For Your Creation, Great Creator, is not perfect, but neither is it imperfect. Your Creation, Highly

Respected Friend, is average. It has much that is good and much that is bad. It is good above all that You gave man free will, otherwise the world would be a machine, without the unpredictability that is the precondition for creativity. But it is bad that free will allows man to abuse Good. And even worse, man often is *not aware* that he is abusing Good, for the sake of Bad.

Did You decide that reality would be as it is?

You, in your infinite wisdom?

Or did reality, among all those possible, choose itself because it had the most qualities that allowed it to be chosen?

Does the world exist simply because there was no better option?

As You can see, Respected Friend, I carry within me a great deal of restlessness, a lot of fear, questions and terrible anxiety that at times do not let me breathe. I live in a permanent present; I find no answer to the questions that obsess me (and often leap at me from ambush like a rabid dog); everything remains shrouded in mist, through which I cautiously feel my way so as not to tumble into an abyss. And I sense the abyss all around me.

Maybe there is more reality in my dreams than in what surrounds me in my waking hours. There are periods when I don't dream at all (or I don't remember my dreams when I awake), but such times are rare; most of the time I have the feeling that my parallel life is unfolding in my dreams and that in its way that life is more real than the one through which I wander during the day. I often dream about beautiful things, about events, feelings, images that are probably the goals of my suppressed hopes, wishes, longings (when I say suppressed, I mean that I have no access to them, although they are interwoven into my spiritual tissue).

Of family walks in autumn woods, for example, with the rustle of fallen leaves beneath our feet – my "family" in this case being my wife, two kids and a dog; or of a big table laden with tasty food and bottles of the best wine, and beside it a lively group of friends in the midst of heated debate about important and intelligent things (but at times also jokes in poor taste and gossip about those who are not

189

present); or of resting in the shade of the trees in late summer beside a river that is sometimes narrow and fast flowing, foaming and jumping over rocks, and sometimes so wide that the opposite bank is almost too far to see, and the water drifts slowly by, calmly and persistently, as if unstoppably carrying all the world's filth to the distant sea.

After such (and similar) dreams, I always wake soothed, even consoled; full of energy, which is so different from the nervous fatigue that accompanies me most of the time on journeys through the world. Such dreams fill me with hope (at least for a few waking hours) that everything will be resolved and that the moment will come when I, too, will flow (like the river into the sea) into a life that no longer consists of jumping and splashing over rapids in a narrow channel, but is endless and calm like the ocean. And in the midst of that ocean I imagine an island that is my home. Where people wait for me. And miss me. My dearest ones, whoever they are.

But I don't often dream about nice things (at least, not as often as I would like). My dreams are usually nightmares that perhaps not even You, Almighty God, can easily imagine. Only Satan has enough imagination to produce the horrors that often throw me from sleep, soaking in sweat and my heart pounding, in the middle of the night and sometimes three times in a row. The content of these nightmares varies, but all are characterised by a scary mixture of extremely painful feelings of fear, anxiety, panic, threat and despair; and in almost every one, someone is following me; I am accused of things against which I cannot defend myself; I am threatened with various consequences for disobedience; I am mocked; my arms or legs are broken; my eyes are put out; I am left alone in the middle of a complete void.

The worst nightmares are those where I am surrounded by a group of uniformed police officers. One of them – evidently the main one – sits at a table writing down the details of my crimes, for which I keep on and on apologising with only one statement: that none of them were premeditated, but were part of a contract according to which the other party, in return for services rendered, would rescue me from the prison of oblivion. From a prison where I would quickly wither and die. You who knows everything, Almighty, would be able to tell me (if my anguish interests You at all) why it is only in dreams that I experience the fear that the police of this or that country will sooner or later track me down and force from me a confession that I am guilty of everything I have been accused of and stick me in a cell with a bunk bed, a toilet and empty walls. Where I will remain until I die.

In broad daylight, when I am fully awake and can think reasonably rationally, it hasn't yet happened (as far as I know) that I have been overcome by fear of arrest, trial and sentencing. (Maybe it has, but I didn't write it down and so I don't remember; but if I record the feelings I experience in dreams, why would I not record similar feelings experienced while awake?) Although in broad daylight I am aware that, regardless of my efforts at disguise and false passports, this could happen at any moment, it leaves me completely cold. As if I knew it couldn't really happen.

When I read through old notes, I see that there appears in my dreams with increasing frequency the image of a small island, on which stands an enormous old house with a half covered roof. I disembark from a small boat at a decaying jetty and make my way along a gravel path towards the entrance. Even from a distance I can see that there is nothing where the doors and windows should be. As if the builders had not installed the doors and windows, or (a more likely explanation, given the age of the building) as if they had rotted away, fallen apart, been removed. I go inside. I enter an enormous empty chamber, from which I can see through the empty doorways into other empty chambers. Half rotten, already partly collapsed stairs lead to the first floor. I dare not put my foot on them. I wander from one chamber to another, thinking how I might get to the first floor without the stairs collapsing under my weight and killing me. I wander and think, wander and think. I realise that the house is empty and that I am on an island. I would like to leave, but I can't.

I have the feeling that I am at home in this abandoned house.

What can these dreams mean, Almighty? And why do they keep recurring? Why with increasing frequency? They fill me with a growing anxiety. How can I reduce it? By believing in Your goodness? I'm afraid that isn't enough. I am a sinner. That's the most I can be.

15.

Dear supremejudge@supreme-court.com, if you really are a supreme court judge and this is your email address (not a joke), then I would like to confide in you regarding one or two matters. At the same time this correspondence is like a draft defence, in case I should ever find myself appearing in front of you charged with the murder, theft, fraud, abuse of trust and similar dishonest practices that I have committed in the past five years. I am an exile, judge, exiled from the home to which I would like to return, but the way back is too complex.

Hence my email. Perhaps it will reach the right person and you will, if I ever appear before you, hand down a lenient sentence. Although I have lost faith in most things, I still believe that the world contains at least some people for whom justice, based on the heart and common sense, not only on the letter of the law, is the highest value. I'm sure you are part of this minority. I have to believe this, otherwise I would not be able to trust you with what follows. And then I wouldn't be able to cite the facts in my defence. Perhaps I need these facts more than you do.

For the court known as conscience.

But you know yourself, judge, that conscience is all too likely to forgive, all too quickly finds excuses. And so I cannot trust the impartiality of my inner judge (although most people in the world do so); I leave you to judge my actions – you will know when to pardon and when to punish in accordance with the law.

Before I start to enumerate the illegal acts I have committed (and which were the toll I paid on my way back to myself) I would like to cite the extenuating circumstances. The first is that none of us is his own master. We are all children of the universe, subject to the influence of the sun, the planets, the stars, the moon, cosmic rays and other invisible forces. Where does our responsibility begin and end? It is not as simple as the lawmakers imagine, for they are (let us not forget) also subject to these influences. And you, judge, how do you know whether the sentence that you give is subject or not to these universal forces?

I know that many would label these words (and similar) as New Age babble and perhaps you think the same. It's good that we at least have science, that divinity that most reasonable people have long worshipped, including the two of us. But of all the divinities, science is still the least dogmatic, the most prepared to deny its own existence and would do so if it could rely on one piece of evidence. Isn't it so, my learned friend?

We can trust science, at least for now.

So please allow me to familiarise you with a selection of universal secrets that are perhaps now known to you. Let's begin with the large red spot on Jupiter. It is roughly as big as Earth and is not stable, but travels about. Astronomers refer to it as an anti-cyclonic storm and it has already lasted more than four hundred years. Is Jupiter too far from Earth for a storm of global proportions to have an influence on the way we feel, our thoughts and actions? It is much further than Venus, which could be called our neighbour. So you will perhaps be less sceptical when I enumerate the secrets of that planet.

If you landed on Venus, judge, you would descend through a freezing cold layer of cloud to a scorching surface (an extreme example of the greenhouse effect), but you would not have the feeling that you had arrived on a planet surface, but at the bottom of an endless basin, around which the whole surface would rise above you on all sides. It would be like landing somewhere in Europe and the whole of Russia, all the way to Vladivostok, plus the rest of Asia, was rising towards the east, Africa to the south and America to the west. Regardless of the fact that Venus is also a round planet, its surface would rise around you in such a way that everything on Venus would be in your field of vision (if you had a powerful enough telescope).

And not only that. If the atmosphere on Venus was completely clear (which it never is) it would seem that all its features – rocks, mountains, canyons and so on – were indefinitely repeating themselves in concentric circles. This means, judge, that at a certain distance you would see another you and then another and another, ad infinitum; you would have the feeling that you had entered a hall of mirrors. Although you were the only person on Venus, it would seem that the planet was really heavily populated. And every inhabitant would be you!

Science fiction?

No, judge, that's what science says.

Of course, regardless of the multiplicity of your presence, you would feel good on Venus only if you enjoyed temperatures of 300 degrees Celsius; I'm afraid you would fry immediately upon landing. And what is the cause of the unusual visual effect on the surface? The simple fact that Venus's atmosphere is thirty times denser than Earth's. This means that sunlight does not bend as it does on Earth, where it bounces back into empty space, but creates a kind of gradually disappearing spiral.

As you can see, supremejudge@supreme-court.com, things in our universe are not as simple as even your most complex case. And then what are things like in parallel universes, which for some time science has speculated are of infinite number!

Credo quia absurdum est!

The Earth, judge, is not a closed system. We think of the atmosphere as some kind of envelope, but this envelope is transparent. It lets through sunlight, X-rays, ultraviolet and infra-red light, radio waves, cosmic rays and showers of subatomic particles that pass through us as if we were as thin as cigarette smoke. The activity of the sun, the phases of the moon, the position of the planets, the movement of the solar system in the galaxy, in spite of their distance, are not separated from the life we live on Earth. Physics assures us that everything in the world is connected, interdependent and inseparable, and even the smallest change on the most distant star has consequences on Earth, in every one of us. Also in you. And me. Nothing, not even the flap of a butterfly's wing, is an event in itself: everything influences everything else.

Study quantum physics, judge, and you will understand my claim that *I am not guilty.*

It has been shown that at times of heightened solar activity, the number of deaths among tuberculosis patients in Hamburg, Copenhagen and Zürich goes up; that the number of accidents in mines increases; that agitation and violence among psychiatric patients goes up: that between 1957 and 1961, the number of new patients in the eight largest psychiatric institutions in New York increased considerably at times of sunspot activity. Activity on the sun's surface is cyclical and reaches a peak every eleven years. In 1930 the Russian professor of history Chiyevski ended up in the Siberian gulag for claiming that a whole series of important historical developments were not the result of dialectical materialism, but were temporally connected with increased solar activity. From 500 B.C. to the start of the 20th century, 72 per cent of wars, revolutions and mass migration of peoples coincided with peak sunspot activity. The same is true of medieval plague, epidemics of scarlet fever and cholera, annual precipitation levels, water levels in lakes, and famine in India and elsewhere in the world.

How is that possible?

Science has also found an answer to that question. Low frequency and low energy electro-magnetic radiation have a noticeable influence on the most widespread substance on Earth – water. Men are up to sixty per cent water, women up to fifty per cent. If extra-terrestrial forces can influence chemical experiments in laboratories (to the extent that sometimes, due to "aberrant reactions", they cannot be completed), why could they not influence the water that makes up such a large part of our bodies? It has been proven that the movement of sunspots across the central solar meridian influences the quality of human blood and that this influence is not halted by castle walls, metal panels or even complete darkness. It can be stopped only by a solar eclipse.

195

And judge, what about the moon? Which waxes and wanes and waxes again? Has the moon ever made you sleepwalk? For the reasons I've already given, I cannot claim that it has ever affected me, but that doesn't mean it hasn't happened. In some countries, as you are no doubt aware, for criminal offences committed when there is a full moon, courts hand out lower sentences. It has been shown, and is relatively widely known, that those whose anti-social behaviour has psychotic causes (pyromaniacs, thieves, robbers, aggressive drivers and murderous alcoholics) go crazy when the time of a full moon approaches. When the moon begins to wane, they calm down again.

You probably know that shellfish open only once a day. At one time it was believed that their rhythm was determined by the tide; now we know it is the moon, which also orders the biological rhythm of every organism on Earth – even menstruation and fertility in women. More than fifty years ago, the Czech psychiatrist Eugen Jonas showed that the time of a woman's ovulation is determined by the moon and that she can get pregnant only when the moon is in the same phase as it was at the moment of her birth.

Do we live in a time of superstition, judge?

No. We live in a time of science.

We live in a world of wonders and miracles. In a world ruled by cosmic forces which, above all – and how could they not – rule each of us, without our being able to resist. And some good news for vampires, if you by any chance have such tendencies: at the time of a full moon and few days before, people bleed much more strongly than at other times. Pass this on: I read somewhere that every one of us has at least one close or distant relative who is a bloodsucker.

Much of what I do on my supposed way "home" demands pretence, play acting, and that comes so easily that I was perhaps in my forgotten life an actor. Although I've noticed that there are few people around who lack this talent. I often think that the greatest actors are those who appear most spontaneous and genuine. And those are precisely the ones I try to emulate, since in the assignments I am given

196

I must create the impression that I am not hiding anything (although I almost always am, and usually not something good).

In spite of this, I cannot be satisfied with the idea that I was in the life I lived before my memory went to pot a professional actor. I resist the idea, although I'm not sure why. Perhaps because what I have been living since my accident seems like a kind of play, a staged, made up story. So I prefer to imagine that in my "previous" life I was something else. And in doing so, I come up with some bizarre possibilities. For instance, that I was a neurologist. Like Dr. Krauthaker. Perhaps even a neurosurgeon. Like the now deceased Dr. X. Perhaps I published a series of articles on amnesia before I became its victim

Hasn't it often been said that God has a sense of humour?

After everything that has happened in the last six years, I decided to pay Dr. Krauthaker a visit. To appear before and confront him. To force him to tell me what precisely he is doing with me. And why he doesn't reply to my emails. Of course, I couldn't remember exactly where he lived, nor in which part of town was his clinic where he tested and "treated" me; I hadn't written any of that down.

But a world renowned neurologist couldn't be hard to find! Do you agree, judge? Even in a city as big as Sydney, a world-renowned neurologist would be widely known, at least in medical circles. And so as not to waste time, I typed his name into Google. Dr. Abraham Krauthaker, Clinic for Neurological Diseases, 25 Wyndham Street, Sydney. Simple.

But at that address I found a Greek restaurant called Mykonos. I sought out the owner and asked him if he had possibly bought the premises during the last six years from a Dr. Krauthaker. No, he replied, he'd bought the place four years earlier, when it was already a restaurant – Vietnamese – from three oriental gentlemen whose names he unfortunately did not recall. And he didn't have time to go home and look at the contract.

No problem, I said to myself. Dr. Krauthaker sold the premises in which he had his clinic and moved elsewhere. The details in Google were simply out of date, as is more than half the information online.

I hailed a taxi and went to St. Vincent Hospital. I looked for the Neurology Department and asked them if there was a Dr. Krauthaker working there. No, they said, there was no doctor of that name on the list. I asked to speak to the head of department, presenting myself as Professor Dr. Sven Lindgren, member of the Nobel Prize committee. The head of department received me without the usual excuses about being too busy and he responded to my questions by saying he had never heard of a neurologist called Dr. Krauthaker, although he had been working in Sydney more than thirty years and he knew all the neurologists personally. Had I perhaps made a mistake with regard to location – should I perhaps be looking for him in Melbourne? Although he knew the neurologists in Melbourne as well, in fact across Australia, since he was the president of the Australian association of neurologists, and there was *no* Dr. Krauthaker on the membership list.

Had I got the wrong name?

Was I looking in the wrong country?

When I got back outside I didn't feel too good. I turned into the nearest park and slumped onto the first bench. Had the person who rescued me on a Bali beach, brought me to Sydney, examined me and then sent me on a risky journey "home" vanished into thin air? Had he disappeared without trace?

That was impossible.

And when I set off on my journey under his instructions (and with passports supplied by him) he even responded to my emails a number of times. He had then broken off contact without any explanation, but I still had his emails stored in a folder.

Perhaps his real name was different and he came up with Krauthaker just for me, so that later, when I came to settle scores, I wouldn't find him? I began to feel dizzy, I thought I would pass out. One of a group of three young girls who went past asked with concern: "Are you alright?" I'm okay, okay, I gestured and waved them on.

I went to the nearest bookshop and asked for the medical department. On the very first shelf I found four books written by

Dr. Abraham Krauthaker. I feverishly looked for his photograph on the covers, but found none. Strange. Truth be told, it wouldn't have helped me if I had found it because I don't remember faces for more than five days. There was still a small chance that someone had got their hands on me who used his name, but who in reality had been anything but a neurologist.

But no, that wasn't possible: the man who brought me from Bali to Sydney had a neurological clinic and four members of staff; I had been to his home, met his wife, stayed with them, and everyone had called him Dr. Krauthaker.

I bought one of the books (*Neurological Features of Retrograde Amnesia*) and returned to St. Vincent's Hospital. Once again, I asked to speak to the head of the neurological department. I got the impression he was slightly shocked to see me again. I showed him the book and asked him if he had ever heard of the author.

I said: "On the cover, in the mini biography, it says that Dr. Krauthaker has a private neurological clinic in Sydney, that he lectures at numerous foreign universities and is held to be one of the world's leading authorities on amnesia. How is it possible that you don't know this man?"

The head of department looked embarrassed.

"It's like this," he finally replied. "We don't talk about Dr. Krauthaker in Australia. He made some serious mistakes in his clinic, which were followed by damages claims worth millions. Dr. Krauthaker quickly sold his apartment and his clinic, and then he disappeared. No one can find him, even though Interpol issued an international warrant. He caused the reputation of Australian neurology, which had been seen as one of the most progressive in the world, irreparable damage. And so we decided to erase him from our memories."

My shock did not quickly subside.

"Why are you looking for him?" he asked.

"Nothing important," I replied with a wave of the hand.

16.

Dear millymolly@yahoo.com, where are you? Have you disappeared off the face of the earth with your husband? Are you mixed up in his criminal enterprises? Was it you who reported him to the authorities? Are you living elsewhere and with someone else? Why don't you reply? What happened between you and Dr. Frankenstein? How many monsters has he created, besides me?

I'm increasingly convinced that in my previous mails I was unfair to you a number of times. I insulted you. Maybe unintentionally, maybe deliberately. Because my memory fades so quickly that I misunderstood quite a few things. If I thought badly of you, it is quite possible that it was your husband who thought that way – the one you never liked. That now seems to me – admittedly a little late – the only possible truth. He (not I) described you as a cow whose only goal in life was idleness, shopping, enjoyment, manipulation, cheating on your husband, cheating on those with whom you cheated on him, taking drugs, both soft and hard, and plotting mischief – mainly on a small scale, perhaps because you are not blessed with much imagination.

I humbly apologise if I have ever created the impression that I don't have a good opinion of you. If we have had (and I think we have) a secret relationship in your house, it must have been consensual, the consequence of mutual attraction, but also probably the fact that you were actually afraid of your husband – that you were (like me) his prisoner. Maybe you managed to escape; I will remain his prisoner for the rest of my life. But I can't understand why it was you in particular who sent me the words "Carry on", the code that compels me to do something that otherwise I would never do. Did Dr. Krauthaker really plant a chip in my head that is activated by the words "Carry on"; a chip that then forces my nervous system to carry out a pre-programmed order? Maybe there's no chip, but the words always trigger the same kind of action; and it was you who sent them.

Are those words connected with a long lasting hypnosis from which I cannot awake? Did Dr. Krauthaker have access to your address and send the emails himself?

As you can see, I am doing quite a bit of wondering, pondering, speculating. If you got in touch, you could clarify some things at least. Wouldn't that help you, as well? I'm tired, MillyMolly, and have begun to think of bidding farewell to the world before fate brings it to an end for me. This is the only freedom I have now as a prisoner of the past authored by your husband. I cannot believe that my life is a hallucination – that it is something I have brought on myself. The things I touch seem real; what I see no less real; what I hear, the same. My head hurts, my teeth hurt, my thumb hurts, I have stomach cramps; I *feel* pain. I'm not dreaming, I'm awake. I know that you live somewhere; I know you exist; I know you're reading this mail.

Answer me.

Of course, you didn't; as you probably never will. But I'd like to tell you something else.

Some days ago in a remote mountain refuge in the Swiss Alps I got talking to a young man who sat down next to me in an armchair in front of the fireplace in which flickered a pleasant fire; I was leaning back, my eyes closed, trying to remember why I came to Switzerland. And why these mountains. And why this remote refuge. He just sat down beside me without saying anything. And ordered double whisky. For both of us.

Before I could open my mouth, he began to speak. In German. But I understand German and speak it very well. He began to say how what bothered him the most was people who came to the mountains without the slightest awareness of their limitations. They are all convinced that they can climb wherever they want, without difficulty or serious effort. When they wear themselves out half way, they are not responsible, they blame him for failing to warn them how demanding the path was. Which he of course did, and not just once.

"I hope that you at least are aware of the dangers lurking in the rock faces," he added.

"Me?"

"Didn't you come intending to climb the Grand Combin?"

"No. But that doesn't mean that I won't do it. Although this is the first time I've been so high up. And I've never climbed."

"I'm a mountain guide," he said. "I thought you were my client." He held out his hand. "Bill."

"Trevor Morris," I said, shaking it. "Maybe I *am* your client and I forgot. It seems to me that I came here to withdraw from the world for a while. Until yesterday I was staying at the hotel Le Grand Chalet. But there were too many people there, so I came here. This place seems ideal to me. No-one will find me here."

"That's true," he said with a nod. "Who are you escaping from?"

"Perhaps myself?"

"I know that feeling," he commented.

"Have you been a mountain guide for long?"

"Not at all," he admitted. "I've been a number of things. I'm always looking for something new. I'm afraid of ending up in a well-paid job where I'll sit at the same desk for thirty years, staring through the same window at the same building."

"That's most people's fate."

"Have you really never climbed?" He looked at me as if he didn't believe me.

"Maybe I have, but I don't remember."

"You never forget things like that."

"Unless your memory fails you. That happened to me. I'm a victim of amnesia."

"Aren't we all," he tried to make a joke out of it. "The whole world has lost its memory."

"No," I said. "I did lose mine. Can you imagine how horrible it is, not knowing who you are?"

And I entrusted this person, who I was seeing for the first time in my life (or was I?) and who I knew nothing about (am I wrong about this?), with the essence of my trauma. And my main goal, the only one: to stop being No-one. To once more become Someone.

"But isn't that Someone," he said after a lengthy silence, "just a construction that doesn't really exist? And which in ways more important than a name changes from day to day?"

"I'm willing to accept that," I said, glad to finally have someone to talk to (in the flesh, not virtual) who knew what I was talking about. "But that Someone, although constructed, is something that I would like to be aware of as a story with a thread and continuity."

"Do you recognise things?" he asked. "Do you know what they are?"

"Things I recognise, but I don't remember faces. Or events. The longest I retain them in memory is five or six days. It's theoretically possible that we met ten days ago and I'm not aware of it. Maybe we've met a number of times. But even if we have, it seems to me that I'm meeting you for the first time in my life."

"Do you think about the future?" he asked.

I shook my head.

"Do you picture it?"

"I can't."

"Because it's a projection of past events. The future is a series of daydreams, nothing more. And if the past is blurred, or even erased, there's no material to project. Then our mind is like an empty film. The projector is turning but nothing appears on the screen."

"Welcome to my world," I said.

"But that is a privilege – you should be grateful!"

"What?! Grateful because I am unable to find the answer to any important question?"

"You're not the only one. No-one can. Maybe illusion is our only sustenance. For those of us who like to think that we know who we are and for you, who are convinced that you do not know."

"That sounds nice," I said. "Philosophical. But I'd like to make contact with life."

"Are you sure that those of us who have not lost our memory have any more insight into the meaning of what happens to us?"

"You *must* have."

"And if we don't?"

"There was a time when I used to read novels," I said. "Identified with fictional characters. I imagined that I was *co*-experiencing their stories. That life was happening to me."

"Now you know it's not like that."

"Now I have a feeling it's not like that."

"Novels are books about events in the mind," he said. "*Everything* happens in the mind. First in the author's, then the reader's. Novels are an *endless* source of an *endless* number of understandings and interpretations. And *intentions* to interpret. We are *trapped* in our minds. Each his own. And each in his understanding of this imprisonment. What is happening to you is just a novel."

"Then we are slaves," I said.

"Not you. You are free. You can live here and now. And nowhere else. Neither in time nor in space. Isn't that the goal of every kind of meditation, of Buddhism, Hinduism – even Christian mysticism? To live here and now? Some strive their whole lives to attain that state. You were granted it by a clumsy surfer."

"Are you joking" I asked.

"I see that you too have succumbed to the law of the matrix."

I confessed that I didn't understand what he was trying to say.

"Every new form sooner or later, sometimes quickly, changes into a matrix. Most people then do not see deviation from the matrix as something new, but as something that, in relation to the encoded pattern, is deficient in some way. And so the world goes round from mediocrity to mediocrity, which the most naïve among us elevate into quality. Which is completely right, for a mediocre world is the only possible one."

"God and I have already come to the same conclusion," I said.

"God?"

"He and I exchange emails."

"So do I," he said, with a sideways glance.

"With God?" I asked in surprise.

"No," he said with a smile. "With you."

"No! Are you… Who are you?"

"Who are you?" he asked in return.

We ordered two more whiskies. "Let's get drunk together," he said. "In memory of our meeting in the Swiss Alps. And at the hospital in Basildon. And everything that happened in the past. And everything that didn't happen."

"I don't remember any Basildon," I said. I looked at him. "I know you from somewhere. Can you tell me who you are?"

"Can you tell me who you are?" he smiled.

And he looked at me.

And I looked at him.

I got the feeling I remembered his smile, which lay somewhere between polite friendliness and barely noticeable scorn. And I remembered that smile when there was no scorn in it, when it radiated only friendliness.

"I'm kleinebilly@yahoo.com," he said.

A minute of silence followed.

"That address does not exist. I never got an answer."

"The answer is in front of you: Kevin Youngson," he said. "Don't you remember what my Swiss mother called me, who you murdered in an outburst of jealous rage? *Kleine Billy*. You had an agreement that she would speak German with me and you English. You wanted me to be bilingual. And I am. Multilingual. Like you. And I cannot find myself in any of the languages I master. I don't know, either, who I am. You left me, father! Vanished!"

"No."

"And what will you do now I've found you?"

"Kill me," I said.

"Why didn't you kill me in Basildon? When you got the order by mobile phone? Carry on, it said. I checked. Did you know I was your son? Is that why you let me live?"

"I don't remember. Perhaps because I decided to resist. Perhaps a voice spoke inside me, saying: You can't, you can't, you can't carry on!"

"A shame it happened just when you should have killed me."

"Why?"

"Because my mother didn't have an affair with a German director named Haidacher, but with me. Not an affair, but a relationship. With your son, father! *That's* why you lost your mind and became a killer. And fled. And forgot me. And everything that happened. You couldn't accept what happened. What you did. You were convinced that the time of Greek tragedy passed two thousand years ago. If you read the popular press you'd know these things still go on. More than ever. Now they seem banal."

"Who is Dr. Krauthaker?" I asked.

"A man with connections, who helped you flee from jail in Sydney, where you were serving a life sentence for my mother's murder. Probably so that he could use you as a guinea pig. Scientists are forgiven everything. You lost your memory in prison."

"So there was no accident on Bali?"

"Is that important?"

"Is anything important?"

"Revenge?" He looked at me.

"Take revenge against me. Turn off the flickering light in my rotten brain."

"I can't. Deep inside I approve of what you did. My mother deserved to die."

"If I really killed her in the heat of the moment, I won't forgive myself."

"What will you do?"

"I'll return to jail."

"I'd like to invite you to a wonderful island in the Gulf of Thailand. Ko Phangan."

"To meet death?"

"Why wait for death and be bored in between? And keep repeating the same movements, the same mistakes? Doesn't it make sense to end a journey that leads nowhere, of your own free will at a chosen moment?"

"Who would choose the moment?"

"Both of us at the same time?"

"But you're young. You've got more than half your life in front of you."

206

"Half a life of memories of sex with my own mother?"

I didn't know how to answer.

"Now that the world has become one, we people are also all one," he said. "Your pain is mine. My malevolence is yours. My hope is as empty as yours. We don't each have our own illusions, they are shared. Our sins are collective. Why should I not accept punishment for your sins? We are vampires, we suck each other's blood. We suck our *own* blood. But we don't know it. Can you imagine how many people do not realise that the world has become one? And that we're all just phantoms. And they each live in their own little garden. In the smallest corner of that garden. The most comfortable one. Comfortable because they master it."

Dear Dr.Krauthaker@amnesia.com, why should I not send my last email to you, the recipient of my first? From the Swiss winter my son and I travelled to the Thai island of Ko Phangan. His wish that we should experience our deaths together as one, as the fusion of two minds that could achieve more than individual ones, offered me an ideal solution for the way forward. To the place where I'd always been heading.

I was no longer alone! After a long time I began to discern within me, alongside fear, the first small signs of hope. Relief. Trust in what to little Billy seemed the only appropriate way. To the son who found his father. And decided to finally take him home. Through a world that had changed so much that no-one recognised it any more. And out of this world.

On the southern part of the Thai island of Ko Phangan (we got there by boat from the neighbouring island of Ko Samui) there was a party going on, celebrating the full moon, a monthly gathering of romantics, drunkards and alternative types from around the world, who have been gathering on this beach for twenty-five years. They bathe, sit on the beach, strum out-of-tune guitars, smoke grass, touch each other, have sex on the beach among the mass of kindred spirits, which does not seem a big deal (and is even encouraged) and of course throw up, because there are more than twenty cheap spirits and no fewer cocktails available, which even someone with an excellent memory would not remember.

"Sex, before we set off?" Billy asked. "No, thanks," I said. "I've become old-fashioned. Sex with love, or not at all."

"I'll adapt," he said, somewhat dissatisfied. He was still young.

"You can," I said, removing the sense of responsibility.

He shook his head. "Now we are one. What one does, so does the other."

On the sandy beach of Haad Rin, a kilometre and a half long, swarmed thirty thousand people and almost all of them were young enough to be my children or grandchildren. The speakers the whole length of the beach vibrated with frightful music (if the noise in hell was at least a little more melodic and at least two decibels lower, then I would *demand* to be sent there). Before these parties began, Kleine Billy told me (and this was before he was born), rabid dogs ran among the few visitors to these beaches and a similar number of robbers. When electricity finally arrived, the regulars yelled "Colonialism!" But progress had its way and now no-one objects, because now in the spotlights the mass can watch you go into the water completely naked.

"We'll try that local drug, yaba," said Kleine Billy. "Or would you prefer ecstasy?"

"You are expedition leader," I replied. "When you are going to the other world, everything is a matter of experience and each one your last."

We found a slightly less crowded part of the beach, sat on the sand and succumbed to the influence of unknown cocktails, yaba and ecstasy (and perhaps something else); we sank into a state that Kleine Billy called "false enlightenment" – the only kind available to man – stretched out on the sand and stared at the full moon above us.

I was struck by a feeling that I'd experienced this before. That I had looked at this moon. That I had lain on this silky sand. That I had heard before this disorder and shouting that someone had just drowned.

"I was conceived on this island," said Kleine Billy. "In 1985. You and my mother were here. She said that the days on this island were the only ones when she really loved you. Isn't it nice that we're dying here, where you gave me life?"

"Are you grateful?"

"No. First I looked for you to kill you. Then to put you back in prison. Then to get to know you. And finally, for us to die together."

"I'm the one who should die. Not you. Help me."

"You face a worse punishment."

He got up, grabbed my shoulder bag with all my credit cards and documents, and rushed towards the water. "Stop him!" I yelled. But no-one paid any attention, they were all wrapped up in the party. They no doubt thought this was part of the party – ours, father and son. Or perhaps two gay guys: the older one buying love, the younger one selling it because he had no choice?

Aren't there as many interpretations as there are pairs of eyes?

In the moonlight I saw that Kleine Billy was already far out, swimming with all his might away from the shore. I went after him. In my clothes. And swam. The water was warm. The beach was full of people half my age, having fun. Strangers to me. Like Kleine Billy. Half my age. Educated, clever, a kindred spirit, a similar outlook, but a complete mystery.

I knew I would not catch him. I knew I would not understand him. I knew that I would never really believe him.

I also knew I lacked the courage to die.

I returned to the beach and collapsed on the sand. Once again I was alone.

And now really No-one. Kleine Billy had taken all my passports into the depth of the sea.

Even as a fake person I had disappeared from the face of the earth.

Or not.

When I got back to the wooden house we had rented near the beach, I looked for my iPad (the only thing I had left) and went on-line. I had decided to write a farewell letter to you, Dr. Krauthaker, and forgive you for all the wrongs you did me. And then to summon up the courage to follow Billy into the depths of the ocean.

And what did I see?

A mail in my Inbox! At first I thought it was from Cassandra – the only one who had written to me during the past five years. But no, it was for Trevor Morris, from kleinebilly@yahoo.com.

"Dear Trevor Morris/Alfred Haidacher/Kevin Youngson/Sven Lindgren/Kostas Asimakopulos. I am not writing to you from heaven or hell (or the depths of the ocean). I'm still here. But when you read this, I'll no longer be among the living. I guessed that you, coward that you are, would not dare to follow me; that you would, as you had before, betray me. And leave me to swim towards life (this time, its last moments) alone. But I don't hold this against you. Nowhere does it say that the fate of father and son should be the same, even if one or the other or both wish it to be. Even those of us who share the same blood are playthings of different gods. When we watch a drama, we each experience it in our own way; when we read a novel, we unconsciously seek in it our own story (and in most cases, fail to find it). It is enough that others do so.

I want to tell you, Trevor Morris etc., that what I brought to your life (which isn't even yours, but belongs to an invisible puppet master) in recent months is not perhaps the complete truth. How much of it is true and how much made up I won't explain, for that would give you one more burden, perhaps the greatest of all. You know yourself that our lives are to a large extent a self-created fiction and that those of us who acknowledge this are not the crazy ones: the truly crazy ones are those who are convinced that everything they consider to be part of their lives is real.

And so you should believe that I am your son; believe that you are the psychiatrist Kevin Youngson, sentenced to life for murdering my mother; believe all that, it won't harm you in any way. In a stormy sea it is good to have at least one anchor. The truth, as we have a habit of calling it, is in every case just a bunch of thousands of flashes of personal vision.

Of which mine is only one. And yours, too.

In the network of tropical islands of the Mergui archipelago west of the Thai coast there lives a nomadic tribe known as the sea gypsies. They spend most of their time in boats on the open sea and learn to

210

swim before they can walk: they are born and die on their boats. How do they live, what do they eat? Shellfish and sea cucumbers. Even children can dive many metres to the sea floor to collect sea creatures to eat. Through many generations they have learned to slow their heartbeat so that they can stay under water twice as long as ordinary people, without diving equipment. Members of the Sulu tribe dive as much as twenty-five metres looking for pearls.

And that's not all! From the age of five onwards, sea gypsies can see under water as well as on land. Without goggles. Most normal people (including us) cannot do that. Their eyes have adapted to their chosen way of life.

Our brains are flexible: each new thing shapes, completes, enriches them.

Become a sea gypsy, Mr. Trevor Morris, etc.

Become something more than a swimmer who, under whispered instructions, crawls on the surface, killing flies. Dive to the depths.

Stop swimming for others, swim for yourself

And Dr. Krauthaker? It would be good to kill him, wouldn't it?

Sadly, that's not possible. Go up to the highest terrace of the highest building in any large city on a Saturday afternoon and look down at the streets below. You'll see thousands of Krauthakers, swarming like ants from one place to another, playing with your life. And mine. And ours."

17.

Dear cassandra@yahoo.com. Perhaps you'll be taken aback that I'm writing after such a long silence. And perhaps your surprise will be even greater when I tell you that this is the last email I am sending from any of my addresses. Why to you in particular, one of the few email contacts I have met in person?

Perhaps because you will not believe (as you did not once before) that I am speaking the truth. This relieves me of the necessity of trying to prove anything to you. Besides which, you are the only person I have met during my six years of wandering with whom – in spite of the lies and deception – I have been able to form a relationship. A paradox, certainly, but what else does life consist of? It seems that, in spite of all our misunderstandings, we understand each other.

I was on holiday on the tropical island of Ko Phangan in the Gulf of Thailand and all my passports and credit cards were stolen. I was left only with a little cash, enough for a few days food and a boat ride to the neighbouring island of Ko Samui, where I had to turn up at an address that I received in a text message from an unknown number: "Pick up a package in the name of Svetaketu Brahman".

At the address I found a tourist agency, where a young Thai woman in glasses was sitting at a desk. When I told her why I had come, without a word she handed over a padded brown envelope. It contained an American passport in the name I had got over the phone, plus a gold American Express with the same name. It was accompanied by a smaller envelope in which there was a slip of paper bearing the words: *Tat twam asi*. In Sanskrit, as you may know, this means *This is you* or *Is this you?*

Dr. Krauthaker (or whoever is guiding me through life) had supplied me with a new identity. And not just that: was he trying to tell me that this was the real me, the one I was before I lost my memory? An American citizen with an Indian name, where Brahman means God and Svetaketu son, who in one of the Upanishads (I think it's called Chandogya and you can find it in one of the Vedas – the Samaveda, if I remember rightly) is sent by his father on six years of learning? A white man with an Indian name (for the passport contained my photograph)?

Of course, this isn't so unusual: many European, American and Australian Indophiles take names from classical Indian philosophy. What was more unusual was that the passport was not a new one: it had been issued seven years previously, a little before my supposed accident on Bali, and the many visas and stamps showed that its owner had visited more than ten countries, including India, Russia, Japan and, of course, Indonesia. Is this my real passport?

Who knows? In an old non-isometric passport it is possible to change the photo. But what did the one who sent me the passport want to tell me with the words *Tat twam asi*? If I ever read the Indian Vedas (and evidently I had, for Hindi, similar to Sanskrit, is one of the foreign languages that I speak surprisingly well), their content had sunk into oblivion with my previous life. So I googled them to refresh my memory.

Svetaketu returned to his father, the sage Uddalaki, feeling very proud because in six years he had learned all the Vedas by heart. Not only proud, but convinced that he, too, was now wise. "Why are you so full of yourself?" his father rebuked him. "Did you learn that which makes the unheard heard, the unknown known or the uncomprehended comprehended?" Svetaketu did not understand, so his father clarified: "From a piece of clay, you can recognise everything that is made of clay. Modifications to clay – effects – are only words. He who knows the cause, knows all its effects, for the cause and the effect are the same. So the body is no different from food, food is no different from water, water is no different from fire, and fire is no different from God. Only God is real and that is you. Your soul is an effect of God, who is the cause of everything, and so God and your soul, your true self, are one and the same."

It sounds complicated, but it quickly became clear to me what the sender of the message was trying to tell me. The last six years, I had lived as an effect, cut off from its cause. And thus from myself, from my soul. How did that happen? What was the purpose of my journey, my six years of agony? Were these years of learning, after which Svetaketu would return to his father – not proud at his knowledge, but wise? As you see, Cassandra, I wasn't rewarded with an answer, but with a greater, the greatest mystery.

I'd like to tell you, Dr.Krauthaker@gmail.com, that I have finally reached the house that I have often dreamed about in recent years. To the house that was probably my home. It stands on a small island that can be reached from the mainland by motorboat in half an hour. Even from far off you can see the house is big, almost a palace, and that the wind has ripped off half its roof. I follow a gravel path to the front entrance. On both sides there are cypresses three metres tall. The sky is clear and sunny, but the air is cold, as if the island is somewhere in the north.

Where are the cypresses from? That question doesn't bother me; perhaps it is one of the puzzles that will accompany me through life – one of the smaller ones, perhaps the smallest. My step is not as firm as it was; I get pains in my knees and hips that are something new for me. Is old age creeping up on me? Even from a distance I can see that there is nothing where the doors and windows should be. As if the builders never installed the doors and windows, or (a more likely explanation, given the age of the building) as if they had rotted away, disintegrated.

I go inside. I enter an enormous empty chamber, from which I can see through the empty doorways into other empty chambers. Half rotten, already partly collapsed stairs lead to the first floor. I dare not put my foot on them. I wander from one chamber to another, thinking.

I wander and think, wander and think. I realise that the house is empty and that I am on an island. I would like to leave, but I can't. I have the feeling that I am at home in this abandoned house. That I have finally reached my goal – where my journey began and where it must end. I sit on the floor (the parquet is distorted, mouldy and decaying) and try to remember life in these draughty spaces.

Was there life here?

If there was not, it is slowly returning. From the adjacent rooms, shadows begin to approach me; unclear at first, but then ever more like people. There are more and more of them, but they pass me by as if they don't see me, lost in themselves, some of them grimacing and gesticulating wildly; now and then, one of them yells, men and women of different ages, suffering faces, like people who have escaped by a whisker a great catastrophe; they surround me, more and more of them, and go past as if they were heading elsewhere, each on their own journey, God knows where, as if they really don't know. They slowly move away and finally disappear, vanish into the air.

The sound of the wind is all that remains.